"What do you want?" he asked.

You, Lydia's heart answered. It hurt that she couldn't say it, so she spoke in a teasing tone. "Not much, really. Just love, safety, security... And someday...maybe my own horse."

Her attempt at levity didn't work.

Jon looked out on the horizon. His expression was pure Rancher Blackwell—grave and determined. But she could also see the vulnerability there. She knew he had feelings for her, too. What she hadn't known was how strong they were. Now she did. And at that moment, all of the reasons why they couldn't be together flew out of her head. *Just say it*, she silently pleaded. Because no matter what happened, she wanted to hear the words at least once in her life from a person she wanted to hear them from.

He faced her, his gray-blue gaze ensnaring hers. "What if I told you that I want those things, too? And what if I told you that I didn't ever want to let you go?"

Dear Reader,

Having friends who share your sense of humor and interests—and maybe even their condo at national conference time—is the best feeling in the world. To rely on them for support, advice and ideas is a gift. To work with them on a project? Well, see above. These four ladies, Amy Vastine, Anna J. Stewart, Cari Lynn Webb and Melinda Curtis, are not only my friends, they are also megatalented writers whose enthusiasm and work ethic inspire me.

So when Melinda approached us with a concept for connected stories, we quickly agreed. Many emails and Skype sessions later and the Blackwell Ranch was born, along with five hot rancher brothers—Jonathon, Ethan, Ben, Tyler and Chance. While these boys love each other, a childhood marked by tragedy has driven them apart and left painful emotional wounds. These guys deserve to fall in love! But bringing them back together is no easy task. In fact, it requires all the ingenuity a clever, enigmatic, irascible— and officially AWOL—grandfather can muster.

And so we are proud to present Return of the Blackwell Brothers.

Carol

HEARTWARMING

The Rancher's Twins

USA TODAY Bestselling Author

Carol Ross

(H) HARLEQUIN® HEARTWARMING™

Recycling programs
for this product may
not exist in your area.

ISBN-13: 978-1-335-63373-6

The Rancher's Twins

Copyright © 2018 by Carol Ross

Printed in U.S.A.

Carol Ross lives in the Pacific Northwest with her husband and two dogs. She is a graduate of Washington State University. When not writing, or thinking about writing, she enjoys reading, running, hiking, skiing, traveling and making plans for the next adventure to subject her sometimes reluctant but always fun-loving family to. Carol can be contacted at carolrossauthor.com and via Facebook at Facebook.com/carolrossauthor, Twitter, @_CarolRoss, and Instagram, @carolross__.

Books by Carol Ross

Harlequin Heartwarming

Summer at the Shore
Christmas at the Cove

Seasons of Alaska

Bachelor Remedy
A Heartwarming Thanksgiving
"Autumn at Jasper Lake"
A Family Like Hannah's
If Not for a Bee
A Case for Forgiveness
Mountains Apart

Visit the Author Profile page
at Harlequin.com for more titles.

For Amy, Anna, Cari and Melinda.

Because it's not possible to thank you guys enough.

CHAPTER ONE

JONATHON BLACKWELL INHALED a deep breath in an attempt to calm the herd of agitated cattle mustering inside his chest. It didn't help. Nothing would, save for getting in and out as quickly as possible. Shopping on a normal day was bad enough. Shopping when he was short on time was downright aggravating. Why weren't items where they should be? And was it his imagination or were products rarely to be found in the same spot twice?

Although he had to admit, Brewster Ranch Supply was more organized than most, and if he had to shop, he supposed this was the least irritating option. Trout, on the other hand, enjoyed a trip to Brewster's, where there was always a treat waiting for him at the checkout counter.

"Almost done, buddy." The black-and-white border collie stood beside him sniffing a rack of vegetable seeds. "Only a couple more things." Jon trudged through Brewster's "home" section, where he puzzled way too long over what kind of sheets a woman might like on her bed—

cartoon cats seemed a little silly and more like something he'd buy for his five-year-old twins, while tiny hearts felt vaguely inappropriate. Telling himself he was overthinking it, he tossed a daisy-printed set into the shopping cart. It was just that any little thing he could do to facilitate a smooth transition for his new nanny, he wanted to do.

Nanny thoughts stirred his already churning anxiety. He needed to get back to his ranch, the JB Bar, because adding to his urgency was a sick calf that needed medicating, a cattle guard that needed fixing at the main gate, cows and heifers in labor and a generator for the calving shed that wouldn't start. Somewhere in between all that he needed to wash the new sheets and make the bed in the soon-to-be nanny's room.

Sofie, the wife of his best friend, Zach, was watching the twins but it felt like bad form not to be there to welcome his new employee and... The word *warn* popped into his head, and he felt a sting of guilt for even thinking that word with respect to his children. A rush of love and affection followed. He adored his girls but the honest truth was that an explanation was only fair where the twins were concerned.

Conscience feeling scratchy, he grabbed a package of those raspberry-flavored fruity snacks the girls liked from the end of the aisle.

Those, he noticed, were always in the same place and perfectly aligned to the sight line of a small child.

"Meds for the calf and we're out of here," he told Trout and headed toward the refrigerated unit. At least he would have no problem finding bovine medication.

Or so he thought.

Frustrating seconds ticked by as he scanned the shelves. A soft voice from behind him interrupted his search. "Hey, Jon, can I talk to you for a minute?" He glanced over his shoulder but didn't budge from his position in front of the display case.

"I'm sorry, Grace. But I'm in a huge hurry. Can it wait until—"

A silk-clad arm snuck in beside him, nimble fingers plucking a bottle from the shelf below the one he'd been searching. "Here." The bottle-holding hand then smacked lightly against his chest.

Taking the bounty, he studied the label. "Uh…" No wonder he hadn't found it sooner. Why were companies always changing label designs and bottle sizes and making things look different? "Thank you." With a final glance at the medication and a shake of his head, he shut the refrigerator door and turned to face the petite blonde now standing rigidly in front of him. "This is it."

Adjusting her glasses, she gave him a brisk nod and an of-course-it-is look. Her gaze seemed to soften as Trout edged closer to examine her shoe. She gave the dog a pat.

"How did you…?"

"Dad said you called this morning."

Dad was Frank Gardner. He and his wife, Alice, owned Brewster Ranch Supply. Grace had recently returned to Falcon Creek and was working for her parents while she established her own accounting business. Jon was her first client.

And what Grace said was true—Jon had called earlier to make sure the medication was in stock. Had that only been this morning? It felt like days ago. Ranching and hard work went hand in hand, but springtime meant calving season, which pushed it to a whole different level. His day had started hours before dawn and wouldn't end until after dark. Technically, it wouldn't end at all, not for a few more weeks, anyway, until his last cow had calved.

Grace was still staring at him. "It will only take a minute."

"What will?" he asked.

"What I need to speak with you about. I know

how busy you are, Jon. You know I wouldn't ask if it wasn't important. Please."

The earnest expression on her face gave him pause. Seeing as how Grace was currently doing his taxes, he felt it imprudent to refuse. Maybe something had come up.

"All right, then," Jon agreed, even as an unsettling feeling began to creep over him. Grace looked...off.

Exhaling a loud sigh of relief, she took off toward the back of the store like a horse for the barn, her heels clicking smartly on the scarred wood floor. The thump of his boots and the tap of Trout's toenails joined in discordant harmony as they followed.

Inside her office, which also doubled as a supply room, he was surprised to see Katie Montgomery already seated in the chair in front of Grace's desk. Katie was the daughter of the ranch foreman on the Blackwell Ranch, his grandfather's spread. Katie and her sister, Maura, had grown up there and, at seven years younger, Katie felt like his kid sister.

She looked up from her phone. The frown she'd been wearing transformed into a tight smile. "Hi, Jon. Hey, Trout." The dog gave her a friendly nudge and an enthusiastic tail-wag. Katie scratched his neck. Strands of reddish hair had pulled loose from her braid and she looked as tired as Jon felt.

"Hello, Katie."

Jon glanced around, considered sitting on a crate marked Farm Cat Tasty Food and then decided to remain standing. Trapped in a cramped room with these two women would normally feel like a treat. That was not the case right now. The air was thick and charged with tension, like that brief, hair-tingling moment of warning right before a thunderstorm came barreling down from the Rockies. You knew it was coming but there wasn't much you could do about it except hunker down and brace yourself. When neither woman seemed inclined to get on with it, he looked pointedly from Grace to Katie and back again.

"What's going on, ladies?"

Grace lowered herself into the chair behind her desk. "This is very difficult for me. I consider both of you friends… I hate having to do this, but I know you both will appreciate it if I just get to the point."

"I know I will." Tasks ticked through his mind again like a slide-show to-do list.

"I can't get a hold of Big E," Grace said. Big E was the name most everyone used when referring to his grandfather, Elias Blackwell.

Jon wasn't surprised, since most of the time Big E didn't want to be gotten a hold of.

"Uh…" Jon wasn't sure how this was his problem.

"Katie needs to order supplies, but the bill hasn't been paid for a couple of months."

That was odd.

"How long has it been since you've called your grandfather?" Katie asked him.

Was it his imagination or was that a twinge of accusation in her tone? Tough, smart, hard-working and honest, Katie also had a way with horses that could turn even the most seasoned cowpoke green with envy. Ranching was in her blood and Jon respected that. He would never say that anyone had an easy relationship with Big E, but Katie's was about the smoothest he'd ever seen. He wasn't quite sure how she managed it.

The phone rings both ways, he wanted to answer. But didn't. His issues with his grandfather had nothing to do with Katie.

Holding his tongue, he looked toward Grace instead. "What do you mean you can't get a hold of him?"

"Katie told me he's not home."

"Did you try his cell phone?"

"I've been trying it for over a week now."

A week? A ripple of concern trotted up his

spine. Jon hadn't known Big E had plans to go anywhere. But he didn't exactly keep himself up-to-date with the comings and goings of his grandfather and his stepgrandmother, Zoe. In a general sense, Jon did his dead-level best to stay away from Big E's fifth wife, while he and Big E's relationship might be described as cordial on a good day and tense on its worst. Thinking back, it had been at least a week since he'd spoken to Big E. And that conversation, like most of their communications, had been ranch-related.

"Huh. Well, Katie, where is he? How long has it been since you've spoken to him? Or your dad?"

Katie inhaled a breath, held it for a couple of seconds and then let it out. "I don't know where he is. Dad hasn't spoken to him."

That troubling feeling gathered a head of steam and galloped headlong through his bloodstream.

"I'm sorry, Jon." Grace's pained expression seemed a perfect reflection of what he was feeling. "Your grandfather, it seems, has gone missing."

"Lydia Newbury, Lydia New-w-bury, Lydia New-bur-r-ry…" Lydia was practicing saying her new last name. Her biggest problem would be slipping up and saying Newton. But Tanner assured her that was the point; it was similar enough to her real name that if she did slip it would be easy to cover.

She studied the ancient map of Montana in the faded, dog-eared road atlas and wondered why—why did she continue to stare at the worn page? It wasn't like the JB Bar Ranch was suddenly going to appear on the paper before her in the form of a little black dot like the quaint town of Billings, which unfortunately was now far, far behind her. Nor was it going to present itself as a pretty, powder-blue squiggle, either, like the winding, picturesque Yellowstone River that she was traveling roughly parallel to.

The view beckoned through the windshield and pulled her focus outside the vehicle again. Awesome, these mountains, but in the truest, most uncorrupted sense of the word. She glanced back down at the map, at the mapmaker's attempt to shade in a likeness of the Rocky Mountains. Ha. Not even a camera could do justice to these peaks jutting from the earth in all their rugged, snow-capped glory.

Philadelphia seemed light-years away. She took a second to be thankful for that and for the fact that she'd made it this far. Every mile felt like a tiny victory, a step closer to freedom. She'd pulled over on the highway because she knew she had to be close. The turnoff was somewhere east of Livingston, but she couldn't remember how many miles. She'd entered the ranch's "address" into her phone at the car lot in Billings where she'd purchased the used SUV. That is if "JB Bar Ranch, Old Tractor Road, Falcon Creek, MT" could be considered a proper address. GPS had recognized the place, so she'd gone with it, but cell service had been spotty and with the constant searching for service, her battery was dead.

Tanner had handpicked this job for her and a few days ago it had seemed like the perfect solution. Working as a nanny and living on a ranch in Montana meant she was virtually untraceable. No rental agreement meant no address and no bills in her name. The perfect hiding place. A bitter chuckle slipped out of her at the irony of a hiding spot so good *she* couldn't even find it.

And if she didn't hide, Clive would find her.

As if Lydia leaving him and taking his money wasn't bad enough, the four dollars she'd left in his bank accounts was going to push him over the edge. A fresh spike of fear left her limbs tingling. Why had she done that? In those last triumphant seconds, she'd gotten greedy. Heady with accomplishment and vengeance, the idea had come to her. A little dig to get back at him after all those months of putting up with his abuse.

"Stupid, Lydia," she whispered and pressed a fisted hand to her mouth. At first, he'd wonder, but it wouldn't take him long to put those twos and twos together and figure out what all those fours meant.

And he would come after her.

Like a fugitive in a crime drama, she'd been flown by a pilot friend of Tanner's to St. Paul, Minnesota. From there, she'd taken a bus to Billings, where she'd paid cash for the used SUV. Now, nearly two days later, she had a burner phone and a vehicle with Montana plates. The signed title and bill of sale were tucked in the glove compartment. The day before she'd left Philadelphia she'd paid every bill, withdrawn all her savings and then closed her bank account. She'd shut down her social-media sites and left her credit cards lying in plastic bits in three different trash cans scattered around the city. She was safe. She trusted Tanner, would never have been able to get this far without her close friend and attorney.

So why didn't she feel safe?

"Don't worry, Lydia Newbury. Your worrying days are over, remember? You can do this. Inside, deep inside, you are brave and clever and honest."

Okay, so she was pretty clever, mostly honest and *trying* to be brave. She really, really needed to be brave. Like right now. The idea of stopping for directions, of showing her face anywhere along this interstate, caused the already taut coil of nerves inside her to tighten.

Flipping on her turn signal, she put the atlas on the passenger seat, inhaled a deep breath and glanced in the side mirror just in time to see the flashing blue and red lights of the police vehicle as it pulled in behind her.

A surge of adrenaline coursed through her bloodstream. "Newbury, Newbury," she repeated, reminding herself. But what if he asked for her ID? This plan hinged on Lydia not using her real name.

In her rearview mirror, she watched a tall lanky man in a khaki outfit get out. His hat was dark brown. She turned off the signal, lowered her window and folded her hands together in her lap so he wouldn't see them trembling.

"Howdy, ma'am." His tone was friendly, but his ice-blue gaze hinted at a cop's shrewdness. When he leaned down she could see freckles sprinkled across his nose and flaming red hair beneath the hat.

"Hi, there." Lydia dredged up her best customer-service smile.

"Did you break down?"

"No, Officer. Thankfully, I did not."

"Then is there a reason your car is sitting here on the side of the road?"

"An embarrassing one." Shrugging a shoulder, she flashed him a cringe-smile. "I think I might be lost. I'm on my way to a ranch where I've been hired for a job."

His mouth pulled down into a frown. His name tag read Deputy Tompkin.

"Not the Blackwell Guest Ranch, I hope? They don't open for another month or so."

Blackwell Guest Ranch? That couldn't be a coincidence. "Maybe. I don't know... I thought I was looking for Jonathon Blackwell of the JB Bar Ranch."

"Oh! Of course." He did the finger-snap-point as his face erupted with a smile. "You're the new nanny. Oh, man, this is great." Sticking out a hand, he said, "Deputy Scooter Tompkin. Pleased to meet you."

Lydia felt a rush of relief. "Lydia," she said, not quite able to bring herself to say her new last name. Shaking his hand, she added, "It's wonderful to meet you, Deputy."

"I can't wait to tell the guys I met you. Jon Blackwell is a friend of mine. And I can assure you, he is going to be one happy camper to see you arrive. He's got his hands full, that's for sure. My sister babysat for him for a spell. A real short one." He shook his head. "He's certainly in need of a professional."

Lydia felt a niggle of concern. She knew Jonathon Blackwell had a fourteen-year-old daughter. As a single dad, she'd assumed he would need more of a shuttle service than a babysitter. She imagined days of ferrying her charge to school and various lessons and activities, providing healthy meals and snacks, and asking the requisite questions about homework completion. At least, that's what her nannies had done. Back when she'd had them, before her parents' divorce. The idea of a troubled teen didn't scare her, though. Having been one, coupled with her years of volunteering at Hatch House Group Home for Teens, meant she was fluent in troubled teen.

"I appreciate the vote of confidence. I'm pretty excited about it myself. If I can figure out how to get there."

"You're real close and it's easy to find. Take the next exit ahead. Follow the signs for Falcon Creek until you come to a four-way stop, where you want to go straight ahead, not into Falcon Creek. After a few miles you'll cross a bridge. Take a right—don't take the spur that heads east. A ways after that, there'll be a fork. You're going to want to go straight, but don't. Stay right and

Old Tractor Road will be off to your left. Then you'll see the sign that says JB Bar Ranch."

"Um, okay, can you let me grab a pen and then start over at spurs and forks?"

He chuckled. "Tell you what, follow me, and I'll take you right to the driveway."

"Really?" Was this guy for real? "Deputy Tompkin, I can't tell you how much I'd appreciate that." Lydia gave him a grateful smile, one she felt to the depths of her toes.

"Call me Scooter."

"Wow. Okay, thank you, Scooter. You're a lifesaver. I will find a way to repay this kindness."

"Ah, it's no problem. I'd do anything to help Jon." Then he tipped his hat and said, "Welcome to Falcon Creek, Ms. Lydia."

CHAPTER TWO

"IT'S OFFICIAL, I'M TERRIFIED of our unborn child. I know Jon's twins are only five, but because there are two of them it's like you can double the devious factor. No, not double—quadruple."

Sofie was speaking to her husband, Zach, in that hushed tone people use when they're all worked up and think they're being quiet, when in fact the opposite is true. Jon could hear every word from where he sat on the long antique church pew that stretched nearly the length of one wall in the mudroom, the rectangular entryway adjacent to his kitchen. Since his foreman, Tom, had fixed the cattle guard, Jon had been able to medicate the calf and check on the pregnant cows and heifers. With the weather holding, he and Tom decided the generator could wait.

The opposite wall was lined with a shoe rack, two boot dryers and a series of pegs and hooks for various layers of outdoor clothing necessary when working daily in the elements of Montana—rain gear, wool jackets, parkas, hats, gloves and the like. The other end of the narrow room led to a half bath, while taking a left brought you into the kitchen.

As always, Trout sat patiently on the thick rug waiting for Jon to towel off his muddy paws and belly. Jon had heard the water running when he entered. That, mingled with the soft music from the satellite radio, the one extravagance he allowed himself, explained why Sofie and Zach hadn't heard him yet.

He tensed at Sofie's comments even though he knew what she said was true. His girls were out of control—"holy living terrors" their last babysitter had called them. She'd lasted three days. He did his best to tamp down the despair eating away at him like a slow-moving but persistent acid. Mercifully, some of that feeling would be alleviated today.

The sound of Zach's chuckle made Jon smile. He removed his boots, not feeling even remotely guilty for listening in on his best friend's conversation with his wife.

Zach said, "They remind me of Brenna and Tess. Trust me, Sofie. They're normal. They're growing up without a woman's influence and thousands of acres of ranch land as their playground. They're a little rough around the edges is all. Our kids probably will be, too. This is good practice for you."

Even if Zach didn't entirely mean it, Jon loved

him for saying it. Brenna and Tess were Zach's younger sisters. Not twins, but at only thirteen months apart, they might as well have been. Jon would be thrilled if his girls grew up to be like the Carnes sisters.

Sofie, on the other hand, had grown up in Seattle. Despite the fact that she seemed to be settling in well with Zach, she didn't get it. Not really. Not in the way that someone who grew up on a ranch did. He said a silent thank-you that he didn't have to worry about that with his new nanny.

She went on, "Oh, they're adorable, don't get me wrong. And they can be sweet, but so can grizzly bear cubs. That's the problem. Cute and out of control is a dangerous combination. I found Gen in the small pasture with the cows and newborns this afternoon. Abby was literally climbing through the fence to join her when I caught up with them. All this, after I expressly forbade them from going anywhere near there. I'm getting too pregnant to keep up with them."

"Sofie, honey, they're fine, though, right? Nothing happened."

"Okay, next time Jon is in a bind you're going to watch them. It will be good practice for *you*. You'll see. If one of the cows would have seen Gen as a threat…" Her voice trailed off. "I don't even want to think about what could have happened. And the scary question is, what were they planning to do once they both got in there? Gen had a rope."

Jon stepped into the kitchen. "I'm sorry, Sofie. There won't be any more binds, or there shouldn't be, anyway. Not with a real nanny on the job." The conversation illuminated why Jon had chosen this particular nanny agency. He'd been able to request specific criteria regarding his new employee. They were sending him a nanny with ranching experience.

He looked around. "Speaking of, I'm assuming she's not here yet?"

"Nope. Hasn't shown." In a softer tone, she asked, "You're sure she's coming?"

"What, you think I've been blacklisted? Like there's some sort of club or network where nannies and babysitters go to talk about their bad experiences? Stay away from those Blackwell cubs. They look cute but they're nothing but trouble."

Zach laughed as he crouched to give Trout a pat. "Hey, Trout. How's the best dog in the world?" Trout's tail went wild as he settled in next to Zach.

Sofie let out a gasp and then clapped a hand over her mouth. "You heard all of that?" Tears welled in her eyes, which made Jon feel terrible for making a joke.

"Jon, I'm so sorry. I'm awful. I didn't mean it. They're wonderful kids it's just that—"

Crossing the kitchen, he wrapped her in a hug. "You've never been awful for even two minutes in your life, Sofie Carnes. I'm teasing. I know they can be difficult."

"No." Her head shook against his shoulder. "No, that was wrong. I shouldn't have said it." The words were muffled as she cried into his shirt. "I'm not myself. I'm a monster."

"You're not a monster. You're pregnant."

Zach grinned and mouthed a thank-you behind Sofie's back.

Sofie lifted her head. Jon handed her a handkerchief from his shirt pocket. She stared at it.

"It's clean, I promise."

"I know." Taking it from his hand, she snuffled out a laugh through her tears. "It's just that I still can't believe I live in a place where men use tissues made from fabric."

Zach reached out and grabbed Sofie's hips, turning and pulling her in close for an embrace. He kissed the top of her head.

Jon smiled, even as the love between these two generated a touch of envy. Had he ever had anything approaching that with his ex-wife? Looking back, he didn't think so. He and Ava's relationship had been fire and ice from the moment they'd met, one extreme or the other.

They'd never seemed to find that sweet smoldering spot in between.

Zach said, "Hey, I've gotta run. I'll see you at home, Sofe."

Sofie gave him a quick kiss and stepped away. "Okay, I'll be along in a bit. Corn bread is still in the oven."

Jon resisted the urge to cringe at the mention of Sofie's cooking. He told his friend goodbye and turned back to Sofie. "I need to go put in a load of laundry. I'll be right back."

"I could have done that. Why didn't you say something earlier?"

"I didn't have any to do earlier." He winked at her and headed to the laundry room to put the nanny's new sheets in the wash.

"Where are the girls?" he asked when he returned. Trout was still in the kitchen, sniffing the room's perimeter for the customary breadcrust bits and cracker crumbs the girls regularly left behind. If Gen and Abby were anywhere nearby, the dog would be hanging out with them by now.

"Tom took them out to see the foal." Tom was Jonathon's foreman and only full-time employee. Since it was calving season, the bunkhouse currently lodged a few extra cowboys who worked for him seasonally. Which reminded him of Katie and the bind Big E had left her in.

She'd told him one of her hands had quit, which meant she was already short on help. Although, thankfully the guest ranch employees wouldn't be arriving for at least another month or so.

While the family's Blackwell Ranch was both a working cattle ranch and a dude ranch, Jon's focus was strictly on cattle. While he disliked the dude ranch, it was his grandfather's methods regarding the cattle ranch that was the source of contention between Jon and Big E.

Which brought him back around to the information he'd learned about his grandfather earlier; Big E was AWOL. Irritation overrode the concern he'd felt in Grace's office when Katie assured him that Big E was fine; he wasn't technically a "missing person" by the legal definition. She just didn't know where he was right at this moment. The week before, he and Zoe had taken off in their motorhome. This didn't surprise him, as Zoe was always trying to talk Big E into anything that would get her away from the ranch, a ranch she was constantly trying to "improve." Meaning, she wanted it to make more money. Jon didn't care. What his grandfather did with Zoe was his business. But during calving season? It was the busiest time of year on a cattle ranch.

Katie had reminded him that no one could sign on the account to pay the bills except Elias or one of his grandsons. In other words, Jon or one of his four brothers had to sort this out. Unfortunately, his brothers all lived out of state. On Jon's promise to take care of the bill, Grace had given Katie leave to purchase what she needed.

The part that chafed at Jon was that Big E had inconvenienced both him and Katie in the process. He was going to have to track down his grandfather. And in the meantime, if Big E and Zoe didn't show up tonight, he would be forced to head over there and figure out what needed to be done so that Katie could keep things running smoothly.

Sofie was peering out the window above the sink. "Wait… Is that a car coming up the drive?"

Jon joined her. The vehicle drew closer and he could see it wasn't a rig belonging to anyone he knew.

The nanny.

A lightness unfurled inside his chest, which had felt unbearably heavy for so long it was like he had an anvil for a heart. Maybe his girls could finally become the kids he knew they had the potential to be, have the life they deserved. Or as much of one as he could give them. What they deserved was a mom, but there wasn't anything he could do about that.

He warned himself not to pin too much hope here. But that felt a lot like trying to push raindrops back into a storm cloud. And besides, he wouldn't want to. He knew it was far from poetic, but he and the girls were like the parched ground after a long drought, eager and hungry to soak up every bit of life-giving water they could get. And this nanny... This nanny was the rain.

LYDIA CLIMBED OUT of the SUV and took in the sprawling, pale gray, white-trimmed home before her. Not overly large, but certainly not small, and everything looked neat and tidy and...new. Huh.

For some reason, she'd been expecting one of those ancient two-story farmhouses with half-finished projects and rusty tools scattered around outside. Inside there'd be faded, gingham curtains, noisy pipes and lots of tiny rooms with creaky floors. Basically, her nana's little farm in upstate New York—the home Lydia had shared with her for the only two truly good years of her childhood.

She had to admit the JB Bar Ranch was storybook pretty with its neatly painted outbuildings in a matching shade of gray and two large, brick-red barns. Some smaller, greener tufts of grass sprouted here and there in the vast expanse of lawn, promising a lush green mantle once spring pushed into early summer. Reddish brown cows dotted the landscape beyond the barn.

Inhaling deeply, she attempted to smooth her crumpled wool skirt and silk shirt. She stared down at her expensive, impractical faux-leather boots and wished she'd had time to purchase suitable clothing for her stint as a rancher's nanny.

"Not that I know what a rancher's nanny wears," she muttered wryly. She didn't know anything about ranching. Although, aside from the basics of sewing and cooking, she hadn't known much about waitressing, hair shampooing, baking, catering, dog-sitting, office assisting, or the myriad of other jobs she'd tackled over the years, either.

Besides, she'd gladly left most of her possessions behind. She didn't want anything Clive had purchased for her with his dirty money, especially that engagement ring.

Shaking her head, she looked around to try and get her bearings and gather her shredded confidence. A lack of options was an incredible motivator and soon had her navigating the neatly cobbled walkway and scaling the steps of the porch.

A surge of nervous tension welled inside of her as she lifted a hand. The door opened before she could knock to reveal a handsome, serious-faced man and a pretty, smiling woman whose eager expression made Lydia think she was going to angle in for a hug. Then she swung open the screen door and Lydia felt her brain stall.

"Um… Hi, I'm…sorry. My name is Lydia… Newbury. I think I must have the wrong place? I'm looking for Jonathon Blackwell of the JB Bar Ranch?"

Jonathon Blackwell was supposed to be a single dad, not one half of an expecting couple. Had there been some sort of a mix-up?

"No, no, you're not at the wrong place." At the woman's encouraging wave, Lydia stepped inside. "Please, come in. I'm Sofie, neighbor and friend." Her honey-blond hair was neatly piled high up on her head and her warm brown eyes matched the kindness in her tone. "It's wonderful to meet you. We've been expecting you. Did you have trouble finding the place?"

"It's wonderful to be here finally. I'm sorry I'm late. I did have a little trouble finding the place, which would have been a lot of trouble if Deputy Tompkin hadn't helped me out."

Sofie smiled. "Oh, good. Scooter's great."

"Even after that I still wasn't sure—"

"Why is that?" the man interrupted, his scowl morphing into more of a glare.

He'd moved a few steps back and now stood in the doorway leading to the kitchen. Lydia could see gleaming silver appliances behind him. Country music drifted softly from that di-

rection. Tall and nicely muscled, he filled the
doorway where he leaned against the wood
frame. He slipped a hand into the back pocket
of his dingy, faded jeans. All that was missing was a cowboy hat to cover his attractively
mussed hair and a piece of straw poking from
between his chiseled lips. Tension vibrated off
him like an overtuned guitar string. A couple of
six-shooters hanging from those lean hips and
he could walk right onto to a movie set about a
gritty, bitter cowboy. He definitely didn't match
up to the nice-guy impression she'd gleaned
from Scooter.

Forcing herself to make eye contact con-
firmed her assumption—he didn't like what he
saw. She wondered if he knew how much his
steely gray gaze gave away.

"Why is what?" she asked, forcing a friendly
smile. Whatever his first impression had told
him, it wasn't good. Lydia needed to change
his mind.

His next words were hard-edged, like it tried
his patience to clarify his question. "Why did
you think you had the wrong ranch?"

"Um, well…" Lydia tried to think of a way
to condense her reasons. *Because a pregnant
woman opened the door and I thought you were
a single dad, and you're glaring at me, and I*

*didn't expect my new employer to be a grouch
who disliked me on sight.*

Sofie blinked wide brown eyes. "That doesn't
matter, does it, Jon? She's here now."

The little shake of his head was almost imper-
ceptible. In a flat tone he conceded, "I suppose
not." He stuck out a hand. "Jonathon Blackwell.
This is the JB Bar Ranch."

"Nice to meet you, Mr. Blackwell." Lydia offered her hand. He gave it a firm squeeze and
then released it like they were playing a game of
hot potato. His stern gaze skimmed over her and
lingered on her boots before he glanced away.

A black-and-white dog sidled up to her, tail
wagging.

"Hello, gorgeous." Crouching, she held out a
hand. The dog came closer and laid his muzzle
on her thigh. Lydia relaxed a little and stroked
his silky ears. At least the dog liked her. "Aren't
you the sweetest thing?"

"This is Trout," Sofie said, beaming.

Blackwell loomed, his face a grim mask.

"How was your drive?" Sofie asked.

"Good. Stunningly beautiful. I've never seen
this part of the country. Or much of rural America at all, unfortunately. Not since I was a kid,
anyway."

"Oh, but I thought you had… Where are you
from?"

"Philadelphia, born and mostly raised." *If a girl can be raised by the age of fifteen*, she added silently.

Sofie's face twisted thoughtfully. "So, you've never lived on a ranch?"

Lydia laughed and gave the dog one more pat before standing. "Nope. City girl through and through." Except for her two years in upstate New York with Nana. But that was a story and Tanner had told her to withhold details when she could. Sofie shot Blackwell another curious glance. He returned it with another head shake and a sigh. What was this guy's problem?

Sofie noticed her watching. Clearing her throat, she focused her bright smile back on Lydia. "Well, I can relate to that, that's for sure. I'm from Seattle."

Trout let out an excited whimper and jogged through the doorway where Blackwell still stood guard. Behind him, the unmistakable sounds of a crowd entering the house followed; voices, laughter, squeals, the clank of what sounded like metal and then the stomping of feet.

"Perfect timing," Sofie said brightly. "The girls are back."

CHAPTER THREE

BEFORE LYDIA'S BRAIN could even register the plural form of the word *girl*, a pair of them rushed into the room. Little ones. Decidedly un-teenager ones. Cries of "Sofie" and "Trout" and "Daddy" followed. Maybe these were the pregnant Sofie's other children? But no, because they were clearly calling Blackwell "Daddy."

Within seconds he was confirming the association. "Girls, I'd like you to meet Ms. Lydia Newbury. Ms. Newbury, this is Abigail." He placed one large palm on a mess of long brown curls before putting the other on the shoulder of a child with lighter brown tangles even messier than her sister's. "And this is Genevieve." There seemed to be a challenging glint in his eyes. "My five-year-old twin daughters."

Lydia's brain was spinning a hundred miles an hour. There must have been a mix-up at the nanny agency. Instead of one fourteen-year-old, she'd gotten placed with two five-year-olds? As much as she wanted to apologize for the inconvenience, walk out to her car, climb in and drive away, fleeing was not an option. This was her flee, so to speak. Images of Clive and his cronies swam before her eyes. Five-year-old twins and their grumpy father versus taking her chances on the open road?

She held out a hand. "It's a pleasure to meet you, Abigail and Genevieve." One tiny, filthy hand and then another reached out and squeezed hers. Adorable, polite, nice-to-meet-yous accompanied each gesture. Lydia studied their dirt-smeared faces and felt a tug of affection working at the knot of terror and anxiety tangled inside her chest.

"I'd like for you guys to call me Lydia, okay?"

"Yes, ma'am," Abigail said.

Genevieve commented, "I like that better. It's faster to say. Like Gen instead of Genevieve, you can call me that if you want." Expression earnest, she flipped a hand toward her sister. "And Abby you can call Abby. Hardly nobody calls us Genevieve or Abigail."

"Hardly anybody," Abigail said, correcting her sister.

"Yep," Genevieve agreed with a quick bob of her head. "That's what I meant, hardly anybody." She hooked her thumbs in her belt loops and seemed to study Lydia's outfit with much less disdain than her father. "Those boots are real pretty. They're tall, huh? I don't think you could run very fast in them. Or ride."

Blackwell let out a sound like a cross between a snort and a chuckle. "Boots like that aren't good for much, sugar plum. They're not even real leather."

Lydia felt her cheeks go hot. Why did it feel like he'd just insulted more than her boots?

"You could wear them to church?" Abigail suggested helpfully. "Or to a party? Not a barn party, though, because the heel part would sink into the dirt." She stomped one tiny cowboy-booted heel as if to show Lydia what she meant.

"Do you like horses?" Genevieve asked.

"Um, yes, I do," Lydia said.

"We love horses. Abby and I have our own horses. Mine is Garnet and hers is Topaz."

"Do you ride, Lydia?" Blackwell asked in a tone that let her know there was only one right answer and he suspected she wasn't going to give it. What was wrong with this guy? Like his first question, she wasn't quite sure how to answer it. Lydia loved horses. But she hadn't been on one since she was fourteen, before Nana died and her dad sold the farm, and Lydia's already uncertain world had completely fallen apart. A painful cramp of longing seized her at the onslaught of memories. She hoped horseback riding was like riding a bike.

She opened her mouth to explain when Sofie stepped forward. "Well, if Lydia does ride, I'm sure she isn't planning on riding in those pretty boots. Lydia, I can't tell you how glad we are that you're here."

She turned toward the twins with an encouraging smile. "Abby, Gen, why don't you girls go wash up for dinner?"

To Blackwell, she suggested, "Jon, why don't you go out to Lydia's car and get her bags?"

"That would be great." Digging into the purse hanging over her shoulder, Lydia withdrew the keys. "You'll need these."

"Of course," Blackwell said flatly. "You locked it."

She dropped the keys into his outstretched palm and watched him stalk toward the door.

Sofie said, "No one locks their cars around here. You'll get used to it. And speaking of dinner, yours is on the stove. Follow me into the kitchen and I'll show you where a few things are before I go."

Lydia already liked this woman and the thought of her leaving now, specifically of being left here with Jonathon Blackwell and this precocious preschool duo that she did not sign up for, left her skin itchy and prickling, probably from the cold sweat breaking out all over her body.

HALF-DAZED AND full-on irritated, Jon headed out to the nanny's vehicle. At least the well-used four-wheel-drive SUV was Montana practical. Although, he noted disapprovingly, it could use some new tires. Opening the back, he wondered how many trips it would take him to haul City Girl's stuff inside. Seemed like kind of a waste since she wouldn't be here long. He was calling the agency first thing in the morning and getting a replacement.

"Huh," he grunted. All he saw was one small suitcase and a bag that looked about large enough for a laptop. He'd expected at least one steamer trunk filled entirely with impractical shoes.

Back inside the house, he deposited the bags in the guest room, which reminded him to take a side trip to the laundry room and put the sheets in the dryer. Still fuming, he headed into the bathroom in his master suite. Normally, he'd just wash up in the half bath off the mudroom, but he needed a second. Several seconds. Days maybe.

After scrubbing his hands, he splashed cold water on his face and stared at his reflection.

"Lydia Newbury," he said and then followed up with a whispered expletive. "It even sounds like a spoiled, city-girl name."

How could this have happened? The agency advertised that they carefully vetted each candidate and placed them in the best possible position. He'd specifically requested a nanny with ranching or farming experience, a rural background at the very least. This woman looked like she just stepped off the subway in her tight skirt and stupid high-heeled boots. Long, silky, chestnut-colored hair shined with expensive highlights, manicured nails clutched a designer bag that looked so soft it would probably melt in the rain.

His marriage hadn't lasted long, but it had been long enough to recognize a woman addicted to the finer things. As if that wasn't bad enough, she'd blatantly given herself away. She didn't want to be here on the JB Bar Ranch. From the window, he and Sofie had watched her, scowling and shaking her head. "I think I must have the wrong place," she'd said, standing right on his doorstep, her expression so baffled and forlorn that once upon a time his younger, naive self might have gone weak with sympathy. That man had died right along with his marriage.

Reality rarely lived up to expectations and he couldn't help but wonder what she'd been imagining? A stately old colonial mansion? A "rustic" lodge-style monstrosity that wasn't rustic at all but was designed to look as if it was, like the guest house at the Blackwell Ranch? Too bad it wasn't open yet—he could move her over there until she could catch a plane back to Philadelphia. Whatever she'd had in mind, it clearly was not Jon's modest-sized rambler.

"How cute," Ava had said the first day he'd brought her to the JB Bar. "A ranch-style home for a rancher. We can add on later, right?" Jon had thought she was joking. By the time he'd learned otherwise, she was pregnant. When it came to material things, Ava had no sense of humor, only a longing that he could not satisfy. Her cravings were the kind that ranching could never cure, not his style of ranching, anyway. He'd built his house and ranch from the ground up with cattle, practicality and comfort in mind. Pretty much in that order.

A nanny like Lydia was out of the question. He'd had enough of coddling beautiful, materialistic, impossible-to-please women to last a lifetime. Besides, he thought as a wave of those bitter feelings washed over him, it didn't work, anyway.

It had taken weeks for this nanny to get here. How long would it take to get a replacement?

AFTER SOFIE LEFT, Lydia remained in the kitchen, admiring the granite countertops, brushed stainless-steel appliances and double sinks. Gorgeous hardwood floors gleamed beneath her feet. A large island made up the centerpiece of the room. Copper-bottomed pans hung from a rack suspended above. Five tall padded comfy-looking stools were tucked under the opposite edge.

She stepped closer to the deluxe five-burner stove with double ovens and felt a spark of joy. A little swirl of hope circled inside of her. If Lydia had designed the kitchen herself, she wouldn't change a thing. Cozy and gourmet utilitarian at the same time. Cooking was an area where she felt supremely confident.

The girls skipped into the kitchen. Genevieve climbed up one of the tall stools at the kitchen's island.

"It's dinnertime, why don't you guys go ahead and sit at the table?"

"We eat here," Abby said, joining her sister in the next chair.

Hmm. Lydia had fond memories of her and Nana sharing meals at the table. "Every day?"

"When we eat here."

"What do you mean when you eat here?"

"Since it's calving time we usually eat in the bunkhouse with the cowboys."

"I see." But she didn't. Was she supposed to cook for a bunch of cowboys, too? Now that she thought about it, the position hadn't come with much of a job description. That had been the least of her concerns. She and Blackwell needed to hash out a few details.

"Tonight, we're going to sit at the table, okay? That way we can see each other while we eat, and I can get to know you guys a little bit."

"Are you going to quit, too?" Abby asked.

"Quit?"

"All our babysitters quit," she explained.

"No, I most certainly am not." For once in her life quitting was not an option.

The girls exchanged glances. Leaning their heads together, they whispered excitedly. After a moment, something seemed to be decided because they sat up straight again, grinned at Lydia and shrugged in tandem. "Okay." They hopped down and darted toward the dining room.

"Hey, you guys want to help me set the table since you're headed that way?"

They turned back toward her, matching gray-blue eyes wide and curious. For a few long seconds Lydia thought they were going to balk.

Abby's face erupted with a smile. "Yes, ma'am."

"I'll get the spoons," Genevieve said.

The three of them were seated and waiting when Blackwell strode into the kitchen. Stopping short, he looked from the kitchen to the dining room and back again. Lydia almost laughed at the baffled expression on his face.

Abby saved Lydia from having to explain. "Daddy, look, we're eating at the table."

"Isn't this neat?" Gen added.

"Uh… Yeah, very…" He walked over and stood before the table for a second, hands on hips. "Neat." He folded his tall length into the vacant chair and Lydia couldn't help thinking that he moved with the graceful ease of an athlete. Or a cowboy. Not that she'd ever known one of the latter. Dipping his head down, he studied the steaming bowl of stew as if trying to decide what it might contain.

Unlike the new kitchen, the oak dining table looked very old. The girls had shown Lydia the drawer in the matching buffet where place mats were kept. They'd seemed excited when Lydia encouraged them to choose a set.

Fiddling with the silverware laid out on his left side, Blackwell looked at Lydia. "We don't usually eat here."

"The girls told me." Lydia unfolded her napkin and placed it on her lap. "Dinnertime is a nice way to multitask, though, don't you think? You get to eat and spend time together as a family. That's what my grandmother always said."

Blackwell's lips formed a grim line while the twins stared at her solemnly.

"You're lucky to have a grandma," Abby said.

"Yeah," Gen agreed. "We have Zoe, but she

doesn't like us to call her Grandma. She doesn't do any grandma stuff, either. One time she painted our fingernails."

Abby added, "We love Great-Grandma Dorothy. But she lives far away in Texas and we hardly ever see her."

"I was very lucky to have a grandma. She died, but I'm glad I had her as long as I did. I'm sorry you guys don't have a grandma." Lydia wanted to ask questions about this Zoe person, but Blackwell's glower stopped her.

She briefly considered calling for a blessing or some other type of predinner ritual, but decided there'd be time to introduce that later. "I think we should eat."

A few minutes later, Lydia decided Sofie might be a paragon of sweetness, but she was a terrible cook. The stew was bland and the corn bread dry. But the Blackwells ate without complaint and there was no way she was going to voice her opinion on a gesture of such obvious goodwill. Nor was she going to comment on the fact that the twins ate like piglets. Not yet, anyway.

"Did you grow up on a ranch, too?" Genevieve asked, scooping up a large chunk of corn bread and shoving it into her already full mouth.

"Nope. I was raised in Philadelphia. That's in Pennsylvania. Do you know where that is?"

Gen shook her head.

"I think Pennsylvania is a state," Abby said, and then licked her fingers.

"It is. I'll show you on a map."

"Have you ever seen a calf being born?" Gen asked.

"No, I have not."

Abby wrinkled her nose. "It's kind of gross."

"No, it's not!" Gen argued. "It's the roof over our head and the boots on our feet, huh, Daddy?"

Blackwell gave her a gentle smile. "Yes, it sure is."

Abby shot her sister an irritated scowl. "I know, Gen. I just meant if you've never seen one before."

"I'm gonna be a rancher, too." Gen shoveled up another too-large bite of stew and then wiped at her face with the back of her hand. "Like Katie."

"I want to be a vet like Uncle Ethan." Abby dipped a finger in her stew and wiped it on the place mat.

Lydia wondered if the girls knew what napkins were for.

They continued chatting through the rest of the meal. Lydia was grateful for the distraction as it saved her from having to talk to her new employer. At least, she noted happily, he wasn't grouchy with his girls.

Dinner complete, the girls hopped up from the table and scampered out of the dining room. Lydia watched them go and felt a mix of sympathy and affection wash over her. What had happened here? Where was their mother? She could feel Blackwell watching her. Turning her head, she saw puzzlement and…something not quite as grouchy splayed across his face.

Standing, he reached across the table and stacked the bowls into a pile. "I'll help you clear the table and then I need to go check on some cows." He carried them into the kitchen.

Lydia gathered the glasses and followed. "Right now? Shouldn't we go over what you expect of me?"

"It's calving season." He pointed this out like a normal person might comment on the obvious state of the weather. He opened the dishwasher, and began loading the bowls inside.

Maybe grumpy, condescending and rude was just his normal state? But how could he have such a nice friend like Sofie? And his daughters might be a bit…unrefined, but they were clearly loved, and they adored their father. Obviously, it was her. What wasn't obvious was why.

"But…"

"It'll be dark soon," he added, tucking the glasses in the top rack.

Lydia felt a bubble of frustration at his cryptic dialogue. "Oh, do they have a curfew?"

The chuckle seemed to escape him before he realized it and left him looking a little surprised. The smile lingered, and Lydia couldn't help but notice how much it transformed him. Jonathon Blackwell was an extremely nice-looking man when he wasn't scowling at her.

"Yes, ma'am, they kind of do. I need to take a look at them and that's easiest when it's still light out. What I should have said is that we'll have a chat when I get back in."

"Oh. In that case you don't need to help with the dishes."

A chime sounded. Lydia watched him pluck a phone out of his shirt pocket. "Just a sec." His expression tensed again, and Lydia wondered how many different scowls the man possessed. He looked up from the screen. "I'm sorry. We may need to have that discussion in the morning. I might need to turn a calf and… I mean, I've got a heifer in labor that needs some assistance. Unless you want to wait up, but it could be late by the time I get back to the house."

Lydia swallowed nervously. Although why she was nervous exactly she couldn't say. "Morning is fine. Should I get the girls ready for bed?"

His eyes zeroed in on her like he was considering the question. At least his eyes didn't have as hard a glint as before. She'd call this expression thoughtful instead of grouchy, which felt like progress.

"I would appreciate it more than I can say." But then he grimaced. "The sheets for your bed are in the dryer in the laundry room. I apologize. I wanted to have it made up when you got here."

"Oh. No worries. Sofie showed me around." Who was this guy? Cranky and ill-tempered with her on the one hand and then full of remorse about sheets on the other? "That's fine. I can do it. Any special instructions regarding the girls?"

"No, not really. They'll guide you through it. Although, I need to tell you…" His voice trailed off thoughtfully while his focus drifted behind her. Gray eyes latched on to hers again and the intensity she saw there had her bracing herself for some truly horrific news. "I probably should mention that they can be kind of a handful."

"A handful?"

"Several hands probably, at least that's what Sofie would say. Their last couple of babysitters would say worse." He sighed. "It's just that they've never had a mom or a steady female influence for…quite a while. Their longtime babysitter, Annie, passed away a year and a half ago.

We've been struggling to get someone regular since then."

"I'm so sorry for your loss. I completely get what you're saying. Kids need structure. Don't worry, I'm sure I can get them tucked in. We'll talk in the morning." No mom at all? Which prompted thoughts of the poor cow mom who needed his help. Waving a hand, she shooed him away. "Go. We'll be fine. Go and do your rancher midwife thing."

She liked the way one side of his mouth twitched like he was fighting a smile. "Rancher midwife," he finally said, repeating the words. "I'll do that."

Lydia forced herself not to fidget and watched, fascinated, as his lips curled and puckered like he was going to... What was he going to do?

An ear-splitting whistle pierced the air.

Lydia yelped and threw a hand over her chest. "Crikey! What the—?"

He winced. "Oh shh-oot. Sorry." Trout dashed into the room. Ears up, tail wagging, the dog skidded to a stop by his side.

Putting a hand on the dog's head, he asked, "Ready, my man?"

Trout answered with a single bark. Blackwell gave Lydia a final assessing look, his gray eyes blazing with an intensity that clogged her throat.

"Good night, Ms. Lydia. And thank you." His voice was soft and deep, the tone sincere.

She felt a little light-headed as she watched man and dog disappear through the doorway that Sofie had told her led outside and to the JB Bar Ranch beyond. Ms. Lydia? A warm flush heated her cheeks and neck. She managed to wheeze out a breathy "Good night" that he probably didn't hear. She was glad because she knew her voice sounded weird. A few minutes ago, she'd wanted to run off and now she wanted to fan herself. What was up with that?

It was just relief, she assured herself. Terror, hopelessness, desperation and anxiety so acute she'd barely slept in days, followed by two days of traveling, would scramble a person's brain. Added to the mix was the sobering realization that her boss didn't seem to like her and the single teenaged girl she'd signed up to ferry around was in reality two busy preschoolers. Exhaustion was setting in. But the thought that she might finally be safe left a small smile on her face.

She'd do anything to stay that way. Wrangling a pair of out-of-control twins and sparring with their irritable father seemed like a cakewalk compared to what she was running from.

CHAPTER FOUR

"You don't look nothin' like a old pear."

Lydia looked at Genevieve. "Excuse me?"

"It's noth-*ing*, Gen," Abby said. "Not nothin'."

"I know that, Abby, but I like the way Tom says nothin'."

Abby rolled her eyes at her sister. "Well, I think you should say you don't look *anything* like an old pear." Face taut with concentration, she studied Lydia. "But she's right, you don't."

"Who told you I did? And are we talking about fruit or boots?"

"Tom," Gen answered.

"Fruit," Abby said.

"Tom said I look like an old pear?" Lydia asked.

Abby explained, "No, Tom said we were getting an old pear. It's a fancy name for a nanny."

Ah. Lydia smothered a laugh. "Actually, it's *au* pair not *old* pear."

Gen frowned. "Oh. What's an oh pear? That don't make no sense."

"It's a French term," Lydia said, choosing not to correct the child's grammar quite yet.

"Like a French fry?" Gen asked.

"Crepes are French," Abby stated knowingly. "They're real skinny pancakes."

Gen gushed, "I *lo-o-ove* pancakes. Buttermilk pancakes are right yummy vittles."

"Let me guess." Lydia looked at Abby, whose eyes had gone skyward again. "Tom?"

"Mmm-hmm. Sofie says he talks like a movie cowboy."

"Who is Tom, exactly?"

"Tom is Daddy's foreman. Gen *lo-o-oves* him."

Gen scowled at her sister. "Only because I'm gonna be a ranch foreman someday. Like Katie."

"Katie doesn't talk that way."

Lydia held out her hands, palms down, fingers spread. She'd herded the girls into the bathroom to commence bedtime preparations. "Okay, hold on." It was already going to be a challenge to become fluent in five-year-old, but five-year-old-aspiring-cowgirl was going to require some serious effort.

"Now who is Katie?"

Abby explained, "Katie is Lochlan's daughter. He's the foreman at Big E's ranch."

Gen fiddled with the faucet. Being still didn't appear to be the child's greatest strength. "But

Katie should take over soon. I heard Daddy tell Tom."

They had already mentioned Big E and Lydia now knew him to be the girls' great-grandfather—Blackwell's grandfather—and he was married to Zoe. Lydia wondered about his parents, but knew introducing yet another topic would only further delay her immediate mission.

"Interesting. Thank you. We'll discuss this more later. For now, let's get back to bath time."

"We like to take showers now that we're five."

"Great. Showers it is. We're going to do this like an assembly line. I'll wash your hair first, Abby. Then you can hop in the shower while I wash Gen's. Then you can shower, Gen. Got it? Use soap, okay?"

Gen groaned. "Do I have to take a shower?"

"What's a *sembly* line?" Abby asked. "Is that French, too?"

"Yes, you do have to take a shower, Gen. It's as-sem-bly line, Abby," she said, enunciating carefully. "And an assembly line is an organized way of doing things. As far as I know, it's not French."

"Why?" Gen demanded, still fixated on the apparent torture of sanitization unfolding before her.

"You don't smell like flowers for one thing, and for another you both need your hair washed."

"Flowers?" Gen repeated, her face scrunched thoughtfully.

"I hate getting my hair washed." This from Abby, whom Lydia had already deduced was slightly more amenable to hygiene and civilized behavior than her sister.

"Why's that?"

"It hurts."

"What do you mean it hurts? Washing your hair shouldn't hurt."

"It's the after part. It gets all snarly like a rat's nest—that's what Daddy calls it—and it hurts to brush it."

"I see. Well, that's no good." Lydia took a moment to scope out the toiletries—soap, toothpaste, toothbrushes and basic first-aid supplies. Another cupboard held fluffy orange and yellow towels. The shower curtain featured brightly colored jungle animals. No razors, shaving cream, aftershave, cologne or other manly potions in evidence. Blackwell apparently had his own personal domain, which was a relief. She didn't relish the idea of sharing a bathroom with him. In the shower, she spotted a single bottle. She picked it up and said, "'Shampoo and conditioner in one.'" That explained it.

"Wait right here. No more rat's nests for you." She started to walk out the door and then stopped as it occurred to her that there was a good possibility they might not be here when she returned. Nibbling her lip, she thought for a second. "I have two important things I need you guys to do while I'm gone. Abby, can you find some cotton balls? Gen, can you gather up all the hair bands in that basket and put them in a pile?" Lydia pointed to a container on the counter, where she'd noticed the hair accessories were kept. "Can you guys do that?"

They both nodded solemnly, neither questioning their assigned task.

Lydia dashed to her bedroom. She'd only brought one small suitcase but it included a travel-sized bottle of leave-in conditioner. Three heads of long hair meant it wasn't going to last long. She added conditioner to the supply list she'd already started. Under *boots* and *jeans* she wrote *conditioner*.

Upon reentering the bathroom, she assessed the work they'd done. "Thank you. Great job, girls. Now, I'll make you a deal. If you let me wash your hair, and you take your showers without complaint, we'll watch a little TV before bed."

"We don't have TV. We can watch movies in Daddy's pickup."

No TV? Lydia thought quickly. There were lots of things that might motivate a five-year-old. The problem was that she'd just got here and didn't know the girls yet or the resources she had to draw from.

"We have internet," Abby announced. "We watch movies on the computer sometimes."

"Perfect." Lydia smiled. "I have a computer. We'll see what we can do."

JON NOTICED TWO things when he stepped inside the house the next morning—it smelled like bacon and it was very quiet. Heaving out a tired breath, he lowered himself onto the bench and pulled off his boots. He took a moment to enjoy the silence, but mostly used it as an excuse to rest his aching back and think about the day's chores ahead.

The calves born last night and this morning put them approximately halfway through the calving. The heavies, or most heavily pregnant cows and heifers, were waiting. Close to labor, they'd been moved into a smaller pasture, where they were monitored by Jon, Tom and his hired hands. Mother Nature had blessed them with a week of mild weather, allowing the cows to give birth outside like they preferred. It also meant less work because they didn't have to cut the cows who were in labor from the rest of the herd and get them into the shed. It was a tedious job because that herd instinct was a strong one and they balked at being separated.

Grabbing a towel, he saw to Trout and then stood. He headed into the kitchen, where he discovered evidence that the nanny had been cooking. He could hear muffled conversation in the next room.

As he neared the doorway, a voice asked, "What about this one? What letter is this, Gen?"

Jon froze and Trout followed his cue, standing at attention beside him. "Um, is it a *P*?" It pained his perpetually raw heart to hear the uncertainty in his daughter's voice. Genevieve was struggling to learn her letters and numbers. Jon knew he needed to spend more time teaching the girls and he planned to as soon as calving season wound down. All the things he needed to do bore down on him like a full-out stampede.

"That's close. It's a *D*."

"*Dagnabbit!* I always get that one wrong. I'm sorry. I'm not smart like Abby."

"You're not supposed to say that," Abby said. "It's almost a bad word."

"Listen here, young lady," Lydia said, "you are incredibly smart. Anyone who can recite every breed of horse on this planet, where they live and what they're used for is completely brilliant. There are all kinds of smarts out there. You'll get this. I promise. Then you can read all about horses yourself. And, just so you know, *dagnabbit* starts with a *D*."

Jon smiled. The words and the encouragement in Lydia's tone eased a bit of his ache. Sounded like she had the teaching skills—too bad she couldn't stay. Jon had already called the agency, but Eileen, the woman who'd handled his application, was on vacation until the middle of April. No one else seemed to be familiar with his situation. He'd been informed he could start the application process all over or wait for Eileen to return. He doubted Lydia could teach Gen to read in two weeks. Doubted she'd want to stay, anyway, after he told her she wasn't suitable.

Jon motioned to Trout and the dog bolted forward into the room. Jon followed, his lungs constricting so tight at what he found that it took several seconds before he could draw a proper breath. Abby was lounging against a pillow on the sofa, an open book across her lap. Gen sat on the floor in front of Lydia, who was doing her hair. Lydia deserved a bonus for this task alone. Little-girl hair was a mystery to him. He had a difficult time even getting a brush through their curls. The ponytails he managed rarely lasted through a day.

"Hi, Daddy!" Gen cried. "How many new calves?"

"A bunch."

"Yay! How are they?"

"Feisty, healthy, hungry fuzzballs. Cute as can be."

"I can't wait to see them!"

"After breakfast."

Abby sat forward, turning to look at him. "We already had breakfast."

"Oh," he said, noticing her hair was already done. Braided and twisted into a pretty little bun on top of her head. Clean clothes, clean face, even clean hands clutching that book in her lap.

"Did you—"

"Yep," she interrupted, "already brushed my teeth. *Seeee*," she drawled, "showing" him the evidence as if he could tell from her clownlike grin.

"Excellent job. Shiny and white, just like the dentist ordered." Which reminded him that they had upcoming appointments. A wave of dread rolled over him. The last one had not gone well.

Lydia looked up and smiled. "The girls told me they usually eat in the bunkhouse with you, but I didn't know what time you'd be back in this morning and we were hungry. There's bacon and pancakes keeping warm in the oven in case you haven't eaten? And I can scramble a couple of eggs."

"Buttermilk pancakes, Daddy," Gen said. "Real ones. And Lydia is doing our hair all pretty like hers."

Jon took a minute to absorb the myriad of feelings churning inside of him and wreaking havoc on both his body and his brain. It had been a long, long time since he'd entertained feelings like the ones tumbling through him right now—relief that the girls seemed to like Lydia, happiness that she seemed to like them and longing so intense it catapulted him back to a place he tried not to go. Why couldn't Ava have wanted this? He immediately reminded himself that he was paying Lydia Newbury to shower this kind of attention on his daughters. And she wasn't sticking around.

"That sounds just fine to me. We can talk while the girls head out for a look at the calves."

"Great." Lydia flashed him another bright smile. "You, sweet girl, are all done." Placing a hand on each of her shoulders, she bent and kissed the top of Gen's head and Jon felt that, too, like a warm surge right in the pit of his stomach. "You want to see?"

Gen took the mirror from Lydia and admired her handiwork. With her other hand, she patted the neat braids. Normally Gen didn't care much about her hair, but the expression on her face right now reminded him a lot of how his daughter looked on Christmas morning. When she wrapped her arms around Lydia for a hug, sweetness dug right into him along with the regret. He'd hoped Lydia would be gone before the girls got too attached.

"I'll text Tom that you're on the way."

"Thanks, Daddy." They skipped over to him and one at a time he scooped them up for a quick hug and set them back on their feet closer to the door. Together, they ran toward the kitchen.

Jon tapped out a text to Tom.

Lydia began tidying up the space around her. "I'll put this stuff away and meet you in the kitchen. There's a fresh pot of coffee."

"All right then."

Jon headed there, poured himself a cup and took a sip. Dang, it was good coffee, too. Standing at the window, he could see the barns, the shop, the chicken coop, woodshed and various other outbuildings. He tried to imagine what it might look like to a woman from Philadelphia who'd never seen it, or any ranch at all. The flower beds needed weeding and the three raised garden beds could use some attention. Cows and their bright red-brown calves stood in the east pasture. That had to be an appealing sight, didn't it?

The reality wasn't like television, that was true, but it was his and he loved pretty much everything about it. At the end of every day he wouldn't trade the long hours he spent blistering under a blazing summer sun, or shivering in a winter cold so brutal it seemed to gnaw right into his bones, for any other job in the world. Not even in the midst of calving season, when he rarely slept more than two or three hours at a stretch and worry was his constant companion.

There were roughly a million things that warranted his attention and concern. In addition to constant monitoring of the cows and heifers before labor, there was the birth itself. Then, would the cow accept her new calf? Was the cow producing enough milk? Was the calf nursing? A ton of health problems could befall a calf, not the least of which was scours, which could race through a herd like wildfire. Inclement weather brought on a host of difficulties, too.

During these few weeks, Jon barely took time to eat. When he did get a moment to shower or change his clothes, there wasn't time to enjoy it because soon after he'd be knee-deep in mud and manure, or shoulder-deep inside a cow assisting with a birth. But every second of this life fed his soul; he needed it, the bad and the good, just like he needed air to breathe.

He wondered what Lydia Newbury needed? What could a woman from Philadelphia possibly think she'd find on a ranch in Montana? Life here could only lead to disappointment.

Sighing, he turned away from the window. Why was he spending time worrying and wondering what she thought? This wasn't the place for her and because of that she wasn't the right nanny for his girls. Not used to being idle, he spotted the eggs on the counter and cracked a few into a bowl.

"Hey, are you doing my job for me?" Lydia asked, hurrying over to join him. Pointing toward the island, she said, "Sit." Beside him, Trout obediently parked his butt on the tile floor.

"Oh, my gosh!" Her grin was pure delight and Jon couldn't help but smile inside. "That's amazing. Does he obey like that for everyone?"

Mustering up his best poker face, Jon shook his head. "He does not. Usually, just me. But when you shout at him like that he's bound to listen." He glanced at Trout, who was giving him an expectant look. Jon signaled his release and the dog trotted over to his water dish.

"I didn't shou—" The furrow in her brow was downright cute and he couldn't maintain a straight face. "Oh. You're joking?"

He chuckled. "I am."

The sound of her laughter filled the room, working into him in a very nice way. Jon kept his eyes on her because she was focused on Trout.

"Did you tell him something with your hand?"

"Yep." He moved around the island to take a stool. Not only had she gotten the girls dressed for the day, but she'd also taken care of herself. Her clothing choice was a sight more practical than her getup of the day before. In her snug jeans, stocking feet and button-down shirt, with a tank top peeking out the top, she could almost pass for a local girl. Almost.

"Incredible. I've never met such a well-trained dog."

"It's not training, not really."

"What do you mean?"

"It's more like understanding. Dogs are special that way. They're like friends. Treat them right and most of them will do about anything for you. Just gotta figure out how to ask."

"Hmm. That's nice. You obviously have good friends." She'd been whisking the eggs, and she poured them into the pan and stirred. She removed the pancakes and bacon from the oven and fixed his plate.

He watched her, mesmerized by the way she moved, fluid and efficient, like a swan or some other graceful, pretty bird.

"You know your way around a kitchen."

"That I do." She paused to look at him like she was going to tell him something important. "And I have to say, yours is incredible. Like my dream kitchen."

"Thank you." He felt himself smiling at the enthusiasm in her tone. He'd designed the space

himself and it was nice to hear a cook appreciate it. "Self-taught?"

"That nana I mentioned last night taught me
the basics and then I had a few restaurant jobs
over the years. I worked for a caterer and a bakery, too, so lucky you." With a wink, she pushed
his plate across the counter and handed him silverware. "I guess I should ask if cooking is part
of my job. I mean, if the girls mostly eat with
you in the bunkhouse?"

"That's expediency, because it's calving time.
I try to cook for us when it's not."

Looking thoughtful, she turned and poured
herself a cup of coffee. When she faced him
again, her expression was twisted up a bit and
he knew she had something to say.

"So now that I'm here, I'll be cooking, and
they can eat with me. I think they need to learn
some table manners. And I'd like to suggest we
have dinner together, or you should have dinner with them at least because…" She added
an earnest look. "Because family dinners are
important."

Did she think he didn't know this about his
girls? It stung a little but at the same time he
appreciated that she spoke her mind. This was
only one small part of the reason he needed her.
Well, not her, but a nanny.

"I agree with that."

"Good." As she leaned against the counter, he caught a nice view of the pale skin of her face and neck. The creamy smoothness was nearly perfect, a testament to the hours she spent indoors. Unlike him.

"This is all delicious," he said, because it was and because he realized she was watching him. "These pancakes might even be as good as Willa's."

"Ha. I'm sure they're better." She added a confident nod. "But who is this Willa competing for my top pancake honors? I hereby challenge her to a pancake throw-down."

Jon laughed even as he wished she'd quit being so likable. It made this so much more difficult. "Willa Carnes, my neighbor. My best friend Zach's mom. You met Sofie last night. She's married to Zach. Willa is her mother-in-law."

"Ranchers?"

"Yep."

"Hmm. Lots of ranching going on around here, huh? Scooter mentioned a place called Blackwell Guest Ranch?"

"Yep, that would be my grandfather's place."

"Big E?"

Jon wasn't surprised she'd already heard his name. The man was, if not infamous, then certainly renowned. "Elias Blackwell is his name but most everyone calls him Big E."

"Does he live there with your parents?"

"He did, and so did I, until they died." Jon managed to keep his voice flat and even, but it still surprised him how much it hurt to say the words out loud.

"Oh. I'm so sorry." Sincerity infused her tone, making Jon suspect she was no stranger to grief herself. "Do you have other family?"

"Four brothers." He scooped up another bite.

"Do they live on the ranch?"

"Not anymore."

"Older or younger?"

"I'm the oldest. Three years younger are Ethan and Ben. Then two years after them, Chance and Tyler."

"Wait, wait!" Hand up, she took a second to absorb that news. "Back the tractor up—your brothers are twin twins?"

"Twin twins?" He chuckled. "I don't think I've heard that one before. Did you make that up?"

"I don't know." Grinning, she shook her head. "There's just so many twins. And you have twins. It's…"

"It is a fact that I have been the odd man out my entire life."

Inquisitive blue eyes searched his before exploring the rest of his face and then traveling down to his hands and back up again. Her voice edged with wonder and maybe sympathy, she said, "Huh. I can't imagine…"

She couldn't. No one could. Being surrounded by twins, and looking after his younger brothers after their parents died, was a unique experience. He knew that. Then, to finally get out on his own, only to accidentally start a family and find out that he would be the father of twins? Honestly, it had felt like a blessing and a curse. And girls, to boot. If there was one area of his life that was his biggest weakness, it would be women. His string of stepgrandmothers hadn't been interested in fulfilling any type of maternal role. He'd been shy in school and there weren't any girls his age hanging around the ranch when he was growing up. Katie and her sister Maura were younger and close enough to being family that he hadn't paid attention in any meaningful way.

He loved his daughters with every fiber of his being, yet his heart was perpetually raw and achy where they were concerned. He knew he wasn't doing right by them. It seemed as if when things were going well in one area, they were lacking in another. Like if he spent too much time cooking healthy meals, he didn't have enough left over to read to them. If he was teaching them about the ranch, there was no time for games. If they were riding horses, there was no book learning going on. He spent a lot of time wondering how other single parents got along. But he didn't want to talk about that.

Shrugging a shoulder, he hoped to throw her off the subject. "It is what it is."

Her sympathetic smile told him she knew it was more than that, yet she let it go. He appreciated that. "So, do you have like a list for me? I reviewed my paperwork last night and all it says is some cooking, which we just covered, light cleaning, child care and other. We need to talk about that other."

"We need to have a different discussion."

Her inquisitive gaze met his. "Oh. Okay?"

"I'm going to get right to the point."

"Please do."

The phone in his pocket alerted him that Katie was calling. "Excuse me a second." He swiped the screen to answer it. "Hey, Katie, what's up?"

"Jon, I know you're coming over later to take care of that bill, but I have a situation. Is there any chance you can move it up?"

"Sure. What time?"

"As soon as possible."

"What's going on?"

He knew her sigh of irritation wasn't directed at him. "It would save us both a lot of time if I could explain when you get here. You know I wouldn't ask if it wasn't important."

Unnerving how he'd heard those same words from Grace the day before.

"I do know that. I'll leave right now."

He clicked off the phone and looked at Lydia. "I'm sorry. I'm going to have to ask that we postpone this conversation again. I need to head out to my grandfather's place."

CHAPTER FIVE

TRAVEL ALONE WOULD slice precious time out of Jon's day. Property lines and gravel roads meant zigzagging and relatively slow-going for miles. And that was before he reached the long driveway to Big E's house and the barns. It would be faster to ride his horse, or an ATV, but opening and closing gates, fencing and cross fencing on neighboring lands would impede him too much this time of year.

The shortest route would have him crossing Double T land. Relations between the Thompsons and the Blackwells had lately been, if not peaceful, then uneventful. But Jon wasn't about to do anything to remind them of the victory Big E and Ben had won concerning water rights. And most importantly, Jon couldn't pack nearly as much gear on a horse or an ATV.

Maybe Big E had given Ethan some clue as to where he was going. Busy as his brother had been with college and veterinary school for so many years, his visits were infrequent and quick. But he'd been back a couple of months ago for

Sara Ashley Gardner's wedding. Sara Ashley was Grace's sister and Ethan's ex. He'd stayed with Jon while he was in town and it had been great spending some real time with his brother again.

Ethan answered on the fourth ring. "Jon, hey, what's up? Everything okay?" As expected, his brother's voice was laced with concern. Ethan knew it was calving season. None of his brothers would expect a call from him now unless it was urgent.

"Ethan. Yep, everything is fine. I think." He paused. "Or not. Have you talked to Big E lately?"

"Just once since I was there and that was two weeks ago. What's going on?"

"Trying to track him down. Big E and Zoe took off in their motorhome about a week ago. The bill at Brewster's hasn't been paid for a while. Katie needs to order feed and supplies, and the store can't extend any more credit."

"Took off? Where did they go?"

"No one seems to know. Not anyone here anyhow."

"Have you talked to anyone else?" Jon knew he meant their other three brothers.

"Not yet. I was thinking we could divide and conquer. I'll call Tyler if you want to call Chance."

"What about Ben? He doesn't want to hear from me."

"I won't fare much better. I'm thinking we both call Ben. Maybe if we each leave him a message he'll think it's important enough to call one of us back. Although I doubt Ben has talked to anyone, and especially not Big E."

Zoe had been engaged to Ben when she threw him over for Big E. Their brother was bitter. Rightly so, seeing as how Jon and Ethan had inadvertently encouraged it. Not the wedding so much, as they'd wanted Ben out of Zoe's clutches. The whole thing had been a mess. Jon wished Ben would give them an opportunity to clear the air. Their brother had to know by now that Zoe was no good for him.

Ethan whooshed out a breath. "Okay, I'll call them both."

"Thanks, Ethan."

"Big E left without paying the bill at Brewster's?"

"Yep. You know that no one can sign on the account except for him or one of us boys."

"Yeah. Did you, uh, talk to Grace?"

"Grace is the one who informed me. Pulled me into her office yesterday. Katie was there."

"Did she mention me?"

"Who, Katie?"

"No, not Katie, Grace."

"Why would Grace mention you?"

"She wouldn't. Never mind."

Jon hoped Ethan wasn't torn up about Sara Ashley's marriage. He'd thought his brother was over that relationship. He didn't have time to ponder that or the sad state of his disconnected family. "I feel bad for Katie. Either let her run the place, or not. I swear, I don't know why she sticks around."

"We both know why she sticks around."

"True." Because the two things Katie loved more than anything in the world were at the Blackwell Ranch—her father, Lochlan, and the horses, many that she'd trained up from colts.

"What are you going to do?"

"I'm on my way there now. Katie called this morning saying she needed me ASAP, which causes me extra concern."

"This is weird. Stupid question, but you've called him, right? Our wayward grandfather?"

"Three times. Two messages. Even called Zoe's phone. Texted her, too."

"Huh. Well, let's hope they're just out of cell-phone range. Maybe he went to see that friend of his in New Mexico. The survivalist who lives in the adobe hut out in the middle of nowhere without power."

"Carl Clutch. Had that same thought seeing as how they took the motorhome."

"But why the secrecy?"

"With Big E? Who knows? I'll let you go. Got some more calls to make before I get there. I'll keep you posted."

"All right. Good luck."

"Thank you. Something tells me I'm going to need it. And Ethan?"

"Yeah?"

"It sure was nice having you back here. The girls are still talking about you. Getting a little tired of all the 'Uncle Ethan this and Uncle Ethan that.' Abby wants to be a vet."

Ethan chuckled. "Thanks, brother. It was good being there. I miss my nieces. We'll talk soon."

Jon called Tom, briefly explained the situation and told him he'd be gone for a good while. They discussed ranch matters. Then he called Tyler and Ben. No surprise, neither one answered, so he left messages. He didn't provide any details, just asked them to call back. It seemed too early to suggest something was amiss. He had no proof anything was wrong, other than the sour feeling in his gut, which settled deeper as he steered the pickup through the grand iron arch.

As far as Jon knew, the large metal sign had arced over the entrance forever; Blackwell Family Ranch. He crept along the lengthy drive that led to his childhood home. All around him was the land—the ranch—where six generations of

Blackwells had lived. A surprising twinge of nostalgia had him wondering what his great-great-granddad had seen and thought when he first stepped foot here. Could he have had even an inkling of all the turmoil this place would witness? The births and the deaths, marriages and divorces, drought and flood, feast and famine, love and hate, and all the accompanying memories both peaceful and painful. It seemed more than any family should have to endure. And for the first time in Jon's life, he wondered if it would be home to a seventh generation. He pondered whether it even should.

LYDIA UNZIPPED HER suitcase and dug a slip of paper out from the lining. Fingers trembling, she unfolded the list and memorized the phone number at the top. She unplugged the phone from the charger, where she'd left it the night before, and dialed.

Tanner picked up on the second ring. "Lydia! Finally! Are you okay?"

"Yes. It's all good. I made it safe and sound. I couldn't call last night because the phone was dead. I haven't had a free moment until now."

Jon had told her that Tom would drop in to take the girls for a ride in the afternoon. Abby was right; he did talk like a movie cowboy. He'd shown up after lunch with a "Howdy, ma'am" and then a "much obliged" after she'd offered him cookies she'd made. He'd collected the girls' helmets from the mudroom and politely invited her out to watch them ride. Concern must have shown on her face because he explained that the riding they were going to be doing consisted of him leading their horses around the corral.

She'd wanted to go. Two things had stopped her, the most pressing of which was this phone call. The other would have to wait.

"That's fine. I'm just glad you're okay. How are things going?"

"So far, so good."

"What do you think of Montana?"

"It's gorgeous." That part was true. No way would she complain about the kid mix-up or her grumpy boss, who possibly wasn't quite as grumpy as she'd thought. "And I feel…safe. Tanner, thank you so much. I would never have been able to get this far without you." Tanner was one of her oldest friends. They'd met through their work with Hatch House Group Home for Teens, where Lydia had once lived before eventually becoming a volunteer. Tanner was the attorney who handled all the group home's legal needs. Clive knew how close they were. It would be one of the first places he went. Tears sprung to her eyes, catching her off guard. She blinked them away.

"We'll get you farther, I promise." When the dust settled, she'd be moving on, hopefully overseas. How long that took depended mainly on Clive and how hard he searched for her.

"Any news? Have you heard from Clive? Have you heard anything about the money?"

"According to my calculations, I should be hearing about both very soon."

"What if he—?" Lydia didn't want to say it but she was terrified of what Clive would do if he suspected Tanner knew something. Or her best friend, Meredith.

"Lydia, he knows he'd never get anything out of me. Assuming I know anything," he joked, like the good attorney he was.

Lydia managed a shaky smile. "Okay. But what about Meredith?"

"She'll be fine. We've been over this. Let's worry about you right now. Just lay low until we figure out your next move."

"That reminds me, I need some stuff. I forgot to pack my ranching clothes."

"Ranching clothes," he repeated with a laugh, and she relished the sound.

"For some reason, even when you told me I was going to a ranch, I never expected it to be this…muddy."

She glanced at her suitcase, still open on the floor. Her boots were sitting next to it. What

Jon and the girls observed was true—the buttery soft, high-heeled boots wouldn't be good for much around here. Certainly not for a horseback ride or that barn party Abby mentioned. They wouldn't even do for a trip out to the barn.

Lydia was dying to see the ranch. Problem was, she'd only packed two pairs of shoes besides the boots, a pair of flip-flops and some supple leather slippers with no lining or traction. The suitcase was packed weeks before she'd ever left Philadelphia. It had been stashed at Tanner's house until the day she'd left.

Stuffing a wide variety of items inside the carry-on had seemed like a good idea at the time. Now, it seemed like a meager and odd mix, very little of which was suitable for life on a ranch. She only had one pair of jeans. Why hadn't she thought to throw in a pair of sneakers? At least she had yoga pants and a few T-shirts.

"I'd prefer you stay out of sight for the time being. Falcon Creek is a small town and people are going to remember you, Lydia. Especially if you go around buying a new wardrobe."

"I know. I don't know if there's much for shopping in Falcon Creek, anyway. And it's a long drive to a city or even a town of any real size."

"Is there internet?"

"Yes, thank goodness." Smiling, she thought of how much the girls had enjoyed the TV show she'd streamed the evening before.

"Order online."

"I don't have a credit card anymore."

"Inside that bundle I gave you, with the documents and the cash, there is a couple of thousand dollars in gift cards. Use those."

"Seriously?" A current of relief flowed through her. "I can't believe you thought of this. Have I told you lately that I love you and you're brilliant?"

"Remember, you need to be untraceable. Speaking of that, it would be best if you only used this phone for communicating with me or for emergencies. And no calling anyone from your old life. Except me. At this number only. If you do use it, don't store any numbers in your contacts and delete everything, every time you use it."

Her old life. Her throat went tight. "Got it. Tanner…" The past few months, with her fear gradually increasing to full-blown terror, it hadn't occurred to her how much she might miss her life in Philadelphia. She had no relationship with her family, she didn't own a home and, because of her itinerant ways, she'd never been one to accumulate possessions. She'd never had any pets, probably for the same reason. Those things made moving on easier. But she loved her two best friends, Tanner being one. Meredith was the other and she couldn't imagine not talking to her every day. They'd been roommates for years.

"Lydia, hon, I'm so sorry. It won't be forever. I just don't know how long it will be. In the meantime, we need to keep you safe."

"I know."

"How's the nanny gig? I'm assuming you have your teenaged charge toeing the line by now?"

"Funny story. Turns out my one fourteen-year-old is two four-year-olds, who recently turned five."

"Five-year-old twins?"

"Yep."

"Yowza."

"Tell me about it."

"I know you're good with teens but what about little ones? Do you have any experience with those?"

"Some." Meredith had a huge family, and Lydia was an honorary member. Meredith's sister Hailey had five kids and Lydia had helped babysit occasionally. And she'd been great with her stepsiblings for the short time she'd lived with them. Never mind that it had been more than a decade since she'd left home and she hadn't seen them since.

"Tanner, please, don't worry about me. I'll

figure this part out. You focus on Clive. Stay safe. Keep Meredith safe."

JON SENSED TROUBLE as soon as he and Trout walked around the corner of the barn at the Blackwell Ranch and saw JT Brimble standing there. The man's back was to Jon but JT's ridiculous hair was unmistakable, even with the long blond curls tied back beneath his cowboy hat. JT oozed a sticky-sweet, good-ol'-boy charm and fancied himself a bull rider. He did odd jobs around the Blackwell Ranch for Big E, jobs that took him too long with mediocre results. Jon had warned his grandfather that the guy was trouble, but he had it on good authority that JT was friendly with Zoe.

Katie stood in front of JT, gloved hands fisted on her hips. With a disgusted shake of her head she said, "JT, I am telling you for the last time, you need to take this up with Big E. He is not here, and I don't want you coming back 'til he personally informs you that he wants to see you."

Of medium height, JT wasn't a big man, but he was muscled and wiry.

"And I'm telling you, Katie—" JT took a step toward her, finger pointed way too close to her face. Jon's blood went hot. If the man so much as touched a hair on Katie's head, the EMTs would have to pick him off the ground with a pitchfork. "—I need to get paid what I'm owed—"

Jon interrupted as he approached, "She's not giving you a dime, JT, or anything else for that matter." He stopped a few feet away. "Now, I'm going to make the following suggestion one time and one time only. Back off and remove your finger from the vicinity of Katie's face or I promise you I will break it off and a couple more appendages, too, for good measure."

JT shot an irritated glance in his direction. "Leave it be, Jon. This isn't your business."

"That was your warning." Jon removed his hat and set it on a fence post off to the side. "Katie, call 911." He took a step toward JT. Trout let out a growl. Katie's cattle dog, Hip, joined in.

JT jumped back, hands raised, palms up in a conciliatory gesture. "Hey, now, there's no need for violence. I'm just here to collect what's owed me."

Jon settled the hat back on his head and asked, "And what is that exactly?"

"Three hundred and eighty-five dollars."

"Katie owes you three hundred and eighty-five dollars?" Jon repeated skeptically.

"Big E owes it to me."

Jon looked at a scowling Katie. "Katie?"

She sighed. "He's owed something, but I doubt Big E would pay him the full amount.

He was supposed to dig post holes and put up fencing for the pigpen, but he's only done maybe half the work."

Pigs? The Blackwell Ranch didn't raise pigs, but that question could wait. Jon wasn't about to air ranch business in front of JT.

"All right. Let's go have a look at the pen."

A few minutes later, Jon could see Katie was right, and he said as much. JT claimed that Big E often paid him before work was complete. "Like a draw," he argued.

"Big E might operate that way, but I don't."

"But I'm telling you, Big E does. We have a deal."

"Do you see Big E here?" Lifting an arm, Jon swept it around for effect. "I'll pay you what you're owed for what you've done and then you're not to step foot back on this land until you're invited by a Blackwell or by Katie. Is that clear?" Jon pulled out his wallet and handed over 150 dollars.

JT counted out the bills and then stuffed them into his pants pocket. Then he smirked at Katie. "You can invite me anytime, sugar."

"JT, I wouldn't invite you to scrape manure off my boots. Now, get out of here."

Jon and Katie watched him head to his pickup and climb inside.

Jon slid a glance at Katie. "Pigs?"

"Zoe says they will add 'atmosphere' to the guest ranch."

"Does she have any idea how much pigs stink?"

Katie belted out a laugh. "Daddy said the same thing."

"Your daddy is a smart man. Big E is okay with this?"

"Yes, he is. Pigs are only one small part of this project. It's going to be a petting zoo."

"A petting zoo?" Jon repeated, not bothering to hide his disdain.

Shrugging, she said, "It's not the worst idea she's had. The tourists will love it."

"I will refrain from commenting."

"Probably best." She flashed him a grin. "We all know your opinions on guest ranching."

On that point, he and Ethan agreed. Unfortunately, ranching was a tough way to make a living. Most every beef rancher he knew supplemented their income in one way or another. In addition to the horse-breeding operation Katie oversaw, his grandfather had expanded into guest ranching. Zach raised horses. Jon did consulting work for ranchers seeking to go "green" and wrote articles on the topic for *Organic Beef Newsletter* and other ranching magazines. Occasionally, he taught a class or gave a workshop.

In a few weeks when calving season ended, a

journalist and a TV crew from a national cable show were coming to interview him for a segment on organic-beef ranching. When they'd contacted him, he'd been reluctant. He hadn't been thrilled about the notion of having his face and life splashed all over TV. Then Bethany Stouffer had called him herself and assured Jon they'd "work together to raise awareness for the industry and shine a favorable light on grass-fed beef." He'd accepted.

Katie pointed her chin toward JT's pickup crawling along the gravel drive. "Thank you for that. Normally I'd be irritated with you for coming to my rescue, taking care of myself and all that, but with everything going on I'm just glad it's done. I was running out of patience."

"I know it. And I know you can handle yourself fine. That guy rubs me the wrong way."

"JT is harmless. I heard he lost a pile of cash gambling the other night. I think he's a little stressed."

"It's possible I may be wound a little too tight myself at the moment."

Katie frowned. "Everything okay?"

No, he wanted to say, thinking about his nanny dilemma. But he didn't. Jon wasn't one to talk about personal matters. He certainly didn't want to burden Katie when she had a slew of her own ranch-related concerns. "Oh, you know, same as you. Too much to do, not enough time."

"For which I'm partially responsible, calling you here and all. I'm sorry about this, Jon."

Jon shook his head. "Don't you apologize to me. This isn't on you. This is all Big E. And likely Zoe."

Katie answered with an affectionate smile that didn't quite reach her eyes. What had Big E been thinking by doing this to her?

"By the way," she said, "JT is not why I asked you here. I need you to make a couple calls for me. The bank and the power company will only speak to you or one of your brothers."

He must have looked puzzled because she explained, "I need to know how much money is in the checking account for the other bills that I'm also going to need you to pay. The power company called today. The account is way overdue and they said they're shutting it off tomorrow if it's not paid today."

"That's odd. Why wouldn't he pay the power bill?"

Katie scoffed. "I think that one is Zoe. She wanted more responsibility, so Big E turned over most of the household bill-paying to her. According to Big E, sometimes she 'forgets.'" Katie's air quotes added a little punch to her wry tone. "Funny how she never forgets when it's something she wants."

"Have you heard from him? Any idea where they've gone?"

"Seriously, Jon?" Katie seemed to ponder the matter over his shoulder, her focus shifting toward the mountains for a few long seconds. "What a mess... Zoe hired Billy's wife, Cindy, to come in and clean once a week. She was here yesterday. Said she went into the master suite to tidy up and Zoe took enough clothes and stuff for a normal person to be away for months, which could translate to weeks for her. What am I going to do? I can't run this place without the funds to do it. I'm not officially in charge but Daddy isn't in any condition to take over again right now."

A mix of sympathy and anger boiled inside of him. Typical of Big E to think about himself first. No, not first—in this case it seemed he'd *only* thought of himself. "How's your dad?"

"Same."

"I'm sorry, Katie." Lochlan had health problems exacerbated by the grief of losing his older daughter, Maura, to cancer a few years previous. Maura had been married to one of Jon's youngest brothers, Chance. Katie had taken her sister's death hard, too. All the Blackwells felt her loss.

Jaw fixed tight, Katie answered with a nod, and that was enough for Jon to know she didn't want to discuss the topic further.

As much as Jon would love to leave his grandfather to clean up this mess when he finally did decide to roll back into town, he couldn't do that to Katie, or to Lochlan, or the other employees who counted on the ranch for their livelihoods. Or to the livestock, for that matter.

"I've got your back, Katie, you know that. Anything you need, just call and I'll be here."

"I do know that, and I appreciate it. But you've got your ranch to run and the girls."

This was truc. How was he going to manage helping here now, too, without child carc?

"Don't worry about that. I plan on sleeping a whole lot when I'm dead. Let's head to the house and see what we can accomplish with those bills. Hopefully, he'll show up soon and we won't have to worry about it for too long."

"Hopefully." Katie nodded, but she didn't look anywhere near convinced.

CHAPTER SIX

THE GIRLS PUT on their boots and coats and headed outside. They were on their way to the bunkhouse to have cookies and hot chocolate with Tom and Dusty. Jon stood at the window and watched them until Dusty stepped out onto the porch and waved them inside. He poured himself a cup of coffee and tried to decide how to begin a difficult conversation.

Lydia stood across the island fidgeting with a dish towel. "So, how is that mama cow you had to help last night? Did she opt for the epidural or did she stick with the more natural *La-mooo-ze* technique?" The twitch of her lips and the twinkle in her eyes added to the jest. She was funny. It was a good thing she wouldn't be here much longer because if he wasn't careful this woman could get right under his skin.

Jon laughed. "That's right, you don't know about the JB Bar Ranch yet. We're an entirely organic, grass-fed, free-range paradise. Only natural childbirth will do for my girls. But she did need a little help getting that calf turned."

"Breech?"

"Wanted to be."

"What?! No way. What did you do?"

"Turned it the right way."

"Which is?"

"Front feet first."

"Holy cow. You really are a midwife."

"Tell me about it," he said flatly. "I'm sure you can imagine how many different ways things can get turned around in there."

A playful grimace on her face, she said, "Yeah, I can think of several right off the top of my head."

He laughed again and she joined him. Why did it feel so nice to laugh with her? Maybe because he hadn't laughed with a woman in a very long time.

"I am *udderly* cow-ignorant. Get it—udder?" She cringed. "That was a bad joke. I apologize. I'm trying to cover up for my embarrassing lack of bovine knowledge."

Still smiling, he said, "I don't imagine there's a lot of cattle grazing around the streets of Philadelphia. I'm guessing at that, though, I've never been there."

"No, you're right. There's not. But I did see a camel downtown once."

That grin of hers was contagious. And it made him curious. What could it hurt to get to know her a bit before she headed back to Philadelphia or moved on to another family? It was possible he was procrastinating but he didn't care.

"Do you have brothers and sisters?"

Eyes shifting, her mouth opened and then closed again as her forehead furrowed.

"I'm sorry, is that a trick question?"

She chuckled. "No. Yeah, um, sort of. I mean, yes, I have a stepbrother, a stepsister and a half sister."

Jon watched her worry the cloth, discomfort splashed all over her face. "Not close?" he asked gently.

"That's one way to put it. They're a lot younger than me and they live in *Florida* with my father and my step—" Changing course, she went with, "His wife."

The "step" aversion he could relate to, but it was kind of funny how she said the word *Florida*. When she didn't elaborate he took it to mean it wasn't a subject she wanted to discuss. That he could also respect. He went with a joke instead. "Yeah, *Florida*."

Her eyes snapped up to meet his and she burst out laughing. "Right? Who would live there? Not a cattle rancher, for sure."

"Actually, the largest ranch in the United States is in Florida."

"It's a gator ranch, though, right?"

He chuckled. "Nope, I meant largest cattle ranch."

She eyed him skeptically. "Is that a bunch of bull?"

"It is not."

"I'm not sure I believe you. You do a really good deadpan."

He grinned. "Why would I lie about that?"

"People lie about all kinds of things," she returned quickly. "For all kinds of reasons."

Leaning against the counter behind him, he studied her. He was struck with the feeling that there was a whole lot more to her than met the eye. Too bad he didn't have time to find out what that was. It reminded him of how he'd felt when he met Ava—intrigued and drawn in by a woman completely different than him. That thought sobered him. Opposites might attract but in Jon's experience that attraction didn't last.

"Not me. I don't lie."

"Really?" Her tone was as skeptical as her expression. "Never?"

"Not about ranching, anyway."

"Well, who would lie about that? Have you always been a rancher?"

"Plenty of people would lie about ranching. And, yes, pretty much since the day I was born. Never wanted anything else."

"Nothing?"

Nothing besides a happy marriage, a wife who wanted to be my partner and a houseful of kids. The words danced across his tongue, surprising him. It was a hard lesson, but he'd learned that not everyone could have it all. Big E, who was on his fifth marriage, was proof of that. Jon was grateful that he learned much quicker than his grandfather. Luckily, she was referring to his career choice and he could tell the truth he'd just claimed he was good for.

"Never wanted to be anything but a rancher."

"Wow. I've always had the opposite problem—trying to figure out what I wanted to do. It must be nice to be so passionate about your work."

"Most of the time." It could also get a little lonely. He had to admit that with Ms. Lydia Newbury around life would probably be anything but lonely. She was like a ray of sunshine standing right in the middle of his kitchen.

That wistful smile was back on her face and it pulled at him like a mystery he wanted to solve. Unfortunately, he needed to get to that work they were discussing, which meant he needed to circle around to the point. He hated the idea of being the one to make that smile fade. "We need to have that talk we started this morning."

She must have picked up on his anxiety because she sobered. "Okay."

Pausing, he struggled for the gentlest approach. Which was not exactly his strong suit. Preferring directness, he decided to give her the same courtesy. "I called the agency to ask them to send a replacement for you."

"What?" Her already pale skin faded to the color of a Montana blizzard. Her palms flattened on the counter in front of her. "You're firing me?"

"I'd rather we agree that I never hired you. The agency gives us both the right to rescind the employment agreement if one party is not satisfactory to the other."

"Not satisfactory? What did I do? I haven't even started."

"I know and I'm sorry for that. I blame the agency."

"What is the problem exactly? I'm sure we can work it out."

"The problem is that you don't have any experience with ranch life. I specifically requested a nanny with a country background."

A long moment drew out between them while her blue eyes traveled over him. Jon wasn't generally susceptible to intimidation, but he found himself feeling uncomfortable. No way to tell if she wanted to cry or hit him with a frying pan.

Finally, she barked out a bitter sound that he wouldn't quite call a laugh. In a tone rife with sarcasm, she asked, "A country nanny? Is that even a thing?"

"I was told it was. Or rather, I was informed I could expect an employee with ranching experience or one who had experience with life in the country." Jon sighed and scrubbed a hand across his now itchy jaw. "I know how it must sound to you, but I need someone familiar with our lifestyle."

"Why didn't you go ahead and order Mary Poppins while you were at it? If this is an April Fool's joke, it's the worst one ever."

"Ms. Lydia, I understand—"

Pointing a finger at him, she bit off the words. "Don't you call me that." Her previously pale cheeks were now pink with what he assumed was anger. He couldn't blame her. She'd come a long way to not even be given a chance.

Stuffing down his guilt was no easy task. "I'm sorry. What should I call you?"

"Lydia," she said through gritted teeth. "My name is Lydia."

"Okay. You can call me Jon."

"That'll be easier now that I don't work for you."

"I understand that you're disappointed. But please try and understand how difficult this is for me. I'm a single dad with a cattle ranch to run. Every minute of my time is taken up with one task or another and I need someone who understands how life works under these conditions. You just told me yourself that you know nothing about cattle. It's not you. I mean it's not personal."

She scoffed. "You have got to be kidding me? This is the first time I've heard the 'it's not you, it's me' speech about a job."

He tried to explain. "You're obviously good with children. In a very short time you've gone quite a long way in proving that, and I admit my children are not easy. I'd be happy to recommend you."

Her glare was formidable. "Recommend me? But isn't what you just pointed out the most important thing? Your children? They like me. And I'm already half in love with them. Can't you teach me the rest?" She gestured around with frustrated hands. "The ranching…country…lifestyle stuff? I'm a quick study and a very hard worker."

Anxious eyes sought his and he couldn't help but feel sorry for her. But he knew what would happen if he acquiesced. He'd seen it with Ava, he'd seen it with Big E's wives. He saw the tendency in the tourists who came to his grandfather's guest ranch. Even if they had the desire, 99 percent of them couldn't handle the kind of stamina and fortitude this life required. Ranching was the center of his world and everything else revolved around it.

"This kind of hard work is not like normal hard work."

Her gaze grabbed a hold of his with surprising intensity. He'd expected her to bow out gracefully. He'd been under the impression the JB Bar wasn't what she'd been hoping for, anyway.

"Listen to me, I've been working since I was fifteen. I've had...a lot of jobs, backbreaking physical labor included. I've never been fired." She paused to add a slow, thoughtful head-tip. "Except for one time but that wasn't my fault. How could I possibly be responsible for a broken water pipe? I promise I can do this." Sincerity mixed with the desperation in her tone. Her eyes were the color of a mountain bluebird and he could feel them pleading.

He cleared his throat. "I believe that you could eventually, but..." He didn't have time for *eventually*. "I don't have time to teach you."

"You have internet. You can learn how to do anything on YouTube these days."

"You want to learn about ranching on the internet?" he asked skeptically.

"Yes! Sort of. I mean not entirely. I would learn as I go, too. And you didn't hire me to be a ranch hand, did you? You just want me to understand ranching life, right? You want like an informed nanny."

"I need a nanny with exceptional skills. It's asking too much of a city…person. Honestly, it's probably too much to ask of a normal person."

"Exceptional how?"

Frustrated by both the situation and the need to let her go, he drew in a deep breath. Then he said, "I need someone who can teach and take care of the girls, cook, clean, do the laundry and manage the house. I need someone who can tend to the yard, the fruit trees, the garden and the compost pile. I want the girls to be a part of this place, to feel invested, so I need a person who can feed the chickens and gather the eggs, take care of the cats, two goats and probably an occasional orphaned calf. I need someone who will make phone calls, order supplies and run errands with two holy terrors in tow. I need more than a nanny. I need an assistant. If you think you can learn all of that on YouTube or wherever in the next two weeks, then you are welcome to try. I'll be happy to pay you for your time." Jon hadn't thought it through before he'd rattled off that challenge. Part of it he'd made up on the spot. He hadn't anticipated that she'd fight so hard for the job.

Fisting her hands on the countertop, she stared at him. No, it was more than a stare. It was contemplation. That look, coupled with her feisty determination, nipped at his resolve. He could only hope that he'd said enough to scare her off. That wasn't entirely true; part of him was trying to convince her not to stay while another piece reminded him that he did indeed need child care. Especially in light of the situation out at Big E's. He didn't even want to think about the time he'd have to spend at the Blackwell Ranch if his grandfather didn't return soon. There was also another slice of him that wanted her around for a reason he didn't want to think about because he didn't want it to matter; he liked her.

"Why two weeks?"

"It's fifteen days to be exact. At least, that's when Eileen from the agency will be back from vacation." The thought occurred to him that that would almost give him enough time to get through calving season and prepare for his upcoming interview.

She tucked her bottom lip between her teeth, and Jon watched, transfixed, as she gnawed nervously for a few seconds. The resolve firing in her blazing blue eyes had him shaking his head. He should have added some truly unsavory tasks to that list, like mucking out stalls and butchering chickens, because she was looking at him and he knew she was going to say exactly what she did.

A slow smile curved into place—it lightened her expression and, despite his misgivings, his mood. "Done," she said. "I can do all of that and more." Then she tilted her chin and seemed to savor his name on her lips when she added, "Jon."

Against every bit of the good sense howling at him like a wolf inside his head, he smiled back. "Fine." He waited a beat and then added his own softly delivered, "Lydia."

SLOWLY, LYDIA SHIFTED out of panic mode. She was safe. For now. Fifteen days wasn't much but she'd learned more difficult jobs than this one in less time. She was sure of it. It was almost like all the work she'd done in her life up to this point had prepared her for this. Well, almost. The one place where she most wanted to make a difference, no matter how long she was here, was where she needed the most help. She poured two cups of coffee and handed him one.

"Now that the matter of my employment is settled, can I ask you a question?"

"Sure."

"What are your thoughts on the girls' education?"

He answered immediately, which told Lydia he'd given the subject some thought. She liked that. "They just turned five, so they should be getting ready for kindergarten, which they're supposed to start in the fall. But I'm afraid they're a little behind academically. Especially Genevieve. She's more than a little."

"Where will they go to kindergarten?" She could get a list from the school about what concepts they should know before then. She knew that states had standards regarding what a child should know for every grade. Specific schools had recommendations as well.

"They'll be going to school here."

"In Falcon Creek?"

"No. Here on the ranch."

The mug she held froze at the halfway point between her mouth and the countertop. She was going to need more than a little help. Then she remembered that she likely wouldn't be here in the fall. But that didn't mean she couldn't do what she could do before the next nanny took over. She carried on with her sip and then lowered her mug. "I see. Is that your plan for their entire education?"

"I'm going to play that one by ear. But the first several grades, yes."

"That sounds good. I have a friend who homeschools her troop and they're the smartest, sweetest kids you'll ever meet." She was thinking of Meredith's sister, Hailey. Tapping a finger on the countertop, she stared out the window and wished she could call Meredith. A bluebird hopped across a branch on what looked like a plum tree in the yard. Tiny buds were popping out along its scraggly branches. She hoped she'd be here long enough to see it bloom. Remembering Nana's plum tree made her long for a hug and a bite of the tree-ripened fruit.

Jon carried his mug toward the sink. Giving it a quick rinse, he moved to open the dishwasher. Lydia said, "Uh-uh. Just leave it there on the counter. I'm going to earn my paycheck."

Ignoring her, he slid it into the dishwasher and then turned toward her. "You sure are. The girls have dentist appointments next week. Dusty goes into Falcon Creek once a week for groceries so anything you need just let him know."

"Sounds good."

"Do you have a cell phone where I can reach you?"

Lydia paused. She didn't want to lie but the way he'd asked the question made it easy to avoid. "I prefer not to use a cell phone if I can avoid it."

If he thought that was odd, he didn't show it. He pointed. "I've got a house phone here, so the girls can call me anytime. The speed-dial numbers are written on the card hanging next to it. My cell phone is one, Tom is two, three is the bunkhouse and so on."

"Got it."

"I'm already mourning the fact that I won't make it in for lunch today. If those pancakes are a sample of what I have to look forward to, it won't be much of a hardship to eat in here with you and the girls whenever I can."

She grinned, already making plans for dinner. "You haven't tasted anything yet. Anyone can cook breakfast."

"I'm not sure that's true. And not pancakes like that, they can't."

"Thank you. It's a treat to cook for people who appreciate it. You know what *I'm* looking forward to?" She answered her own question before he had a chance. "April fifteenth."

Frowning, he joked, "Well, that's just wrong, Lydia. No one likes filing their taxes."

She fought a smile. "Including me. But it will be special for me this year, Jon, because that is the day when you beg me to stay here on your ranch."

"I hope you're right about that. But I don't think two—"

"Shh." Her hand shot up to cut him off. "Don't say it."

He chuckled and shook his head. "All right then. I'm getting to work."

Trout had been lying on his dog bed near the mudroom doorway. At Jon's comment, he was up and ready to go. Unnerving how the dog seemed to understand everything he said. She swished a finger from Trout to Jon and back again. "What happened here? Is it the word *work*?"

"Maybe. That and body language probably."

"Huh." After a last admiring look at Trout, she brushed him away. "Get out of here, then. I have things to do—a lot of things apparently. My boss has superhigh expectations and until I came along he was impossible to please."

His eyebrows edged up in an I-warned-you gesture, but he was fighting a smile. Without another word, he and Trout headed into the mudroom. Only when she heard the door close did she exhale the breath she'd been holding. How in the world was she going to pull this off?

CHAPTER SEVEN

LATER, LYDIA WOULD blame the bee for the chicken incident. Gen blamed Lydia's shoes. Abby blamed her technique.

With the girls flanking her and a feed pail in each hand, Lydia cautiously approached the chicken pen. She noticed all the chickens moving toward them, running actually, wings flapping. A feathery mass of noisy clucking. Why had Nana never kept chickens?

She opened the latch and pushed the gate forward with her hip. Abby said something, but it was too late, she was being chicken-mobbed. That's when she saw the bee zipping toward her face like a tiny, buzzing, heat-seeking missile. As she ducked and swiveled, her right foot slipped off the bed of her flip-flop right into slick chicken poo, causing that leg to shoot out from under her and slide beneath the fence. She landed on her butt with a thump, chicken feed spilling on and around her. Only vaguely did she register pain in that foot. Chaos erupted. A chicken riot. Chickens running over her.

Chickens squawking, lurching and weaving all around her.

"Hey!" she cried as one pecked at her toe. "Umm, hi." A pretty gray-and-black one hopped right into her lap.

"Shoo, shoo." Gen waved away the bird.

Abby grabbed one of the overturned buckets. She plunged her hand inside and tossed some grain toward the far side of the coop. The chickens scattered. Sweet relief.

"You should wear boots," Gen said, staring down at her feet with a knowing expression.

Lydia found herself giggling. Nothing like the most obvious answer to a problem. Five-year-old logic was awesome.

"Thank you, Gen. That is wonderful advice. And I plan to just as soon as I can get some new ones. You've seen my boots. I don't think they'd do too well out here in the chicken pen."

"Nope. You'd get stuck for sure." Gen held out a foot. "We get our boots at Brewster's."

Gingerly, Lydia climbed to her feet. She examined the scratches on the top of her foot from where it had slid under the wire fence. Thin lines of blood were forming. Not overly painful, but they'd need a good disinfecting.

"Brewster's, huh?"

"Yep. Brewster Ranch Supply. It has lots of other stuff, too. It's the greatest store there is."

Abby helpfully offered, "You should always throw a handful of feed in the back of the coop before you open the gate."

"That is also incredibly wise. I will do that from now on, thank you, Abby."

Abby grinned and held up the basket in her hand. "Come on, we'll show you how to gather the eggs."

It was a chore Lydia knew involved more than scooping up a cardboard container from the refrigerated section. As it was a specific task her new boss had listed, Lydia nodded with much more confidence than she felt. "Let's do it. Do we need gloves? Those beaks look pretty sharp."

GATHERING THE EGGS had proven to be a relatively simple task. And chickens, she discovered that evening, were all over the internet. The pecking-order phenomenon was fascinating and a little brutal. She learned about their nutritional needs and what made their eggshells hard and how to properly store the eggs.

The goats were cute and docile. Their job was to eat the grass and brush that grew up around the house and barnyard during the spring and summer months. All Lydia had to do was feed and water them, let them out in the morning and put them in their stall in the evening. Jon often accomplished the latter on his way to or from the cattle.

Funny how dramatically footwear could impact a person's life, though. Studying the calendar, she placed several orders online, which included teaching supplies, items for the girls and clothing and boots for herself. The rural address precluded the express shipping option and she could only hope they arrived quickly. In light of the chicken-coop incident, she knew she needed shoes with traction before she could tackle the gardening or venture out any farther than the chickens and goats. Flip-flops just didn't cut it.

Each night, after getting the girls tucked in, she headed to her room and spent a few hours researching—goats, cows, chickens, cattle ranching, composting, gardening in Montana and especially child development and pre-k education.

Of all the things Jon had rattled off on his list of demands, it was the teaching one that caused uncertainty to gnaw at her insides. Working at the group home, she'd spent untold hours tutoring teens. Lydia felt confident she could shift to kindergarten, but she needed some knowledge and the right tools.

Lydia found construction paper, pencils and crayons as well as a bucket of craft items, glue sticks and kid-friendly scissors. As the girls drew, cut, colored and glued, Lydia quizzed them on everything from letters and numbers to shapes and colors. Both the girls were incredibly bright and so inquisitive Lydia suspected she was going to learn as much as them when she tried to answer all their questions. But Jon was right about Gen; she was behind when it came to her letters and numbers. She'd developed a habit of letting Abby take the lead and supply the answers for her.

Early one afternoon, a few days into her trial period, Lydia sketched out a couple of bunnies and left the girls to color them while she headed into the kitchen. She was making a large pan of macaroni and cheese when she heard the door open.

"Hey, anyone home? Lydia?" Sofie poked her head around the corner.

"Sofie, hi! Yes, we're here. Come in. You look gorgeous. I love your dress."

Bunching her skirt, she gave it a flutter. "Oh, this old tent."

Lydia laughed. "It's funny how so many of you pregnant women think you look fat but all I see is precious baby and glowing mommy."

"You are sweet. But just wait. I used to think that, too. But it all changes when it happens to you. Pregnancy does ungodly things to your body. Zach, bless him, tells me I'm beautiful every fifteen minutes and he seems to mean it. Crazy cowboy that he is. And he talks to the baby every day."

Lydia couldn't help but smile at the dreamy expression on her face. A surprising jolt of longing flooded through her. Lydia had never been in love like that. She wanted kids, but tried not to think about it too much, because for her, love was a prerequisite. After her parents' volatile marriage and nasty divorce, she'd never bring a child into this world without being certain that love would last.

"Hey, girls!" Sofie called out as she strolled into the dining room, where the twins were working on their projects. The girls greeted her, showing off their artwork. Sofie's enthusiasm warmed Lydia's feelings for her even more.

A few minutes later, she reappeared. Pointing to where she'd just been, she whispered, "How did you manage that?"

"Manage what?"

"Getting them to focus like that."

"I don't…know. They don't normally focus?"

"I can't ever get them to sit down long enough to try."

"Huh." Lydia lowered her voice and said, "Jon told me they can be a handful. They're energetic but I haven't seen the rest."

"I guess that's why you're the professional.

And you can cook." Sofie drew out a sigh. "I'm so envious. That looks delicious. It's obvious that you have years of experience, just like Jon was hoping for."

Lydia felt a twist of guilt. She wasn't a professional anything. She was competent at a lot of things and what she'd told Jon about being trainable was accurate. Meredith always said she had job-lust, like wanderlust but with jobs. She never stayed at any job long enough to claim years of experience at any one of them. At a year and three months, her longest stint of employment had combined with her longest relationship and equaled her biggest mistake. The group home was an exception, although it was volunteer work.

Sofie gestured toward the dining room again. "That must mitigate some of his disappointment in your lack of ranching experience, huh? The look on his face when he realized you were from the city." She gave her head a little shake. "I thought he was going to send you away on the spot. Ava did such a number on him."

Ava? Lydia slipped the casserole into the oven and realized that not only was Sofie a potential friend, but she could also undoubtedly provide some insight into her new employer. Stuffing down another bout of conscience at the notion of prying into his personal business, she told herself she needed to use any means available to keep this job. Jon Blackwell had given her this opportunity and Lydia needed to succeed. Besides, she could use a friend. Or as much of one as she could have under the circumstances.

"You're welcome to stay for lunch."

The woman's eyes lit with delight. "I'd love that."

"I should warn you, though. We're going to have a lesson in table manners and you won't be exempt."

"Great," Sofie said with relief. "It's about time someone tackled that. I'll be on my best behavior."

"NEW NANNY WORKING out all right?" Zach asked Jon when he'd finished tamping in the last fence post. Zach was giving him a hand after he'd gotten behind from spending part of the last few days at the Blackwell Ranch helping Katie. They were repairing a stretch of fence in the east field, where a herd of elk had busted it up the night before. Trout was busy sniffing their tracks.

Stepping back, he eyed the plumb of the post. "Mmm. So far."

"What do you mean 'so far'? Sofie says she's wonderful. Has the girls under control, cooks like a celebrity chef. Sofie couldn't stop talking about her mac and cheese. And she sent home a loaf of the best pumpkin bread I've ever eaten. Pretty sure there was something addictive in that frosting."

Jon kneeled and snipped a length from the coil of barbed wire they'd retrieved from where they were kept hanging at intervals along the fence line. "Honeymoon phase."

"Honeymoon? Don't tell me you pulled a Big E and married her already?" Zach quipped as he grabbed one end of the wire and began splicing it to a broken strand.

Jon rolled his eyes. "I can't believe your wife thinks you're funny. No, I mean it's only been a few days. I'm reserving judgment."

"A few days?" Zach repeated flatly. "That's a lifetime in your world. Do I need to remind you, buddy, that the longest babysitter you've had since Annie died was one week? And she threatened to quit after two days. Only reason she stayed is because you paid her an exorbitant amount of cash."

This was true. He'd been desperate. Beavers had dammed the creek and the lower fields flooded with water. It wasn't safe for the girls to be with them while they were trapping beavers and dismantling the dam.

Annie had been a friend of his grandmother's—his actual grandmother, Dorothy, Big E's first wife. Annie had been like having a tiny piece of his grandmother looking after the twins. She'd suffered a stroke and passed away a year and a half ago. It still hurt to think about it, but he was grateful they'd had her that long. Since then, Jon had hired babysitters on and off. Mostly, he carted the girls around the ranch with him. Tom helped. Sometimes Dusty would keep an eye on them in the bunkhouse. Occasionally Zach's mom, Willa, would take them for an afternoon or even a sleepover. As much as Jon enjoyed having the girls with him, they'd gotten increasingly out of control. Willa said they needed a schedule, regular meals, a bedtime and such. Jon agreed, but it just wasn't feasible. It had been Sofie who'd encouraged him to give the nanny thing a try.

"Tell Sofie not to get too attached. She's only going to be here a couple of weeks."

Zach paused where he was splicing another strand of wire. "What do you mean? You spent a lot of time trying to find a good, qualified person. I thought it was supposed to be a long-term gig."

"It was but she's not qualified."

"Sofie said the girls made it through the entire meal without playing with their food."

"She's good with them." Jon snipped some barbs from the section he was working. "It's not that."

"Is it because she's from the city and didn't grow up on a ranch or whatever you were harping on about before?"

"Don't start." He didn't like the way his feathers were feeling all ruffled. "I know what I'm doing. Her city-girl ways will catch up with her and I'll be the one to suffer. The girls will suffer."

"Sofie didn't—"

"Sofie is an isolated case. An anomaly. And I know you don't like to be reminded of it, but it almost didn't work out for you guys." Zach and Sofie might be a sticky-sweet example of true love now, but their relationship didn't start out that way.

"Way I see it—" Zach squinted at him "—the only relevant point you're making is that it did."

"Which isn't relevant at all in my case, is it? I need a nanny, not a wife."

"I don't see what's wrong with keeping your options open," Zach muttered.

Jon ignored him and hooked up the fence stretcher.

LYDIA STARED OUT the window. Tapping a finger on the sill, she thought it through. The chances of Clive bugging the phones of the multimillion-dollar computer-tech company where Meredith worked were slim. Meredith always talked about how the company's security was top-notch, grumbling that she was constantly being forced to change her passwords.

Before she could talk herself out of it, Lydia dialed the phone. After pressing the number for her friend's extension, Meredith's unmistakable voice came on the line. "Meredith Blumen."

"Hey, Meredith."

"*Omigosh!* Lydia?" Lydia squeezed her eyes shut at the sound of her friend's tone, which was happy, frantic and hushed all at the same time. "Where are you?"

"I can't tell you that. Can you go somewhere where you can talk? And not on your cell."

"Um, I can borrow Dillon's cell phone and go outside." Dillon was Meredith's coworker who had a monster-sized crush on her.

"Perfect."

"I'll call you back in three minutes."

Two minutes later, the phone buzzed in her clenched hand.

"Clive is looking for you, that fatheaded jcrk-face. But, of course, you know that. As if I would tell him where you are even if I knew."

"I'm sorry, Meredith. I hoped to keep you out of this."

"This? What *this*? What is going on?"

"I can't tell you that, either. At least, not now." Probably never, Lydia realized, and felt a painful stab of grief at the thought that she'd never see her friend again. No more lunch dates, or nights listening to music and eating ice cream straight out of the container. No more going out dancing, or perusing the employment section looking for Lydia's latest career venture and then giving up and doing the crossword puzzle together instead. She'd miss the Blumen family gatherings, too, where they all made Lydia feel like a sister, daughter, aunt.

"I'm so sorry you had to deal with Clive."

"Oh, sweetie, I know. It's okay. Tanner warned me. I was prepared. I threw a plate at him and accused him of murdering you. I demanded that he tell me what he did with you. You should have seen his face when I threatened to call the cops."

Lydia couldn't help but laugh, despite the seriousness of the ordeal. It gave her a measure of peace knowing her best friend had this protection.

"It was comical. It was like it never occurred to him that anyone would suspect that he'd done something to you. I wish I would have thought to film it. Guaranteed five million hits online. When are you coming home?"

"I don't know. I'm not sure..." She couldn't bring herself to say the words that she might never see her again. New feelings for Clive swirled inside her. Hatred and contempt, she re-

alized, were mixing with the fear that had been
dominant for so long.

Lydia expected an argument, but Meredith
remained quiet for so long Lydia almost asked
if she was still on the line. "Yeah, I got that impression from Tanner. I want to ask you what
happened, but I know I shouldn't."

"Yeah, don't."

"Can I just say that I knew he was trouble
from the moment we met him."

"That you can say. In fact, you've already said
it. Many times."

"Well, you broke our cardinal rule."

"Not technically. I didn't go home with him."

Years ago, she and Meredith made a pact—
they would keep their nightlife separate from
their real life. Going out was strictly about their
shared love of music and dancing. It had nothing
to do with meeting men. Neither of them could
ever leave a club with a guy or leave the other
alone under any circumstances.

They'd met Clive at a club. Without introducing himself, he'd bought drinks for "you and
your friend," the server had told her. He'd continued to do so all night. Near the end of the evening, Lydia had asked the server if he owned the
place, or if he was buying drinks for any other
women. "Nope," she'd said. "He comes in here
all the time and I've never seen him buy any-

one else a drink. Not until you." Lydia was intrigued. When they were ready to depart, she'd gone over to his table to thank him. He'd stood and guided her away from his friends. Unable to resist, she'd asked him why he'd done it.

He'd answered, "You and your friend were having such a good time. I wanted to be a part of it without spoiling it. The way you dance... It's... I don't even know..." He'd shrugged helplessly and said, "Sublime. Thank you for making me believe that people can be happy."

That had done it. She'd asked for his number. All the way home she and Meredith had argued about it. Meredith maintained it was nothing but a clever pickup line, but Lydia had felt something...different. Between them, they'd heard a lot of lines over the years. None of them had ever gotten to her like that.

Unable to stop thinking about it, she'd called him. Clive had been charming at first, generous, attentive and thoughtful. She'd just quit yet another job and he'd begged her to work for him. It had taken her too long to realize the "different" she'd felt was actually danger.

"Ugh. I want to hurt him for doing this to you because whatever happened, I know it's his fault..."

She let her friend vent. Even though Lydia felt like it was a lot her fault, too, for not being stron-

ger, for not leaving Clive sooner. By the time
she discovered who he was, and that what he
was doing with an investment fund was cheat-
ing people while not technically committing a
crime, it was too late to simply leave. He knew
that she knew. And the longer she stayed, the
more he pulled her in, until she had reached a
point where she couldn't *not* curtail his plans
without feeling culpable herself.

But her options were limited. She could wait
for him to do something actually illegal, and
then report him. But Clive was clever when it
came to technicalities and skirting the rules.
What if there wasn't enough evidence to pin
anything on him? Removing the money from
the equation seemed like her only answer. Without knowing how much and to whom the funds
should be returned, she did the only other thing
she could think of. She gave the money away.

"Wherever you are, are you okay?"

"Yes." Saying the word cemented how much
she felt it. She felt safe at the JB Bar Ranch, safe
and needed. For all the bravado she'd felt and
shown Jon, when the day came, she wanted him
to ask her to stay. She knew it wouldn't be an
easy task convincing him. Sofie had inadvertently told her that. Without providing much de-
tail, she'd alluded to the trauma he'd experienced
at his ex-wife's hands. Ava had hated the ranch

and everything that went with it. Lydia couldn't quite wrap her brain around the idea that she'd left her children, but it wasn't her place to judge. And certainly not a miserable, unhappy woman whom she'd never met. Lydia felt a tiny stirring of sympathy for the fact that she'd been so desperate. Lydia knew desperation all too well.

"That's part of the reason I'm calling. I'm, uh, I'm working with some kids and I could use your expert aunt advice."

"Oh, that's awesome. You're great with kids."

"Yeah, well, I *love* kids. I'm good with teens. But these kids are preschoolers. I need some help."

"How old?"

"Just turned five."

"They're not that much different than teenagers really," she joked. "Smaller vocabulary but less attitude and way more common sense."

Lydia laughed. "They should be ready for kindergarten this fall, but they're behind. I found some guidelines on the internet, the basics they should know and stuff."

"That's my favorite age. Their brains are like sponges. Molly is four and Scotty is six. You've helped me babysit lots of times." Meredith's sister Hailey homeschooled her six kids. Molly and Scotty were the youngest.

"Yeah, but when we babysit, it's all fun and games."

"Exactly. That's the way learning should be, right? Hands-on. Engaging. Keep them busy and tell them everything while you do it. Dance, do crafts, science projects... And bake with them, they'll love that."

"Okay, yes, been doing all of that." She was glad she'd called. She was already feeling better.

"Ooh! Make some slime. You can do science and colors and letters... I'll call Hailey and have her send me links and stuff. Or even better, can I have her text them to this number if I don't tell her who they're for?"

Lydia hesitated for a second. Tanner had been adamant about the phone. But it was his job to be paranoid. And this was, if not an emergency, then extremely important. Chances seemed slim that Clive's tentacles would spread as far as Meredith's family. "Yeah, sure, that will work. I appreciate it, Meredith. Now, remind me how to play that counting game with the buttons..."

CHAPTER EIGHT

JON HAD NO trouble admitting how nice it was to walk into his own house and be greeted by the smell of a home-cooked meal, especially one he hadn't had to cook after ten or twelve hours of ranching. The meals Dusty prepared in the bunkhouse were just fine, but the food was plain, made to appeal to a wide range of hungry appetites. Sofie hadn't exaggerated to Zach about Lydia's cooking. Every day he found himself anticipating mealtime. He would miss it when she was gone.

Between the soft music playing in the background, the giggles and the clanking and banging of kitchen sounds, nobody noticed him and Trout when they stepped around the corner. Perched on stools at the island, the girls were elbow-deep in some sort of mushy green gunk.

"Hope that's not dinner," Jon joked, stepping closer to examine the mess.

Abby giggled. "Yep, it's dinner all right. Here, try a bite, Daddy." She held up a gob for his inspection. The girls erupted into fits of laughter.

"It's called slime." Gen pulled a handful of the goop through her fingers.

"Are you sure it's not called disgusting?"

More laughing. Abby said, "No way. It's awesome. Lydia says all the kids in Philadelphia play with it."

Hmm. Jon was seeing a pattern here. The girls seemed almost always to be having fun when he came inside. So much so that he suddenly wondered when the learning was going on.

"Oh, hey." Lydia came out of the pantry carrying a sack of flour and a can of corn. "Didn't hear you guys come in. Dinner will be ready in about fifteen minutes. I didn't want to cook the vegetables until you got here. I know the chickens get all the fruit and veggie leavings, but can Trout have table scraps?"

Hair up in a high ponytail, eyes sparkling, she seemed to be settling in so easily. Too easily? Jon glanced over at the girls and then back at her. "Yes, he can have a bit. Can I speak to you in the other room for a second?"

"Sure." Setting the supplies down on the counter, he caught sight of the I Love NYC T-shirt she wore. Who in their right mind would love any city? He couldn't believe his brother Ben chose to live there.

He followed her into the living room, where she spun toward him. "What's wrong?"

"Why do you think something is wrong?"

"You've gone all Rancher Grouch-Face on me again."

"Rancher what?"

"You're scowling like you were the day I got here."

"Oh." Shifting on his feet, he made an effort to compose his features. "It's not that I'm upset so much as it is that I'm concerned."

"Okay. About what?"

How to word this exactly? "It seems like you're always having an awful lot of fun with the girls."

She stared up at him and Jon was struck once again by how pretty she was. "I would say thank you but I'm sensing there's an issue buried in there somewhere."

Jon sighed and scrubbed a hand across his jaw. "I guess I'm wondering what you're teaching them. When are they learning? Whenever I come inside, you're rarely sitting down and teaching them anything. Except for bedtime with the reading, which I do approve of."

"Sitting down?" she repeated. "Have you met your daughter Genevieve? She can barely sit still through a meal. Abby isn't all that much better."

"I understand they're busy girls—that's why I hired a professional."

Nodding slowly, she seemed to be pondering his words. "Mmm-hmm. I see."

Jon felt relieved. She was taking this surprisingly well. "Even though you're not going to be here all that long, I think every minute you can, you should spend teaching them and preparing them for kindergarten."

"Can you follow me back into the kitchen?"

He wasn't quite through explaining himself but she took off without giving him much choice.

Stepping toward the radio, she turned it way down. "Hey, Gen, what color is that slime?"

"Green."

"And what rhymes with green?"

"*Mean, clean, preen*—chickens do that, Daddy, did you know that's what it's called when they pick at their feathers? *Jean, keen... Bean*!"

"What letter does *slime* begin with?"

"*Es-s-ss*," she hissed it out and then formed a string of slime into the letter's shape. "Same as *snake*. And there's an *S* in *horse*, too, but it starts with an *H*."

"How about *slime*? What rhymes with that, Abby?"

"*Lime*! The same color as our lime slime. *Time, dime, mime*. Mimes are those white-faced guys who don't talk but do this with their hands." She held her own dripping green ones up for effect. "Have you ever seen one, Daddy? Lydia has."

"No, I can't say that I have," Jon said, wishing he'd been one when he'd gotten the big idea to critique Lydia's teaching techniques.

Lydia grinned. "Right on, girls."

"Abby, do you know your dad's phone number?"

She rattled it off. Jon had never thought to teach the girls his number. It had seemed too complicated, especially when they could just pick up the house phone and press one button.

"Gen, what is Tom's phone number?"

Gen recited it. Of course, there could be a time when they weren't in the house and might need to call Tom.

He swallowed around the tractor-sized lump of shame in his throat. "Wow. You girls have been working real hard. I'm so proud of you."

The girls beamed at him and went back to playing with their lime slime. He could feel Lydia watching him and he had to force himself to make eye contact. Anyone would expect a glare or at least a frown in return—Jon knew it was what he deserved. That's not what he got.

Lips flirting with a smile, mischief dancing in her eyes, she said in a voice as gentle as a breeze, "We're having one of your favorites for dinner tonight. Pot roast with baby potatoes, carrots and brown gravy. Peach cobbler for dessert. At least the girls told me it was your favorite."

At his nod, she went on, "They helped me make it while we learned how to count and measure from a recipe."

"A teep-spoon is real small," Gen volunteered. "Like this." Reaching across the counter, she retrieved one and held it up.

Abby corrected her sister more gently than Jon had seen in a good long while. "It's a *tea*-spoon, Gen. Like Sofie drinks."

"Yep, that's what I meant, teaspoon." Brow furrowed, she added, "Ssss-poon. That's an *S*, too, huh, Lydia?"

"Yes, my s-s-s-weet, it certainly is."

The girls giggled. Jon's stomach felt like a knotted mass of bailing twine. He leaned over and kissed the girls, one smooth, grinning cheek at a time. Standing straight, he cleared his throat and offered Lydia a sheepish smile. "I think I'll, uh, go wash up for dinner."

"Why don't you do that. We'll have dinner on the table when you get back. Maybe you could ask the blessing for us tonight?"

WASHING UP FOR DINNER, Jon decided that was undoubtedly the softest and smoothest yet most thorough chastisement he'd ever received. He liked the notion that Lydia was using a similar technique on the girls. He felt stupid for even thinking what he had. But the sting of his pride could no way compete with the smell of pot roast.

Bracing himself, he headed to the table. The girls were already seated, napkins in their laps. Lydia walked out of the kitchen with a platter in one hand and a gravy bowl in the other. Her smile seemed genuine, his gaffe all but forgotten. Jon realized that he didn't entirely trust that reaction. He knew people who did not necessarily forgive and forget. They could appear calm and collected on the outside and all the while be coiled like a rattlesnake on the inside, waiting and ready for the right time to strike. Ava's memory had been like that—long and vengeful.

The girls kept up a steady stream of chatter through dinner, in between bites, because they seemed to be making a concerted effort to chew with their mouths closed. Lydia corrected them a few times, but gently. She'd say their name and then show the proper way to use a utensil or wipe at her own cheek with a napkin.

When they'd finished, they asked to be excused, a habit Jon had never established. Lydia reminded them to take their plates into the kitchen. "The show is ready for you to watch. Just hit the button like I showed you."

After depositing their dishes in the kitchen, they headed out to the living room.

Lydia gestured at his plate. "Would you like dessert?"

"Yes, but I can—"

"Jon," she interrupted, standing and scooping up the plate. "I appreciate the way you don't expect me to wait on you. But I know how hard you work. I can see how tired you are. My fetching you dessert doesn't have anything to do with women's rights or you treating me like a servant. I'd do it for anyone. Besides, I'm getting some for myself, too. Would you like ice cream with the cobbler?"

"In that case, then yes, I would."

Flashing him a warm smile, she headed into the kitchen.

Jon enjoyed the sound of the girls talking and giggling. Music from the program drifted into the room. They quieted.

Bowls in hand, Lydia returned. That's when he noticed her feet. They were bare, but the right one sported a big Band-Aid on the top and a smaller one around her big toe.

She set a bowl in front of him and he peered a little closer. "What happened to your foot?"

"Oh… It's nothing."

"You've got Band-Aids on it."

"It's pretty well healed."

Jon realized he was staring again when she said, "I probably should have asked you about allowing them to watch a show. Do you not have television because you don't want the girls watching it? It's an educational program about animals. And they said they're allowed to watch movies."

"Oh, no…yeah, I mean it's fine. I trust you. I don't want them sitting in front of the TV mindlessly. And to answer your question, I'm not a TV watcher myself and it's an unnecessary expense."

She nodded and scooped a bite of dessert.

"Lydia, I'm sorry about earlier. I don't know what I was thinking. I shouldn't have doubted you. Or at least I should have gone about it differently. Or at least, more, uh, stealthily."

"I understand. I didn't make an effort to share with you what we've been learning, or how. I've been meaning to, of course. I've been assessing where they're at academically, so I haven't finalized my lesson plans."

"Nice of you to try and let me off the hook."

She shrugged a shoulder. "So you want to be involved, consulted?"

It seemed strange to be having a conversation about raising his girls, a task he'd been wholly in charge of since Annie had died. But that relief he'd been hoping for with a nanny's presence overrode it. "Yes, I would."

"Great. I feel confident about teaching them academics and more practical matters like table manners, personal hygiene, making their beds, et cetera."

He felt himself scowling and made an effort to correct it. The fact that they were lacking in so many areas made his heart hurt. Was he that bad of a father?

As if sensing his doubts, she said, "They're wonderful, amazing girls, Jon. Kind and bright and curious and thoughtful. You've been doing a fantastic job. I can't imagine how difficult it's been for you being a single dad and running a ranch. And now with your grandfather... I'm getting a sense of how thinly you've been stretched. But there is one area I'm concerned about..." Trailing off, she nibbled on her lower lip and Jon realized this wasn't the first time he'd been staring at her mouth.

Forcing himself to look away, he scooped up another bite. "This is the best peach cobbler I've ever tasted. I'm getting spoiled. What has you concerned?"

"I'm glad you like it. It's my nana's recipe. I'm afraid... I'm wondering if they might not be getting enough socialization."

"They see people here on the ranch every day."

"Horseback riding with Tom, eating in the bunkhouse and talking cattle with cowboys is nice but I think they need more. They need to see some other kids."

"Oh." She was probably right. Willa had recently raised this subject as well. Jon used a thumb to scratch his cheek. "They, uh, *we* have church on Sundays. Normally. We're not going this Sunday because I gave some of the boys the day off, so I need to be here."

He was fascinated by the little dip that formed between her eyebrows when she was thinking.

"So, there's Sunday school," he added.

"Sunday school?"

"Yep."

"Mmm." Her expression hinted at longing, like she was remembering a happy place. "I like church."

Why did that surprise him, that she liked church? "You're welcome to join us. I assumed you'd want Saturdays and Sundays as your days off, but we usually have dinner over at the Carnes place after church. Big family. Lots of kids. It's fun. And you already know Sofie."

The brow-dip was back. "Does Sofie cook this dinner?"

He felt a stirring of amusement at the question.

"She helps. They live with Zach's parents, Pete and Willa. Not with them in the same house, but right next door. Willa does most of the cooking. She's an excellent cook. Zach's brother and sisters come, too. Everyone brings a dish."

She grinned and this time her twinkling blue eyes spoke loud and clear. "That's good. About dinner, I mean."

He winked at her, but he didn't know if she was blushing because of that or because she felt bad about insulting Sofie. "I knew what you meant."

"She's a lovely woman."

"I knew that, too."

She pointed her spoon at him. "If you repeat what I just implied, it will not be good for you. I think she's becoming my friend."

He chuckled. "Hey, I agreed with you, didn't I? It wouldn't be good for me, either. So that's a yes to church?"

"Absolutely." And she looked so genuinely happy about the notion that Jon knew she meant it. He'd never had a woman go to church with him before. *She's not a woman, Jon*, he reminded himself. Not in a bring-a-lady-to-church kind of way. *She's your nanny. And she's leaving in a week.*

Lydia scooped up a bite of her cobbler. "How are the cows doing? Tom said you're more than halfway through the calving now and it's going well. But it's supposed to rain tonight. Will they be okay?"

And that's when something occurred to him. Lydia had been here a week, but she hadn't seen much of the ranch, hadn't ventured out to see the cows or the horses. To his knowledge, she hadn't been farther from the house than the chicken coop. Surprisingly enough, he hadn't heard one word of complaint about that chore or seeing to the goats, housed right next door. He'd popped in there every day to make sure all was well. Eggs had been gathered, animals had been fed and watered.

"They should be fine. We had to move a few of them into the calving shed, which is never fun. I promised the girls I'd take them out to see the new babies tonight. You don't want to, uh… You wouldn't want to join us by any chance, would you? There's not much cuter than a new calf." *Nice, Jon, you sound like you did back in high school, when you asked Marilee Inez to the spring dance.* But unlike Marilee, Lydia did not look eager. She looked more like a scared calf herself as she stared back at him.

"Oh, um…thank you so much for asking. But not tonight."

Even though he'd expected as much, disappointment churned inside of him. The words came out before he could stop them, "Seems kind of tough to learn about something that you won't even take a look at."

"What? No, that's not it. It's not that I don't want to. I…"

"You what?" Now he felt like a fool. Why had he asked? Cattle had to be so boring compared to what she was used to in Philadelphia.

"Um, I would, except… I need to prepare some stuff for tomorrow. The girls have dentist appointments and I wanted to make some worksheets and…"

Standing, Jon let her off the hook. "I understand. I'd better go round them up so I can get them back before bedtime." It was obvious she was lying. And now they were both uncomfortable.

"I'd appreciate that. It'll make our day go so much smoother if they get enough sleep." Her voice was soft, her big blue eyes wide. He had the feeling she wanted to say more, but Jon didn't need to hear it. He knew all the excuses; about the mud, the dust, the heat, the cold, the smell. The animals might hurt her or she might break a nail, she didn't want to get her jacket dirty, and didn't one cow look like all the rest?

CHAPTER NINE

STANDING AT THE island in the kitchen, Lydia studied the supply list she'd made and tried to decide what she should go ahead and purchase in Falcon Creek and what could wait until her overdue packages arrived. She wasn't even sure what she'd be able to find in town.

A knock sounded on the back door.

She opened it to find Tom standing on the porch. He was reading a slip of paper. Looking up, he removed his hat to reveal sandy-colored hair curling around his ears. "Good morning, Ms. Lydia." Lydia had liked the handsome foreman from the first moment she'd met him. *Talkative* wouldn't be a word she'd use to describe him, but she liked his quiet confidence, respectful manner and especially his gentle way with the twins.

"Hi, Tom. How are you?"

"Just fine. Jon said you're headed into town?"

"Yes, the girls have dentist appointments."

Piercing green eyes met hers. "I feel confident that will go real smooth for you."

That seemed like kind of an odd remark, but Lydia had the feeling he was trying to convey something to her. She smiled and said, "Thank you."

"Jon and I need a few things, if you please?"

"Yes, of course."

Tom handed over a list. Lydia scanned it, her spirits sinking as she realized that most of the items she'd never heard of.

"Um, what's a—"

Tom said, "You can just hand that paper to Frank at Brewster's. He'll collect it for you."

"Great. Thank you, Tom. That should save me time." About three or four hours, she wanted to joke. But didn't. She couldn't risk that Tom would report to Jon that she was clueless. Not that he didn't already know it, but she was trying hard not to advertise.

"You're welcome. I, uh, I added something on the back there you might want to consider."

Lydia flipped over the list. The word *boots* was neatly printed, and beneath it, he'd written a brand and style. Like a thermometer dipped in hot water, she could feel the heat rising in her cheeks.

"Brewster's has a real nice selection. These are the best for you."

She brought her gaze up to meet his. "Did you see—?"

"Yes, ma'am."

"Does Jon—"

"No, ma'am, just myself."

Lydia stared at him, wondering why he would help her. He was Jon's foreman, his friend and, from what she'd seen, his most trusted employee.

Her face must have betrayed the question because he cleared his throat. "Gen and Abby are real special to me, like my own family. I've known them since they were babies. Walked the floor with them more than a time or two." He paused, adjusting his stance. Lydia felt for him as he struggled to explain without saying too much. "What I'm getting at is, I know they're good kids. But it's been a long while since they've had the chance to prove it. With you, they..." Tom's gaze dropped to the ground. Taking a breath, he looked back up. "They're doing just fine, Ms. Lydia. And I'd like to do my part to see it on. Sorry for the sermon."

Lydia's heart went light. She wanted to hug the man but knew instinctively he'd be uncomfortable with that. Instead, she reached out and squeezed his forearm. "Thank you so much, Tom."

SPIRITS BOOSTED BY Tom's confidence in her, Lydia and the girls set off toward Falcon Creek. She hadn't even driven through the town on her way to the JB Bar. Now, she turned at the four-way stop and headed toward downtown. She counted three church steeples dotting the immediate horizon. How refreshing to discover that they seemed to be the tallest structures around. In the back seat, the girls discussed the merits of dill pickles versus sweet. Lydia had no idea how the topic had come up, but she enjoyed their chatter.

Falcon's Nest Hotel seemed ideally located on the edge of town with the Clearwater Café across the street. On the right was White Buffalo Grocers. Up to this point, Dusty had been supplying her with groceries, but she was thinking they could start sharing the duty.

There were no cars behind her, so she inched into downtown, taking it all in, trying to absorb the magic that the town's history had fashioned all around her. Old, old buildings of brick and stone and wood stood side by side, all apparently still in use by someone or something. Lydia was charmed.

On the right, a stately, redbrick structure appeared before her like something out of a movie set. Captivated, she glanced in her rearview mirror and stopped. Right there. In the middle of the street.

"Hold on, girls." Getting out, she stood by the car and gaped at the Falcon Creek National

Bank. It wasn't hard to imagine robbers busting out the door and firing guns while jumping on their getaway horses. Turning her head, she noticed Pots & Petals Flower Shop, Mountains Past Antiques and Bee Balm Gifts. Down the street she saw the red, white and blue barber pole, just as Sofie had described.

Whoop. One short burst of a siren had Lydia spinning around, pulse pounding, hand on her chest. Cop car. Before she could even move, a familiar cap of red hair appeared out the window of the vehicle.

"Mornin', Ms. Lydia."

"Scooter, you need to quit sneaking up behind me like that."

With a loud guffaw, he climbed out of the car. "Not hard to do when you're always parking in these odd places. You lost again?"

As he approached, Gen and Abby cried, "Hi, Scooter. We're going to Brewster's."

"Hey, girls. Aren't you lucky? Brewster's is always a good idea."

Lydia explained, "We have dentist appointments today. Then we're going to do some shopping."

"And something led you to believe this was Dr. Beazley's parking lot? Boy, they sure do things different in Philadelphia, don't they?"

Lydia laughed. "Sorry. Getting my bearings.

It's my first trip to town and I was doing a little gawking."

Scooter held out a hand. "Wait right here." He walked back to his vehicle, ducked inside and returned with a paper in his hand. Standing beside her in the middle of the street, he took a moment to look around. "Yeah, kind of pretty, isn't it? Can't give you a ticket for gawking so I'll give you this map instead."

Handing her the paper, he pointed down the street. "This is Front Street and Brewster's is down past the drugstore. If you want to see it all, turn left just beyond Brewster's, and then left again. That'll be Back Street." Leaning toward the SUV, he said, "You girls have a nice day."

To Lydia, he said, "I'm sure I'll be seeing you parked askew again real soon."

"Thank you, Scooter. You are like the north in my compass."

Chuckling, he walked away and got into his car.

Lydia climbed into her vehicle and kept driving. A giant silver dollar on the side of a dark brown building advertised the Silver Stake Saloon. A lighted ice-cream cone in the window of a large, redbrick building on the corner caught her eye. The sign above said South Corner Drug & Sundries.

Brewster Ranch Supply would have been difficult to miss. A large, freestanding building with attractive, weathered gray siding, it reminded Lydia of a general store from an old television Western. Convenient, she thought, as she spotted the dentist's office across Front Street. There was a law office next door to that.

Gen piped up. "Lydia, can I show you the saddles at Brewster's?"

Lydia smiled. Five-year-old translation—can we look at the saddles? How was it possible to already adore these little ones as much as she did? "As soon as you girls rock your dentist appointments we can look at whatever you want."

Lydia turned left where Scooter recommended, turned left one block later and toured Back Street. Businesses here included a quilt shop, a veterinarian and a bookstore, as well as the fire station. A row of older well-kept homes, with their picket fences and tidy flower beds awash with early spring color, had Lydia fighting the urge to pull over again.

"Bear claws from Maple Bear Bakery are the best," Abby commented as they passed the shop. In the window, a carved wooden bear displayed a pie in one paw and a rolling pin in the other.

"I like the maple muffins," Gen said.

"Those both sound delicious to me," Lydia commented.

Misty Whistle Coffee House looked fun, too,

housed in the old train station. The bronze steam whistle displayed out front reminded her of a café she and Meredith adored back in Philly.

She turned at the credit union and then again onto Front Street. Lydia parked near the barber pole. Sofie had told her about Jem Salon when Lydia had wondered if there was a place in town that offered printing services.

"It's a beauty and print shop?" Lydia had asked, trying not to laugh.

"And a nail salon, yes. Trust me, it's not what you're thinking. The owners, June and Emma, relocated here from Los Angeles. We're so lucky to have them. People are coming from all over to get their hair done. June's also a graphic designer. She has all these cool printers and stuff in the back."

Now she told the girls, "We need to make a quick stop here at Jem Salon." She'd filled a flash drive with worksheets, ideas, crafts and activities that Hailey had sent her. She'd supplemented those with others she'd found online.

"We love June and Emma. They cut our hair sometimes. And Daddy's, too."

The girls unbuckled and climbed out. Holding hands, with Lydia in the middle, they walked inside. She could see what Sofie meant. Classy and tasteful meets vintage Montana country. Old red brick and mortar made up one entire wall. She wondered if it and the distressed wood floor were original to the building. To the left was the waiting area with an espresso-colored leather sofa, two matching chairs and a round table, which had stacks of neatly arranged magazines on top. Black-and-white photos hung on the walls.

An antique display case served as the reception desk. Beyond that was the busy salon, where a gorgeous vintage barber chair stood ready. Lydia and the girls took a few steps forward and the room went silent.

At least seven women looked in their direction. Two were seated in the black-and-silver styling chairs situated in front of large mirrors. An apron-wearing stylist holding scissors and a comb stood nearby. Another woman was perched on a chair in front of the shampooing sink, a white towel twisted on her head like a dollop of soft-serve ice cream. Under the dryer was an older woman, her silvery hair coiled tight with blue curlers.

Two fancy pedicure chairs were positioned near the back corner. Lydia loved a good pedicure. Might be fun to treat Sofie one of these days. At the manicure station a pretty blonde was filing another lady's nails.

"Hello, there. I'll be right with you." A slender woman with long black silky, straight hair came hustling out of a doorway in the back. She carried a stack of fluffy white towels. Glancing their way, she set the bundle on the counter and approached them.

"Well, if it isn't the Blackwell beauties." She wore skinny jeans tucked into tall boots. Her brown-eyed gaze flicked from Abby to Genevieve, back and forth a couple of times. Shrugging helplessly, she added, "Looking extra beautiful today. And girls! Your. Hair. Is. Gorgeous!"

"Thank you, Emma." Abby beamed. "Lydia does it for us now."

"You must be Lydia?"

"I am."

"I'm Emma. Excited to meet you." Emma reached out a hand. Over her shoulder, she called out, "June, come over here and take a look at this."

Lydia had braided Abby's hair and then twisted it into an intricate updo on top of her head. She'd threaded in a sparkly ribbon she'd found in the basket of hair supplies. Gen preferred French braids, so Lydia had parted it on the side and braided around each side of the crown, arranging the ends into a bun.

"Hi, June," Abby said.

"Hey, Abigail and Genevieve. How are my favorite twins?"

"Good," Abby said.

June beamed at Lydia. "Hi, I'm June." June was shorter than Emma with a chic blond A-line cut, moss-green eyes and bow-shaped lips. Both women looked hip and stylish enough to work in an upscale salon anywhere.

"Genevieve, let me look at you." June took her gently by the shoulders and guided her into a slow circle while she examined Lydia's handiwork. "I love this!"

"Thank you." Gen smiled shyly, her hand coming up to touch the braids. "Lydia can braid real good."

"She sure can."

The women traded knowing glances, silently communicating in a way that reminded Lydia of herself and Meredith. Emma said, "This is excellent work. Any chance we could hire you to work for us on prom days and maybe an occasional wedding? We do hair for a bunch of different proms now. People are driving hours and we're getting booked for this season already."

Lydia smiled, grateful for the stint she'd done at Luxe Salon as a shampoo girl. Marta, one of the stylists, had taken Lydia under her wing and instructed her in the fine art of braids and updos. "I could maybe be persuaded to work out a trade. The girls and I are all going to need a trim one of these days. And I understand my boss gets his hair cut here, too?"

June looked at Emma, who clapped her hands together. "Done. But you don't have appointments today, do you? I'd remember if the Blackwell beauties were on our books."

June pointed a finger at Lydia. "You called about having some printing done, didn't you?"

"That was me." Lydia fished the flash drive out of her bag.

June waved her forward. "Come on back and we'll get you set up."

"Great. I bet you ladies carry a good leave-in conditioner here, too."

"Finally." Emma sighed. "I told Jon he needed to get one."

Lydia laughed. "I don't think he understood. He's been using shampoo and conditioner in one."

"Shampoo and conditioner in one," Emma repeated with a resigned shake of her head. "On hair like these girls have… I'll leave some up at the counter. Part of the deal."

June informed her she could pick up her order in a couple of hours. Lydia thanked her, and they went on their way. Approximately three minutes later, she was parked at the office of Dr. Richard Beazley, DDS, DMD. Lydia silently extolled the virtues of running errands in a small town.

"Okay, girls, we're here. We talked about what's going to happen but before we go inside, do you have any questions?" It was just for checkups and the girls had been here before, yet Jon had seemed concerned when they'd discussed it, even offering to bring them himself.

Gen looked troubled. "It's not going to hurt, right?"

"Nope." She reached back and gave Gen's hand an encouraging squeeze. "And I'll be with you. Abby?"

"I'm ready, I guess."

Inside, the receptionist checked them in and directed them to the waiting area. Another woman joined her. They spoke in hushed tones and kept glancing toward the waiting room. Lydia wouldn't have thought much about it if they hadn't been the only ones there. Removing crayons from the bag she'd brought, she handed them to the girls along with the worksheets she'd made. She instructed them to color all the images that began with the letter *A*.

"Ms. Newbury?"

Lydia looked up to find one of the women now standing in front of her. "Yes. Please call me Lydia."

"Hi, I'm Nell. Can I speak with you at the front desk?"

"Sure. Girls, I'll be right back."

Nell led her beyond the reception area, out of earshot, but with a clear view into the waiting room. She said, "So, we worked out a strategy this time."

"A strategy?"

"Yes. Last visit was a little...chaotic. We weren't prepared. Although..." Nell looked toward the girls, a curious expression on her face. Lydia followed her gaze to where they were both serenely coloring away.

"Although what?"

"Abigail and Genevieve, right? Jon Blackwell's daughters?"

"Yes."

"Hmm. Maybe things have changed now that you're, um..."

"Nell, please feel free to speak openly. What happened last time?"

"Genevieve bit the hygienist and Abby knocked over a cart of instruments."

That explained a lot, Lydia thought. "I can go back with them, right?"

"Yes, of course. We prefer that."

"I can assure you that neither of those things will happen today."

Nell heaved out a relieved breath. "Great."

An hour later, dental appointments complete, the girls were in the waiting room rummaging in their goodie bags, excited about their new toothbrushes and stickers. Lydia was checking out when Nell and the hygienist appeared beside her.

Tara, whom she'd learned was the Gen bite victim, reached out and squeezed her arm. "Thank you. I can't believe the transformation. Whatever you're doing, keep on doing it."

The receptionist whispered, "Are you from one of those nanny emergency shows?"

Nell grinned. "Does Jon know how lucky he is? If he isn't paying you a million dollars a year, you need to ask for a raise."

"Thank you, ladies, but I'm the lucky one. They're really wonderful kids."

After stowing their bags in the car, they walked up the street and crossed to the drugstore, before venturing back to Brewster Ranch Supply.

A wide porch stretched across the front of the building. An elderly man with the craggy face of a wind-swept cowboy lounged in one of the four wooden rocking chairs arranged there. A chessboard sat beside him, midgame from the look of it.

"Hi, Blackwell twins," he said, the fondness in his eyes immediately winning her over. If Lydia had time to kill she'd settle in for a chat.

"Hey, Pops," Gen and Abby answered.

Keen eyes shifted to Lydia. "You must be Jon Blackwell's new nanny. I heard you're working

out real well and that you can cook like a professional."

"Yes, sir. I'm Lydia. Word travels fast around
here, huh?"

"Pleased to meet you, Lydia. My name is
Pops. And hurricane-force winds don't blow as
fast as gossip in this town."

Lydia laughed.

Pops grinned before turning serious. "But the
important question is, do you play chess?"

She'd learned at Hatch House and she and
Tanner played often. "As a matter of fact, I
do." With a deliberate lift of one eyebrow, she
reached out and moved a knight.

Pops studied the board for a moment before
looking up and winking his approval. "'Bout
time Jon Blackwell was blessed with a good
woman in his life."

Lydia grinned. "I agree, Pops. Thank you."

"Intriguing move. Come on back and play
some time."

"I'll do that."

"See you later, Pops," Gen said. "We're going
to look at the saddles."

Abby squeezed her hand. "Lydia, can we look
at the bunnies, too?"

A trio of bunnies was featured on the sign
hanging in the window. *Bunnies are here! Just*

in time for your Easter celebration. Abby stared up at it. "I mean, please, if we have time?"

Lydia wondered if Jon realized that he'd invited her to church on Easter Sunday? Yet another reason she needed those packages to arrive.

"Of course, we'll see everything while we're here." Might as well. Because if she'd learned one thing on her first trip to Falcon Creek, it was that there was no point in trying to hide in this town.

"I HAVE THAT exact same pair."

Lydia glanced up from the bench in Brewster's surprisingly large shoe section, where she was trying on boots. A woman smiled down at her, pointing at the boot on Lydia's right foot.

Long, loose, dark curls framed a pretty round face. Lean and trim in a pair of snug blue jeans and a form-fitting T-shirt, she had the look of a person who, unlike Lydia, regularly skipped dessert and never blew off morning boot-camp class. She'd noticed her earlier by the chicken feed, flirting with a cowboy whose curly blond hair was nearly as long Lydia's.

"Do you?" Lydia looked down. On her left foot was the rubber boot hybrid Tom had recommended; high-topped, waterproof, but not nearly as stiff as a typical rain boot, plus they had a nice comfy insole with a thick fleece lining. Lydia was already sold and felt like wearing them out of the store. The one on the right didn't fit nearly as well and cost almost twice as much.

"Yep, that one on your right foot is the way to go."

"What about cowboy boots?" Lydia asked, noting the gorgeous pink-and-gray leather boots gracing the woman's tiny feet.

"Cowboy boots are good for dressing up and for riding. But those ugly old things you've got on are the only ones I wear for barn chores. You need some traction when it gets muddy."

"That's a fact about the traction. No way to get an all-purpose ranching boot, huh?"

The woman laughed. "I'm afraid not. I don't even ride in these because they're too fancy. These are my dress-up boots. For riding, you need a smooth-soled boot that will fit in the stirrup and come up higher than the hobble strap. A regular old cowboy boot is best." She pointed at a plain brown pair Lydia was considering.

She frowned thoughtfully. "You're not from around here, are you?"

"Um, no."

Stepping closer, she reached out a hand. "Marilee Compton. Oops, sorry, that's Marilee Inez. Recently divorced and took back my maiden name."

"Lydia Newbury."

Marilee's eyes went wide to match the "ohhh" that escaped her lips. Lydia bit back a laugh as yet another person pieced together who she was.

Gen and Abby appeared with the salesgirl, Belle, who'd graciously offered to show the girls a batch of new chicks while Lydia tried on boots.

"*You're* Jonathon's new nanny?"

Jonathon? Lydia hadn't heard anyone call him that, which made her wonder about this woman's connection to her rancher boss.

"Yes, ma'am, she is," Gen answered, coming over to stand next to Lydia. She placed her tiny hand possessively on Lydia's knee. "She's the best nanny ever." The gesture and the words stirred the affection already firmly planted inside of her. Lydia covered Gen's hand with her own. Abby positioned herself next to Gen and took her sister's hand.

"Hello, girls. How are you?" Marilee's voice sounded chipper, but her gaze roamed over them for so long Lydia began to wonder what she was looking for.

Abby answered flatly. "We're fine, Marilee. Thank you for asking. How are you?"

Lydia smiled inside at Abby's recitation of the manners lesson they'd reviewed that morning. But her tone and stance told Lydia she didn't like this woman. Confident, talkative Gen stood tense and silent beside her.

Marilee seemed caught off guard. "Well, I'm good, Abby. How sweet and so polite. And don't you girls look...pretty?"

Abby stared up at Marilee, her stony expression so much like her father's that Lydia felt something catch in her chest. Gen's hand gripped Lydia's fingers even tighter as a fierce protectiveness gripped Lydia's entire body.

Lydia slipped the boots off her feet. "Well, we'd better get going. Nice to meet you, Marilee. Thanks so much for the boot advice."

She boxed up Tom's recommendation and handed the boots to Belle. "I'll take these."

Marilee appeared to be watching her carefully. Voice overly friendly, she said, "It was nice to meet you, too, Lydia. And you're welcome. Maybe we can get together sometime after you're all settled in?"

"What a nice offer," Lydia replied, purposely keeping it noncommittal. The girls didn't like this woman and that had Lydia's alarm bells ringing.

Marilee beamed. "Consider it a date then. Abigail, Genevieve, we'll see you girls in church," she said, and sauntered away. The girls didn't relax until the woman was well away.

Lydia added a pair of cowboy boots to the

cart already loaded with other items on her list and the list Tom had given her. Between what she'd found at the drugstore and here at Brewster's, she could get by until her orders arrived, as long as they were here by Easter.

She crouched in front of the twins. "Thank you, girls, for being so good. I'm so proud of you I can barely stand it."

They beamed at her. Gen gave her a hug.

"Now, let's go take a peek at those bunnies."

CHAPTER TEN

WHERE WAS EVERYBODY? Jon and Trout entered a quiet kitchen. Evidence of a craft project littered one end of the table—macaroni, string, bits of fabric and what looked like Mason jar lids. A cursory check of the living room, family room and the girls' bedroom revealed no hints of their whereabouts, either.

He'd wanted to spend a few minutes with the girls before he headed out to the Blackwell Ranch. A note on the edge of the counter caught his eye.

Jon, the girls and I headed into town for their dentist appointments. We also need to pick up a few things in addition to what was on the list Tom gave me. We're hoping we'll be back in plenty of time that you won't even have a chance to read this note. P.S. Abby wants me to add that we made cherry pie for dessert. Gen wants me to remind you that you promised to take them out to see the calves again tonight.

Lydia had signed it but his throat went tight when he saw the two signatures scrawled under hers across the bottom—Genevieve Dorothy Blackwell and Abigail Louise Blackwell. He'd never seen Gen write out her entire name before. Smiling, he considered tucking the paper in his pocket.

Picking up the pen, he added a message of his own:

Lydia, Abigail, Genevieve; Sorry I missed you girls this afternoon. Had to run out to Big E's again. That pie looks like perfection. I'll try to be home for dinner to help you eat it. Love, Dad

He added a *Jon* in parentheses. He'd just slipped his boots on when he heard the doorbell ring. Instead of removing them or tracking mud through the house, he went out the back door. He made it to the front in time to watch a delivery truck pulling away.

Climbing the porch steps, he discovered the packages had his name on them. He hadn't ordered anything. Could this have something to do with Big E? A surprising bout of concern chased the question. The front door was locked, so he carted the packages around to the back and deposited them in the mudroom. Using his pocketknife, he slit the top of one box open. Pink velvet and satin glowed ominously from the depths. Lydia. He closed the box.

Jon's blood went cold. Memories coursed through him, leaving him tense from a potent combination of latent anger and fresh disappointment. Ava had nearly brought him to financial ruin with her shopping habits. She'd used secret credit cards and drawn money from his savings accounts, and he was still digging himself out of the hole she'd left. He'd been honest with Lydia when he'd said the cable bill was an unnecessary expense. He just hadn't told her how tight his budget was. Anxiety churned inside of him as he thought about the interview marching closer by the day. He needed it to go well.

Jon told himself this was another good reminder of why he couldn't keep her on. Not only was Lydia not interested in the ranch, but she also loved to shop. Irritation bubbled inside of him. It was not a habit he wanted her teaching the twins.

LYDIA UNLOCKED THE front door, noting once again the absence of her packages. She was going to have to go online and see if she could track them. But that would have to wait. Right now, she needed to finish dinner. In addition to making a cherry pie, she'd put soup in the slow cooker that morning. She wanted to make a batch of biscuits to go with it.

"Girls, please take your bags to your room. Then meet me in the kitchen, okay?" Lydia had learned not to give Gen too many tasks at a time. She tended to get distracted and forget, which is when mischief happened.

Lydia dropped her bags in her room and headed to the kitchen, where she spotted the note Jon left. Reading the words made her insides go warm.

Gen and Abby joined her.

"Hey, your dad saw our note. He left one for you guys, too. You want to read it with me?"

They climbed their stools. Lydia asked them if they recognized any words on the note. Gen picked out *Dad* and Abby spotted *pie*. Then Lydia slowly read the message, pointing to each word as she read.

"Does that word say 'love'?" Gen asked when she'd finished.

"Yes, it sure does."

"I love Daddy."

"He loves you, too. I bet you could write that now, couldn't you? You know how to write all of those letters. All you have to do is put them together."

Gen looked up at her, gray-blue eyes shining bright and clear. "I love you, too, Lydia."

The words pierced her heart so forcefully that tears sprung into her eyes. And for the first time, she truly comprehended the painful truth of this situation. In the beginning, she'd been so focused on being safe, and then on convincing Jon to keep her on. Teaching and caring for the girls felt like second nature. She'd failed to see the reality underlying it all. She was, in fact, going to have to leave someday. Not at the end of these two weeks, hopefully, but no matter when, it would be way too soon. How cruel that she'd finally found a job she could imagine doing for the rest of her life and it could only be temporary.

Reaching out, she gathered the girl for a hug. "I love you, too, Genevieve."

"We wish you could be our mommy," Abby chimed in with another slam that stole her breath.

Oh, boy. She had no idea how to handle this. She wasn't prepared for this emotional attachment to happen so quickly. It felt like her heart had been taken apart and then reassembled, with the girls solidly at the core. Lydia couldn't think of a single thing she wouldn't do for them.

Throat thick with emotion, she gave Abby a tight hug, too. "Well, I might not be your mom, but I love being your nanny. And I love you girls, too."

There weren't any rules about nannies loving the kids they cared for, were there?

LYDIA WAS REMOVING the biscuits from the oven when the phone rang. She allowed Gen to answer it because she recognized Jon's cell number on the caller ID. She told her dad a little about their trip to town and answered questions about the dentist appointment. Then she listened for a moment and said goodbye. She turned to Lydia. "Daddy told me to tell you not to wait on dinner. He's stuck out at Big E's."

Lydia pondered the interesting mix of disappointment and relief this news evoked but hid it from the girls. They were so excited about the evening schedule of checking out the calves with her, it wasn't difficult. On one hand, she wanted Jon to show her the ranch he was so proud of. But on the other, she was nervous that it would illuminate what he already disliked about her— that she didn't know anything about ranching. She'd been doing research and had a hundred questions about cattle and raising beef. She'd even prepared herself for the harsher aspects, so she wouldn't act like a novice when faced with the hard truths of the industry.

"Okay, girls, let's go ahead and eat."

Lydia dished up their food and carried it to the table.

When they were almost finished Gen asked, "Are we still going to go out to see the calves? We want to show you the horses, too."

"I'd like to. But since your dad's not here I'm not sure we should." Although she didn't know why not, the girls went out there every day, but either with Jon or Tom. She assumed she'd count as an acceptable chaperone, but the trouble was she didn't know the rules.

"We can call Tom," Gen suggested.

Lydia looked at Abby, who nodded like this was a viable option. Lydia didn't want to bother him, but it suddenly seemed like the answer she'd been looking for. She could quiz Tom and add to her knowledge without reminding Jon of the extent of her ignorance. Plus, she had the items he and Jon had requested from Brewster's. She headed to the phone. Tom picked up on the third ring, which Lydia thought might be a good sign. At least he wasn't helping with a delivery. She briefly explained without revealing her personal motives. He sounded cheerful and told her he'd meet them in front of the barn.

"Okay, girls, we're all set. Let's gear up."

After fetching her new boots, she found the girls waiting in the mudroom gathered around a stack of boxes.

"Lydia, look, it's your packages!" Abby said when she joined them.

"Finally!" she exclaimed. "What a relief. You haven't put your boots on yet. You girls each grab a box and I'll take two and we'll stash these in my room."

"What's in them?" Gen asked shyly.

Lydia flashed her a grin. "School supplies and other important things. You'll see."

FOR THE SECOND time that day Jon and Trout entered to an empty house. But this time there was no note. The oven was still warm and the slow cooker was set to low. Lydia's SUV was in the driveway, so he knew they'd returned from town. The packages had disappeared from the mudroom, too. Maybe she was in her room trying on her expensive new clothes, he thought cynically. A quick trip down the hallway coupled with Trout's disinterest told him no one was inside.

He tapped out a text to Tom: Have you seen Lydia and the girls?

Jon paced in the kitchen and waited for a response, which came two minutes later: They're out here looking at the cows.

Did he mean Lydia was out there, too? He must have, because where else would she be? Yesterday, he'd asked her to go out with him and the girls and she'd refused the offer. What had changed?

"Come on, Trout. Let's go see what the girls are up to."

He could hear them all laughing before they ever reached the pasture. Trout ran ahead. The girls' enthusiastic greetings made hiding his sour mood easier.

Tom said, "Hey, Jon, look who came out here to fall in love."

Lydia said, "It's true. You were right. There's nothing cuter." When she turned those bright blue eyes on him there was so much eagerness reflected there he could almost believe she meant it. But the problem here was that he didn't believe her. And that was partially his fault, he realized. He never should have pointed out that she hadn't seen the ranch. He was forcing her to do things and lie for this job that he never intended to let her keep, anyway. Disappointment, anger and guilt mingled inside of him.

Abby approached Lydia and slipped her tiny hand into hers. Lydia lifted it and planted a kiss on the back like she'd done it a thousand times.

Beside him, Gen said, "We're going to show Lydia the horses next. Do you want to come?"

He did. And he didn't. Frustration and longing constricted his chest so tightly he could barely breathe. Why had he agreed to let her stay for this bogus trial period? Two weeks hadn't seemed very long at the time. He'd been desperate for child care and taken in by her enthusiasm and charm. His heart suddenly felt cold, like it was packed in ice. The girls were falling in love with her and he was falling in love with the idea of a woman he knew didn't exist. She was only playing a part to keep this job. Although he didn't see how she could fake the affection building between her and the twins. He needed to figure this out.

"I'm going to pass on that because I have a few more things I need to do." Avoiding eye contact with Lydia, he said to the twins, "I'll see you girls back at the house, okay?"

"Okay, Daddy. Come on, Lydia." Gen took her other hand and led her toward the horse barn.

Resisting the urge to watch them walk away, Jon turned and headed back to the house.

JON WAS IN the office when Lydia and the twins returned to the house. The girls went in and visited with him for a few minutes, but they reappeared quickly. Lydia played a game. Then they got ready for bed and each picked out two books for Lydia to read. Usually, if Jon was in the house, he'd take over for the last story or two. Not tonight. She kissed them both and promised to let their dad know they were ready to be tucked in.

Lydia lightly knocked on the partially open door of his office.

"Come in."

He was seated behind his desk.

"I'm sorry to interrupt but the girls are waiting for you to tell them good-night."

He glanced up but didn't quite make eye contact. "I'll be right there."

"Before you do, can I talk to you about something?"

"Sure."

"Abby wants a bunny."

"A bunny?" he repeated flatly.

"Yes, and I know Gen would love one, too. We looked at them today in Brewster's. I know you have a lot going on, but they sell cages and I wouldn't mind paying for them out of my own pocket and I could give them each a bunny for—"

"Lydia, hush."

"Hush?" she repeated, casting him a playful scowl. "Did you just hush me?" He frowned, and Lydia saw the tight lines around his eyes. He looked upset.

"Yes, you don't need to lay out an argument so my girls can get pet rabbits. I'm not opposed. Except…" He studied her carefully and that's when Lydia realized that something was wrong. He looked exhausted. Probably because he was. She knew he only slept a few hours a night. But this was...different.

"Except what?"

He opened his mouth, shut it again and finally answered, "Nothing."

"Great. Thank you. I've already done some bunny research. They make great pets and they're relatively easy to care for."

"More YouTube?" His smirk rubbed her the wrong way.

"Yes."

He blew out an impatient sigh. "Don't buy a cage. Tom and I will build something."

"Okay, I'll call Brewster's and see if they can hold the bunnies for a few days."

"They'll do that. Ask for Grace or Alice and mention my name."

"Thank you. Abby is going to flip."

His expression was so intense it made her nervous.

Lydia walked closer to his desk. "Are you okay?"

"Yep." He reached around to grip the back of his neck. "Just...trying to figure out what I'm going to do."

Lydia froze while her heart clawed its way up into her throat. Was he talking about her?

She still had several days left to prove herself. "Can I help?"

"Not unless you know a detective."

Her pulse raced. "A detective?" Had he somehow found out the truth about her?

"My grandfather is still gone. He won't return my calls. Three of my brothers won't return my calls. My step—" One side of his mouth formed a sardonic curve. "Zoe won't answer my texts."

"Are you worried something happened to them? Should you file missing-person reports or something?"

"No. I'm not worried like that. They took off in their motorhome. They've been…seen. Sort of. Evidence of them has. I'm—I'm about at the end of my rope here."

"Maybe I could—" She moved to step around his desk.

"No." He stood so fast his chair hit the wall behind him with a thud. "I don't want you—" He stopped to clear his throat and when he continued his tone was tight. "I'll figure it out."

Lydia was struck with the feeling that he was deeply displeased, possibly angry. With her? She didn't know. For the life of her she couldn't imagine what she'd done.

He moved around the desk and it took a second for Lydia to realize she was standing in his path. She waited until he looked at her again.

Her spirits plummeted. Rancher Grim-Face had officially returned.

"Jon?" Reaching out a hand, she touched his forearm. "Did I—?" The jolt to her bloodstream combined with the look of revulsion on his face made her words skip like a scratched vinyl record. Lydia withdrew her hand and before she could get the needle back on track, he sidestepped her as if she'd burned him.

"Lydia, please…" Looking away for a moment, she watched him draw a few deep breaths. When he looked back at her, his eyes were like ice chips. Voice tight, he said, "What would help me is for you to keep your focus on the girls for the next five days, okay?"

Lydia felt her face heat like a blowtorch. What in the world had she been thinking trying to comfort him? And touching him? Then the meaning behind his words sunk in. Five days? He'd already decided to let her go?

"I'm sorry."

He sighed. "Please stop apologizing when you're just being yourself. You shouldn't have to do that."

"I don't know what that means." The knot of anxiety tightened in her belly.

"I know." He shook his head and glanced up at the ceiling for a moment. "I know you don't." He nudged his chin toward the door. "I'd better get in there. Abby won't fall asleep if she knows I'm coming."

Lydia tried to smile but her face felt immovable, like a plastic mask. She wanted to cry but for a reason so much deeper than her humiliation. "No, she won't."

Jon strode out the door and that was the last she saw of him that evening.

A FEW DAYS LATER, Lydia and the girls were on their way inside from visiting the horses when a pickup pulled up. Lydia was expecting Sofie and she couldn't wait to see her friendly face.

"It's the Carnes!" Abby cried.

Lydia and the girls closed the distance and they all exchanged greetings. Gen and Abby hugged them both and then asked if they could head inside. Lydia knew they were anxious to finish a project they'd started the day before.

Sofie said, "Lydia, I don't think you've met my husband, Zach, yet. Zach, this is Lydia."

"Ah!" Zach took a step toward her, arms spread wide. He was wearing a smile Lydia could only describe as roguish. "Finally! It's such a pleasure to meet Ms. Nanny Fantastic."

"Zach!" Sofie cried.

Lydia let out chuckle of surprise. "Who?"

"What, Sofie? She's gonna hear it eventually.

Lydia, that's what people are calling you all over town."

"All over town?" A flurry of nerves erupted inside of her. "I've only been to town one time and that was three days ago." Three days since she'd gone to town, three days of Jon acting displeased. Rancher Grim-Face was worse than Rancher Grouch-Face. At least when he was grouchy he still spoke to her. She was convinced she was getting fired. "Why would they call me that?"

Zach laughed and shook his head. "You really don't know what you've done, do you?"

"What I've done?"

"How you've tamed the Blackwell twins. It's currently the talk of Falcon Creek. You're fast becoming a legend."

"Tamed them?" Lydia said, feeling her temper rise. She was getting tired of these false notions where the girls were concerned. "I didn't have to *tame* them. They're sweet, intelligent, amazing, wonderful kids who just needed some direction and attention."

Zach tossed his wife an amused grin. "Sofie, I think you need to clue her in on exactly what she's accomplished."

Lydia scowled at the man. "I don't think Jon would appreciate you talking about his children that way."

Zach laughed. "It's okay. Jon is my best friend. Trust me when I tell you, he knows how difficult the twins are."

Words and statements came floating back to her. Jon warning her, calling the girls "holy terrors." She thought about the women in the beauty shop, Dr. Beazley's staff, Marilee studying them in Brewster's, the clerk Belle gushing about their good behavior. How Mr. Rennick at the drugstore had seemed nervous when they came in and kind of followed them around. Lydia had thought he was being kind. Even the normally stoic Tom had commented on their good behavior.

"Well, I adore them. And whatever difficulties they may have had in the past need to stay there, in the past. And I would appreciate it if you wouldn't use words like *difficult* and *tame* when referring to them. Often those kinds of monikers stick with a person and affect them their entire life." Didn't Lydia know the truth of that? *Spoiled, difficult* Lydia, who exasperated her father and couldn't get along with her stepmother. All she'd needed was a little understanding, someone to listen and maybe give her the attention she'd no longer received after Nana passed away.

Zach removed his hat. "Yes, ma'am. I can see how that might be the case. I apologize."

"Good." Lydia had startled herself with the vehemence behind her speech. Maybe she was a little distraught, between Jon's behavior and her impending dismissal. But she meant every word. Zach surprised her with the abrupt turn-around. "Apology accepted. I'm sorry if I seem a little, um, over-the-top."

"You heard the woman, Zach, apology accepted. Now, if you're done standing around and gossiping like an old hen I could use the help that you're here to give me."

Lydia turned to find Jon standing behind her. Perfect, she thought as her stomach took a dip. How long had he been there? Long enough to hear her give his best friend a piece of her mind. Everything had been going so smoothly until three days ago. She couldn't take this anymore. She needed to talk to him.

At that moment, Abby stuck her head out the door. "Lydia, we're ready for our fashion show."

"Fashion show." Sofie clapped her hands. "That sounds fun. I brought it, by the way."

Jon focused his scowl on her and Lydia could feel the hostility radiating from him. In a tone rife with sarcasm, he repeated, "Fashion show? That sounds constructive." He added a disgusted shake of his head. "I hope that's not all you have planned for today." He looked at Zach. "Let's go." Then he turned and stalked off toward his pickup.

Zach shrugged at Sofie, gave her a quick kiss and followed Jon.

CHAPTER ELEVEN

"Wow. That was rude. What is the matter with him?" Sofie asked after the men were out of earshot.

Lydia felt horrible. Tears burned behind her eyes. "I don't know. He's been like that for a few days now."

Sofie shook her head and was about to comment but Lydia headed her off. "Is it in the back seat?" She couldn't talk about this. She was too close to breaking down.

"Yes," Sofie said drily. "I was going to have Zach carry it inside before they left but apparently there's a fire burning somewhere and Jon's been elected fire chief. Seriously, Lydia, I can see you're avoiding this subject, but I'm tempted to take off after him myself and give him a piece of my mind."

"I can get it." Lydia headed over to the pickup and opened the back door. She gathered the portable sewing machine and supplies sitting on the floor behind the seat.

"Why didn't you lay into Jon like you did Zach? That was awesome, by the way."

"Because I really want this job."

"He doesn't deserve you if that's the way he's been treating you." Sofie shook her head as if trying to puzzle it out. "I mean he wasn't happy that first day but I thought he was over it."

"Me, too."

"Him and his city-phobia."

Lydia chuckled. "Is that a thing, city-phobia?"

"It is where Jon Blackwell's concerned," Sofie said. "Falcon Creek is the only *city* he doesn't mind going to."

Once inside, Lydia put the kettle on to make Sofie some herbal tea. While it was brewing, she poured a cup of coffee for herself, took a fortifying sip and then set it down.

"The girls are anxious to try on their dresses. If you don't mind, I'll just get them pinned and then they can work on their puzzles while we visit."

"Of course."

Lydia had ordered the dresses for Easter, but they didn't quite fit. The girls were so slender, she needed to take them in a bit. She herded them into the bedroom and helped with the buttons and zippers. Together, they came out to show Sofie.

Abby touched the soft velvet. "It feels kind

of like a bunny. It's the prettiest dress I've ever had."

Gen seemed fascinated by the tulle, sticking her arms out and spinning.

Sofie oohed and aahed appropriately while Lydia plotted and pinned. She and the girls headed back to the bedroom. Lydia helped them remove the dresses to avoid the sharp pins. She got them started on their puzzles and went back to the kitchen.

Sofie was sipping her tea. Gesturing toward the sewing machine, she asked, "You can do this? Work that machine and make them fit?"

Lydia laughed. "I can."

"Who taught you how to sew?"

"My nana. Lucky for me, it landed me my first job. I worked as a seamstress for a while."

"And you were a cook?"

"After I was a dishwasher and a waitress, yes. Then I worked for a caterer."

"And a bakery?"

"Yep, among other things."

"Like what?"

"Let's see… Shampoo girl, babysitter, dog-walker, barista. Then I graduated to receptionist, office assistant, bookkeeper. There were other even more glamorous jobs thrown in there, too," she added drily. "Like maid and car detailer."

"Wow, I wish I would have done all that."

Lydia answered with a doubtful look.

"A sociology degree doesn't translate well to ranching life. In college, I worked at a bookstore. I could barely toast a bagel when Zach and I got together." Holding up a finger, she added, "I can still barely toast a bagel, to be honest."

Lydia smiled. "Yeah, I didn't go to college, but I've got mad practical skills." She didn't particularly want to discuss her colorful job history. She couldn't bear the thought that this job would soon be just the latest in a long list.

Changing the subject, she asked, "How did you and Zach meet?"

Sofie let out a snort of laughter. "Zach and I met at a livestock auction."

"A livestock auction? I thought you said you were from Seattle?"

"I am. I was there for a college project. It's a long story but I accidentally bought a bull from Zach."

"You what?!"

Sofie laughed. "I know, and I couldn't afford it. I tried to return it, but Zach didn't offer a return policy. He offered me a deal where I could work for him on his ranch and pay it off."

"And you took it?"

"Heck, yeah, I had an ulterior motive, I needed to ace that project. Against Jon's advice, Zach invited me to stay at his ranch. It didn't go well initially. But it didn't take long before I fell in love with the place and once Zach turned on that cowboy charm… I was a goner. The rest is history." She shrugged and pointed at her belly. "Technically, I guess it's more like the future."

"That is quite a story."

"Someday I'll tell you the entire thing. Jon didn't like me. Didn't think I was right for Zach. Or more like, he doesn't like people from the city in general. That sounds bad, but he's not, I swear. He's a really good man."

Lydia did believe that last part. Already, she could see he was a wonderful father, an incredibly hard worker and a great boss. He was fair and kind to his employees. She couldn't even say that he'd been unkind to her the last few days.

"I think you're saying I shouldn't take his bad mood personally. Believe it or not, aside from that first day, he hasn't been like this… The first week and a half was…great."

Sofie heaved out a sigh. "It's all Ava's fault."

Lydia glanced down the hallway to make sure the girls were nowhere near. She lowered her voice, anyway. "The girls' mother, where is she now?"

"London, as far as I know. She's a broadcast journalist."

Lydia felt a bolt of shock go through at those words. She wasn't sure what she'd expected but that wasn't it. Somewhere in the recesses of her mind she'd been speculating that maybe the woman had serious personal issues that made parenting prohibitive. Why else would she leave Jon and her babies?

"So, she just voluntarily gave them up?"

Sofie's expression was pained. "Yes. Zach says she never wanted them in the first place. She and Jon barely knew each other when they started dating. Jon was in Bozeman for a few months teaching a class on organic beef ranching. They met. Ava got pregnant. Jon married her and brought her here. He was still building up the JB Bar then. That's why he'd taken the teaching job, to make some extra money. Ava hated ranch life almost from day one, missed her job, her friends, the city... Anyway, she left when the girls were only a few weeks old."

Lydia felt her blood go cold. She said a silent thank-you that the girls hadn't been old enough to feel the full force of that abandonment. Because Lydia knew it well. Her parents had divorced when she was twelve, about the worst age imaginable. At least Jon wanted them. Neither of her parents had wanted her.

"She never sees them?"

"Nope. She relinquished all custody, gave up her parental rights."

Lydia heard a noise. Gen poked her head inside the door. It was so darn cute the way she waved when she noticed Lydia watching her. A rush of affection flowed through her. She couldn't imagine loving her own child more. And one thing was for sure—if she was ever lucky enough to have her own children, she would never leave. No matter the circumstances.

"We're all done with our puzzles. You want to come see?"

"You know I do."

"WHAT IS THE matter with you?" Zach asked from his spot in the passenger seat of Jon's pickup as they bumped along the edge of a field. They were going out to dismantle the dam the beavers were rebuilding.

"Nothing."

"Nanny trouble?"

"No," Jon scoffed, scrubbing a tired hand across his unshaven jaw.

"Really? 'Cause you seemed a little grumpy with her."

Jon shook his head. "She's just the nanny. Why would she care if I'm grumpy?"

"Just the nanny, huh? The woman has managed to corral your twins and she's only been here two weeks."

"Twelve days," Jon muttered, and then realized he'd given ammunition to Zach's argument.

He couldn't help but feel a surge of affection at the way she'd defended the girls to his best friend. "And you're not supposed to talk about them like that anymore."

"Yeah, I caught that." Zach laughed. "If you tell her I said it I will call you a liar. Sofie said Genevieve is learning her letters and writing her name?"

"Her entire name—first, middle, last," Jon said proudly.

"Yeah, she's just a nanny, all right. You know she has a nickname in town already, right?"

Jon shook his head.

"The whole town was stunned after their trip to Falcon Creek the other day. Scooter and Cody Goode both told me she's being referred to as Nanny Fantastic."

Despite his personal misgivings, Jon felt a stirring of pride. "She's an excellent nanny, I'm not denying that. She's some kind of a…twin whisperer. That's not the problem."

"Exactly what is the problem?"

"It's complicated."

"How so?"

"I don't want to talk about it."

"Me, either, if it makes you all prickly like this. Is it because you like her?"

"How is this not talking about it? And I like her fine."

"I'm your friend, who else are you going to talk to? And you don't like a woman like that *fine*. She's so gorgeous it makes my eyes burn to look at her. She talks like an angel but acts like a mama bear where your girls are concerned. The house is tidy and smells good. And I don't even want to mention her cooking, you lucky dog. I hate you a little because of it. Good thing for you Sofie is my soul mate."

Jon scoffed. "You're using terms like *soul mate* now? Really? You're going soft, are you aware of that?"

Zach gave him a silly grin. "The only thing I'm aware of is how much I worship Sofie. And how much you're acting like I did before I figured out I was in love with her."

"Please, stop talking. You know very well I could never be interested in another woman like Ava."

"Like Ava? What are you talking about? Lydia isn't anything like Ava. Other than the fact that they both happened to have been born in urban environments."

Jon awarded him the "exactly" expression.

"One last comment and then I'll shut up for real—you didn't think Sofie and I would work out, either. Based solely on your experience with Ava, which was hellish for sure. But Jon—"

Jon interrupted, "Not just Ava. There are plenty of other examples."

Zach shook his head, giving up the argument. "Still no word from Big E?"

"Not a one. Nothing from Zoe, either. And you know how that phone is attached to the tips of her fingers."

"This is strange."

"Irritating is what it is." Jon's concern for Big E had slowly evaporated, leaving a thick residue of frustration. If there was anything seriously wrong, they would have heard about it from Zoe or the sheriff by now. Which meant this was likely about something personal and Jon didn't have time to care what that was. He just needed Big E to get back to the Blackwell Ranch. Because his conversation with Zach reminded him of a fact he didn't want to think about—tourist season began in roughly a month. He was already running back and forth spending time he didn't have paying bills, accepting deliveries, meeting with the vet while Katie tended to the cattle, or vice versa. Then there was managing the construction of Zoe's ridiculous petting zoo.

It annoyed him having to confer with Katie about decisions that should be hers alone. Just the thought of having to help with the guest ranch in addition to the rest sent his blood pressure to heights that could not be healthy. That's all he needed right now, more city folk to contend with.

"It'll be nice having Lydia over for dinner on Sunday. Mom is dying to meet her. You know Brenna's friend, Nell Smith? She works at Dr. Beazley's office and she told Mom and Brenna that the girls acted like perfect little sweethearts in the office. Mom and Brenna and Tess are beside themselves to meet Nanny Fantastic. The only reason they haven't shown up at your place already is because it's calving season."

Jon couldn't help it, but he loved hearing this about the girls even as the information coiled the anxiety even tighter inside of him. It wasn't going to be easy to let Lydia go. But he was done discussing her with Zach. How could he talk about it when he didn't even know what was going on himself?

"I'm sorry he has to spare you today, Zach. I hope he knows that."

"He does. Besides, Matt got home yesterday so he's on duty now, too."

"Matt is home?" Jon stopped the pickup and shut it off.

"Yeah. Mom is so excited that he'll be here for Easter."

Easter? Jon wouldn't have guessed his mood could get any blacker. He'd known the holiday was coming up but with everything going on

he'd forgotten it was this Sunday. Which meant
the girls needed baskets and candy and dye to
color eggs and about a hundred other items.
Maybe Lydia could help. He could watch the
girls for a few hours while she ran into Falcon
Creek and picked up what they needed. Thankfully she'd be here until after Easter, at least.
Guilt and anxiety churned like a nasty whirl-
pool inside of him.

Zach climbed out of the pickup.

Trout let out an impatient whine, eager to join
Zach.

Jon stared out the windshield.

Zach stuck his head back inside. "Hey, Jon,"
he teased, "how 'bout you stop thinking about
your just-a-nanny so we can get to work?"

HAPPY CHATTER GREETED them as he and Trout
came through the door. Trout let out an impatient
whine, anxious to join the fun. Jon toweled him
off and let him go. Lowering himself onto the
bench, he took a moment to gather his thoughts.
Abby's high-pitched giggle almost dredged up
a smile. He knew what he'd find when he went
inside. It didn't matter if they were reading stories, writing, drawing, cooking or making paper
airplanes—the girls would be having fun…and
learning.

They still had their rough moments; Gen

didn't want to go to bed, Abby didn't want to brush her teeth, neither of them wanted to clean their room. Fits were thrown, tears were shed, giggling got out of hand, but Lydia managed all their moods like a seasoned expert.

Jon hated the way he felt. Tense and guilty and needy. He wanted to join them and yet being around Lydia made him uneasy and unhappy. Zach was right—he liked her. The girls loved her. The bottom line was that he wanted her to be different. He didn't want her teaching the girls how to shop and have fashion shows. The twins would not be materialistic and pretentious like their mother. He wished... With a frustrated exhale, he shed his jacket.

"That sounds like the sigh of a troubled man."

Jon looked up to find Lydia watching him from the doorway. She sure didn't look like a city girl anymore. He admitted to himself that aside from that first day, she never had. No makeup, and like she did with the girls, her long hair was always up and out of the way in some style that made him want to unwind it and see how the parts fit together.

He was rapidly reaching the conclusion that this was his curse in life—being attracted to exactly the wrong woman. Shifting on the bench, he busied himself with removing his boots.

"It's nice how you always take your boots off. Sofie says not all cowboys are so gracious."

She walked closer and sat down beside him. Jon inhaled a breath. Big mistake. The scent of her filled his lungs and addled his brain. He couldn't quite identify it, but it made him think of a spring morning when the lilacs first started blooming.

"This is my home and it will be for as long as I live. I'd like it to last, so I take care of it."

"That's nice." She nodded and gripped the bench beneath her. Jon could feel her tension now. He waited because he knew the unpleasant conversation that had been simmering between them was about to boil over.

She inhaled a breath. "Jon, if I did something to upset you I wish you'd tell me. Gen and Abby are doing so well. They've learned so much and I—"

"I know," he interrupted. "I know, and I appreciate what you've done. I should have said so before now. It's just that…" He paused and then decided not to hold back. She deserved for him to be honest. "I have issues, Lydia. They might seem silly to someone like you, but like I told you when I agreed to temporarily keep you on, I need someone who will be an example for the girls in a lot of ways."

"In what ways? I know I don't… I didn't know

about ranching, but I'm learning. I promise. I'm reading and watching videos."

"And going out to the barn?"

"Well, yeah." She gave him a little grin. "I like your ranch, Jon Blackwell. I can't wait to see more."

"That's convenient."

She frowned. "What is that supposed to mean?"

"It means you never went past the chicken coop until I pointed it out. Seems to me you're pretending to like it so you don't get fired."

"Are you serious?"

He shrugged a shoulder.

Her head tipped back to look up at the ceiling. She spent a few seconds muttering under her breath. When she turned her eyes on him they were flashing with emotion. It reminded him of the day he'd almost sent her away, the day he'd agreed to this frustrating mistake of a two-week trial.

"I didn't have any boots."

"What?"

"I didn't have any boots," she repeated flatly. "Appropriate boots, I mean. That's why I only went as far as the chicken coop and even that wasn't easy in my flip-flops. That's why I had bandages on my feet. There was an episode in the chicken pen and I slipped… Anyway, when you asked me to go out and see the cows the other day I realized I couldn't stand it anymore. I was dying to get out there and look around. When we went to town I bought some boots. I'd already ordered some but they were taking forever to get here. All my packages were taking forever. Funnily enough, when we got home the packages were here so now I'm flush with boots." She added a bitter laugh. "I'll be sending a few things back."

"Why didn't you just tell me that? That you didn't have boots? When I asked about your feet? Or when I asked you to go out and see the cows?"

Her head dipped down. "Because I only had those stupid boots that I was wearing the day I got here. You were right about those. I certainly didn't want to put them on, and I didn't want to admit that I didn't have anything else. It felt like flashing my ranching incompetence in your face."

"Speaking of that, why would you come here, to a ranch, without boots? For that matter, why did you come here with only one tiny suitcase?"

A few long seconds passed while Lydia fidgeted beside him. "Um, it's a very long story. Suffice it to say that I needed a new start…" Her shoulders bunched as she turned to look at him again. "I figured I'd just buy whatever I needed when I got here."

Jon's thoughts were shuffling through his mind like a deck of cards in a dealer's hands. The pink velvet and satin popped into his mind. "All those packages were boots?" he asked doubtfully.

"No, of course not. I ordered Easter dresses for the girls. That's what the fashion show was about. They were too big, but there's not enough time to send them back and get new ones. Which is why Sofie brought me Willa's sewing machine. So I could alter them."

Jon swallowed but his throat was so thick with the ball of regret and shame lodged in it, it was difficult. "You ordered Easter dresses for the girls?" His *thoughts* hadn't even reached as far as dresses.

"Yeah."

"And you know how to sew?"

"I do." She shrugged a shoulder. "I also ordered Easter baskets and toys and candy for them. I didn't know what you already had but I figured I could send stuff back. And I needed school supplies. And hair conditioner, but I was able to find that in town so now we have plenty. I hope the Easter stuff wasn't overstepping. I've been meaning to talk to you about all of this, but I wasn't sure what my role was in this situation.

You're busy and then... Honestly, lately, you've been kind of...moody. I know you're worried about your grandfather and the family ranch and...everything."

The skin on his back itched like he'd gotten into poison ivy. But he deserved the humiliation. He also owed her an apology.

Reaching out, he tried to take her hand. She wouldn't let him, so he attempted to pry her fingers from the bench seat. After a struggle that made him smile, she produced her hand. Her skin felt just as creamy and smooth as he'd imagined. Heat shot through his bloodstream and he wanted to lift her hand to his mouth and kiss the palm. Touching her, he realized, was a mistake, just as it had been the other night when she'd touched him. But he wouldn't let go now and risk making her feel worse.

"Lydia, I owe you an apology. I am sorry. I was thinking things, assuming things, about you that were unfair."

Those bluebird eyes studied him, wide and uncertain. "Why?"

"I... It's a lot to tell. In a nutshell, I haven't had good luck with women and relationships." He felt his eyes drift to her lips. *Especially beautiful city girls who make me forget my manners and tempt me to kiss the sadness from their eyes.* Pulling his gaze back to hers, he said, "Not that ours is that kind of relationship. But I entered into this agreement not trusting you, not believing that you could handle it. That wasn't fair to you."

Her voice was soft as a summer breeze. "Is it because of Ava?"

Jon froze. Gently, he released her hand and spread his fingers over his knees. Sofie must have said something. Or Zach. But what had they told her? What should he tell her? Some of it she should know if she was going to be caring for the girls but...

Lydia went on, "Sofie explained a little bit to me. Not that much, but enough for me to know it didn't end well."

A loud squeal erupted from the other room and saved him from having to answer. Like Jon, Lydia glanced toward the doorway, assessing the nature of the noise. Trout let out a happy bark. Giggling followed.

Curling her fingers around his forearm, she gave it a squeeze. "Thank you for the apology. I'm glad to hear it's not anything I did. On purpose, anyway."

Then she stood and flashed him a smile so sweet it left him weak in the knees. He'd never met a woman who was so forgiving. Or so appealing. He had to acknowledge that fact, too, because he was running out of reasons not to like her. His next challenge was going to be keeping these feelings in line for a few more days. Which only strengthened his opinion that he needed to let her go. He couldn't be harboring romantic feelings for the nanny. But how was he going to do that when all he wanted to do was beg her to stay?

CHAPTER TWELVE

EASTER MORNING, LYDIA walked out the back door holding a large, steaming pan and promptly stopped in her tracks. The sunrise was painting the horizon with pastel streaks of orange, yellow, purple and pink on a background of blue that seemed too bright for this time of morning. Silvery mountains jutted out of the earth. She could see cows and calves milling around in the field, their fur shimmering in the morning light. Two deer eyed her warily from the edge of the yard. She didn't think she'd ever get tired of their morning visits.

Happiness unfurled inside of her. She'd never been so moved by the sheer beauty around her. *This place.*

A rooster crowed, startling her out of the moment and prompting her to resume her mission. The day before, she'd borrowed a large pan from Dusty in the bunkhouse. This morning, she'd risen extra early. The lights were on inside, so she knocked on the door.

Tom answered, coffee mug in hand. Surprise

blossomed across his handsome features. "Good morning, Ms. Lydia."

"Good morning, Tom. Happy Easter. Did you see the sky this morning, by any chance?"

"Happy Easter to you. I've been admiring it myself."

"I swear I've never seen anything so beautiful in my life."

"I'd have to agree."

"Not even my new boots can compare."

"I've noticed," he said with a trace of a smile.

Dusty appeared behind him, also looking a little startled and rather bashful. Gray hair a bed-head mess, he attempted to pat it down.

"Hey, Dusty. I'm returning that pan you loaned me but it's full of sticky buns. Hope that's okay."

Dusty came closer. Lydia slipped off the loose foil covering. "Son of a biscuit…" He dipped his head and took a whiff. If a person could sniff reverently, Dusty managed it. "Those look exactly like the kind my granny used to make. Are those pecans?"

"Yes, they are. Here you go."

Carefully, he took the pan from her. "Thank you, Ms. Lydia. Even though it pains me to do so, I will share these with the boys. But I will also hide an extra one, possibly two, for myself and Tom. These guys are pigs."

Lydia laughed. "That seems fair. I wanted to thank you two again for helping with the bunnies."

"That was our pleasure," Tom said. "Can't wait to see Abby's face."

Lydia grinned. "Me, either. Jon will text you before we head outside so you don't miss it. Will we see any of you at church later?"

Dusty said, "Tom and Grady will be there. The rest of us will tend the herd. But it's light duty for everyone today—except the heavies, of course."

Lydia chuckled at his cow joke. "I understand. At least the rain has stopped. Will it be dry enough for them to birth outside now or will they have to go in?"

Tom answered, "I was just heading out to check on that. But I suspect it's going to be a good day to be born on the JB Bar."

"That's great news." She'd learned how the cows disliked having to go into the shed to give birth. It tugged at her heartstrings to hear their bellows of distress. They chatted for a few more minutes before Lydia told them goodbye and headed back to the house.

"Mornin'." Jon was standing in the kitchen when she returned. He raised the steaming coffee mug in hand. "It is not a hardship to wake up to hot coffee in the morning. Thank you."

"Good morning and you're welcome," she said, flashing him a grin. When he wasn't grumpy with her, he was so easy to please. They seemed to have rounded a corner during the last two days. The night before, after the girls were asleep, he'd helped her fill their Easter baskets. Then they'd tiptoed around the house trying to decide on the best hiding spots. Abby's was in the hall closet behind some linens and Gen's was stashed inside the dryer.

"You're up even earlier than usual. What were you doing outside? The chickens aren't even awake yet."

"Oh, trust me, that rooster is awake. I nearly dropped the pan of sticky buns I was carrying to your cowboys."

"Sticky buns?" One eyebrow nudged up. "I hope my cowboys didn't get them all."

Chuckling, she crossed the kitchen to fetch her own cup of coffee. "Don't worry." She pointed to where the other pan was cooling. "There's plenty to go around. All my life I've dreamed of having double ovens. Yesterday I made brownies for Easter dinner and cookies for Scooter at the same time." She had it on good authority Scooter would be at church and she wanted to thank him for his kindness toward her with a basket of goodies.

"That was thoughtful of you, to take some to the guys."

She shrugged. "They work hard. I appreciate their taking the time to help you get that bunny housing complex done so quickly." She didn't mention Tom's hand in the acquisition of her boots.

His phone chimed, and he pulled it out of his pocket. "Zach wants me to ask the girls if they'd like to go for a ride at his place today after church. After dinner and the egg hunt."

"I'm sure they'd love that. I was going to bring them a change of clothes, anyway. I'll pack something they can ride in. And their boots."

"Do you... Would you like to ride, too? I'm a pretty good teacher."

There was an eagerness to his tone that Lydia couldn't resist, not that she wanted to. "Sure. Yes, I'd love to go for a ride."

"So, I guess that's a change of clothes for all of us."

Lydia heard the bedroom door open. She grinned eagerly at Jon. "This is going to be so much fun. I thought they were never going to get up."

The smile that split his face told Lydia he'd been looking forward to it, too. "It's nice how much you seem to enjoy them."

"I think it would be impossible not to."

The look he gave her heated her from the inside out.

The girls ran into the kitchen. "Did the Easter Bunny come?"

Jon lifted his hands and let them fall. "I have no idea. I guess you'll have to hunt around and see."

After plenty of giggling, a fair amount of searching and a few hints, they finally found their baskets. Chattering and excited, they examined every toy and trinket. Lydia wrangled them into the dining room for a breakfast of fruit and yogurt and sticky buns. When they finished, Lydia gave Jon an encouraging eyebrow-raise. He took out his phone, studied the screen and then tapped out a text.

Feigning bewilderment, he said, "Tom thinks maybe the Easter Bunny left something outside for you girls. Should we go check it out?"

A few minutes later the girls, coats on over their pj's and wearing barn boots, stood in stunned silence as they laid eyes on two fuzzy bunnies. Abby burst into tears. First, she hugged Jon. Then Lydia and Tom. Beaming, Gen cuddled one of the fluffy bundles to her chest.

Tom, Dusty and Jon had constructed a better bunny setup than Lydia could have ever imagined. They'd built it against the woodshed with the overhang offering protection. There was a hutch raised up off the ground, complete with a "burrow" for the critters to sleep in. A door could be opened onto a ramp that led down to the ground, where a grassy patch provided daytime grazing.

"Bunny paradise." Lydia shook her head in wonder.

Jon grinned. "We'll have to figure something out come winter, but this will do nicely for now."

Lydia watched the girls for a few minutes, her heart full and a little achy. Somehow, she needed to remember this moment and every other second of whatever time she had left here. She smiled at Jon. "It's going to be a challenge tearing them away from here for church."

His gaze meandered over her, leaving her skin tingling and her belly tight. "I understand the struggle," he said, his deep voice soft so that no one else could hear.

She opened her mouth and then closed it again. Was he flirting with her? Lydia's instinct was to flirt right back. Not a good idea, she told herself. A few days ago, she'd longed for him to like her. But his grumpiness had provided a natural distance. This playful sweet side was way more dangerous, and impossible to resist. Now she realized this situation might be easier if they didn't like each other quite so much. Because the problem was that even if she stayed for now, it wouldn't be forever. It couldn't be.

Lydia forced a smile. "I'd better get back inside and finish that potato salad."

A FEW HOURS LATER, Jon walked into the church and tried to decide what he enjoyed more, the sight of his girls in their dresses with their hair done up so pretty, or the fact that they seemed to like it so much.

Congregants were filing inside, many already seated in the pews. It wasn't difficult to spot Scooter's bright red hair.

"There he is." Jon pointed.

"I'll be right back," Lydia said, and headed up the aisle.

It took effort not to stare at her. The dress she wore was cut conservatively, almost to the point of being prim, but it clung to her curves in all the best ways. Lydia approached Scooter, shook hands with him and his parents. Laughter rang out. Jon smiled as he watched the back of Scooter's neck go red. He could relate. Lydia had that effect on people.

Jon and the girls slipped into a pew near the back. He braced himself for an exhausting hour of hushing and scolding the girls. Lydia returned and took her seat. The choir started singing. The girls were between them, and to Jon's astonishment, the twins were mostly quiet and barely fidgeted. A few times they whispered a question in Lydia's ear, to which she'd issue a brief gentle response. At one point, Gen drifted off while tucked in close to Lydia's side.

Lydia seemed oblivious to the stares and curious glances coming from every direction of the congregation. When the service was over, folks swarmed around wanting to meet her. Jon performed introductions. Lydia was gracious, kind and funny. The girls stood serenely next to them. With Lydia holding Gen's hand and one of Abby's enfolded in his, the girls politely accepted compliments about their dresses, their hair and exceptional manners.

Jon grew impatient and tried not to scowl when Emmet Baker sidled up next to Lydia. Emmet was an excellent cowboy. He was also a renowned womanizer and Jon didn't want him anywhere near his nanny. His nanny? He wasn't sure exactly when he'd decided to keep her on, but he had.

Knowing they could be stuck in church all day, he finally took Lydia's elbow and moved them toward the door. They were skipping coffee hour to head out to the Carneses' for the Easter festivities.

"I hope I didn't drag you out of there too quickly," Jon said as they crossed the parking lot toward his pickup. Trout barked a greeting from the open window. Jon ruffled his fur before opening the back door so the girls could climb inside.

"Not at all."

Closing the door, he turned toward her. She was so beautiful. It was no wonder the men inside had buzzed around her like bees to honey. But she was also…radiant. She'd probably always been that girl at parties that everyone wanted to talk to, sit by, dance with. The fact was he wanted her all for himself and the girls. But was that fair? If she was going to stay in Falcon Creek, she would want to meet people.

"Everyone is curious about you. You haven't been out much since you got here. We could go back inside if you want."

"Why would I want to do that?"

"I want you to have a nice day."

"I'm already having a nice day," she countered cheerfully.

"But it's supposed to be your day off and here you are spending it with us."

Lydia met his gaze headlong. "I can't think of anyplace else I'd rather be."

Her answer caused a burst of heat to shoot straight through his bloodstream. He fidgeted with his keys. "Okay, then. We best get going before someone else sidles up to meet my Nanny Fantastic."

WILLA CARNES PULLED Lydia in for a tight hug. "Lydia, it is so lovely to meet you. I've heard nothing but wonderful things from Sofie and Zach."

"Thank you, Mrs. Carnes. It's an honor to meet you as well. I've heard the same about you from Jon and Sofie and Gen and Abby. Thank you again for letting me borrow your sewing machine. Jon is bringing it in."

"Call me Willa. And it's my pleasure. Especially seeing my little peanuts in their Sunday best." She turned toward the girls, who'd followed Lydia inside. "Why, those are the most beautiful Easter dresses I've ever seen." She hugged them both in turn.

Abby beamed. "Thank you, Willa."

Gen looked at Lydia. "Is it okay if we keep our fancy dresses on until after dinner?"

"Sure, if you want to."

"We do. Thank you, Lydia." The girls skipped off.

Lydia turned and found herself facing two strikingly pretty women and a handsome young cowboy who could only be Zach's siblings.

They all looked so much alike it was difficult not to gawk.

The shorter of the women wore her tawny brown hair in a messy bun. She stuck out a hand. "Hi, Lydia. I'm Tess."

The other, hair in a long braid, followed suit and introduced herself. "Brenna, youngest." *Brenna Braids*, Lydia repeated silently to herself, so she could be sure and tell them apart.

Zach clone held out a hand. "Hello, gorgeous. Matt Carnes." Lydia shook it, but instead of releasing her hand, he lifted it high and held it there. He blew a soft, low whistle through his teeth. "And here I thought everyone was calling you fantastic because you were a great nanny."

"That was so bad." Brenna groaned. "You're such a dork, Matt."

Tess gave her brother a horrified look. "Does that kind of line work for you?"

"Ladies, I'm a bull rider. I don't even need lines."

"That's a relief, because I think all the good ones have been bucked out of you," Tess quipped. She removed Lydia's hand from Matt's and led her into the kitchen. "Come on, Lydia, let's go give that hand a good scrubbing."

They walked into a kitchen filled with organized chaos reminiscent of the Blumen family. Laughter, teasing and bickering abounded.

The smell of roasting ham and onions permeated the air. Lydia jumped right in, stirring the green beans, washing dishes and making dressing for a salad.

Zach's older brother, Derrick, and his wife, Raelynn, arrived with their three kids, Georgia, Ellen and Michael. Gen and Abby greeted them and soon they were all playing in the family room at the other end of the house.

When the ham came out of the oven, Pete set about carving it while they carted the rest of the food to the large dining room table. Everyone filled their plates, buffet-style. The day turned out to be as lovely as the sunrise had promised so they ate outside, where three picnic tables were pushed together.

Lydia enjoyed listening to talk of people, cattle, horses, weather and speculation about when they would drive the cattle to their summer grazing areas. Everyone, it seemed, helped with the cattle drive. It sounded like a blast. Lydia silently hoped she'd still be around for that.

The egg hunt commenced immediately after the meal. The kids delighted in discovering one brightly colored plastic egg after another hidden in the yard, garden, orchard and around the assorted outbuildings. While the kids sorted and admired their bounty, Lydia helped Sofie bring out dessert. Coffee was served. The kids scattered to eat candy and play a game of horse-shoes.

The adults visited until Zach announced it was time to go riding.

"Maybe I should stay and help with dishes?" Lydia offered, even though she wanted to ride.

Willa said, "Lydia, honey, you are a guest. You've done more than enough already. That was hands-down the best potato salad I've ever eaten. Pete made me promise I'd get the recipe. And please don't ask me how many of those brownies I had. Now go riding and have fun."

Sofie agreed. "There's plenty of people not riding. Don't worry, Willa won't have to lift a finger. Derrick and Raelynn have to leave soon so they're not going, and I can't ride anyway." Sofie patted her belly.

Lydia acquiesced and went to fetch the duffel bag she'd brought containing their spare clothes. Sofie showed her a room where she and the girls could change. When they came back outside, Jon, Zach and Tess were waiting. Brenna joined them.

Zach said, "All right. Let's go. Matt's already out saddling up the horses." He and Jon led the way to the barn.

Stomach fluttering, Lydia trailed behind, hoping she'd be able to bring up the rear, but Jon circled back and joined her. "Are you nervous?"

She managed a shaky grin. "How did you guess?"

Leaning over, he lowered his voice and answered, "You nibble on your lip when you're nervous."

Lydia glanced up to find him staring at her mouth. "No, I don't... Do I?"

"Yes, ma'am, you do."

His attention wasn't helping her nerves. Lydia swallowed. An enormous building loomed in front of them. "Wow. That is like the biggest barn I've ever seen."

"It's pretty fancy. I call it Zach's Equine Castle. This is just for his horses."

Several horses were already saddled and outside the entrance. A cowboy she hadn't met was helping Matt with the preparations. Zach introduced him as Dale.

"Jon, can the girls ride with Brenna and me?" Tess asked as she took the reins of a horse. "Then you can help Lydia. Matt and Zach will catch up when they're through."

"That would be perfect, Tess. Thank you."

Lydia had packed the girls' riding helmets. She made sure they were snug and secure. Matt lifted Gen to sit in front of Tess. Jon settled Abby with Brenna. Soon they were moving off across the pasture.

"You ready?" Jon asked.

The comforting scent of hay drifted from the barn and combined with horse and leather to calm her nerves and boost her confidence.

"Which one is mine?" she asked.

"This one. Her name is Cheyenne." Matt patted a brown rump. Then he quirked a rakish brow in her direction. "Do you know how to mount a horse, Lydia? Or would you like me to give you a little boost?" Eyes twinkling, he held out his arms like he was going to hug her.

Zach shook his head.

Jon rolled his eyes.

Lydia chuckled. "I think I can get that far, Matt. But thank you, that's a sweet offer."

Jon looked pointedly at Lydia. "Now, you don't want to hold the reins too tight, but you don't want them too loose, either. I'll show you after you get—"

"Hey, there, Cheyenne." Lydia slipped a foot in the stirrup and, with her heart threatening to jump out of her chest, swiftly mounted and settled into the saddle, reins quickly in hand. Before Jon could give further instructions, Lydia shifted slightly forward and clicked her tongue while giving a slight leg squeeze. "Let's go, Cheyenne." They headed across the field.

Behind her, laughter rang out, and Matt said, "Wow, you're either a really great teacher or she's a superfast learner, huh, Jon?"

CHAPTER THIRTEEN

THE RIDE WAS SCENIC, and exhilarating at moments where the trail snaked along the edge of the river. But her horse was a pro and Lydia relaxed into the saddle better than she'd dared hope. No surprise, the company was entertaining with the Carnes siblings teasing and insulting each other. Zach pointed out landmarks and relayed interesting tidbits to Lydia. Jon kept casting her sidelong glances and she wondered what he was thinking. She hoped that maybe, finally, she had a ranching skill he'd approve of.

On the way back, she allowed the others to get ahead of her and Jon. Where the trail led out of the brush into the open field, she halted her horse and dismounted. She could see the barn just over the rise.

As Jon stopped beside her, nerves left her trembly and a little breathless. She briefly considered moving on but wanted to have a private word with him. She needed to know what he'd decided and if he'd be placing a call to Eileen.

"Wow," she said. "That was fun. Can I talk to you for a minute?"

Jon dismounted and faced her. Lydia felt her spirits plummet. He was wearing his grim rancher face. Trout darted off to chase a squirrel.

"I'm glad you enjoyed it."

"You don't look happy."

"I wonder why that is?"

"I'm wondering, too. What did I do this time?"

He exhaled a breath like he was trying to hold on to his patience. "It's more like what you *can* do that has me in this state."

"What does that mean?"

"You can ride." The compliment warmed her even though it sounded a bit like an accusation.

"A little, but it's been a long time."

"More than a little, Lydia. You ride very well. How long has it been?"

"Roughly thirteen years."

"You let me give you instructions and make a fool of myself."

"I didn't mean to. I appreciated all of the advice."

"You told me you didn't ride."

She pointed a cautious finger at him. "If you think back, I never said that. You asked but I didn't answer. You assumed, and I didn't correct you because it had been a long time."

He muttered under his breath.

"I'm confused about why this has you so upset. I'm sorry I didn't tell you. I didn't know it would all come back to me like this."

"Don't apologize to me," he snapped. And then cursed. "You need to stop apologizing when you haven't done anything wrong."

"But you're mad at me."

Taking a step closer, he softened his tone. "Lydia, I am not mad at you. I'm mad at myself. Beyond angry. I'm seeing red. And stars. Red flashing stars."

"I don't understand. Why would you be that angry with yourself?"

Shaking his head, he stared over her shoulder for a few long seconds. His eyes met hers again and the intensity shooting from the gray depths almost made her flinch. "For hiring you. For letting you stay these two weeks. I never should have agreed to it. I should have given you money for a hotel and sent you away that first night."

Lydia grimaced. When she'd worked at the bakery, she'd once been hit from behind with a twenty-pound bag of flour thrown from a truck. It had knocked her to the ground. That didn't even compare to this kind of pain. Tears pooled in her eyes. Blinking them away, she tried to speak but her throat was on fire.

She rasped, "I'm sor—" And then swallowed

down the *sorry* she was going to utter. Pointing toward the barn, she turned away. "I should go."

Jon curled his fingers around her wrist. "Wait, please." When she faced him, he let go of her and took a small step back. "You're nothing like I assumed. I thought you were a spoiled, snobby shopaholic like my ex. I thought... But you're not. At all." Squeezing his eyes shut, he inhaled a deep breath before opening them again. "You're so much worse."

Lydia couldn't speak past the emotions constricting her lungs—anger and sadness and disappointment, and yes, there was a little fear there, too, because what was she going to do? Where was she going to go? But way beyond that, and so much more painful, was how was she going to leave the girls? She had so much she wanted to teach them, do with them, see them accomplish. She wasn't ready to say goodbye to them or to Jon. Hot tears flooded her eyes.

Her voice was a breathy whisper. "So, this is it? You're firing me?"

Removing his hat, he tossed it aside. One lightning-quick step brought him right into her space. She gasped as his arms went around her and he buried his face in her neck. "No, heaven help me, Lydia. I'm not firing you. I'm kissing you."

Then his lips were on hers and Lydia melted

against him. She was struck with the thought that he kissed like he did everything else. He was confident, bossy and so expert at it she could barely stand it.

When he moved like he was going to pull away, she slipped one hand behind his neck. He groaned against her mouth and kissed her again deeply.

After not nearly long enough he ended the kiss but stayed where he was. Cheek resting against her temple, Lydia liked how he sounded as out of breath as she felt. Angling his head, he trailed his lips across her cheek to her neck. He paused and she could hear him inhale a deep breath.

Shifting, she hugged him tighter and he made a sound like a cross between a growl and moan. Urging his lips back to hers, she kissed him this time. And for a moment, Lydia glimpsed a world, a feeling, she'd never dared dream existed.

The high-pitched squeal of a child's laughter brought Lydia back to her senses like a good hard shake. Placing a hand on Jon's chest, she gave him a little shove. "Oh, no! What are we doing? That's Abby."

Jon took a quick step back. Eyes wide, he stuttered, "I—" And gave his head a little shake. "I have no idea. The girls… You're the nanny. We can't do this. I don't want to confuse them or have them thinking—"

"Don't." Lydia lifted one hand stop-sign style. A bubble of panic welled up within her, flooding her bloodstream with adrenaline. "Of course we can't. And right now, we need to get back. The girls are probably exhausted, and I don't want them having a meltdown for the Carneses."

Nodding, he raked a hand through his messy hair. His expression suggested he was as flummoxed as she was. "You're right. You're going to have your hands full tomorrow as it is."

"Tomorrow?" Lydia repeated. Despite her churning emotions, the meaning behind that word sunk into her like a dip in a nice warm bath. Was it fair to bring this up when he was clearly still reeling from what had just happened? But then again, so was she. "Wait. Does this mean you're not firing me? I can stay?"

Jon snatched his hat up from the ground and settled it back on his head. "Even though we've just complicated matters exponentially...yes, this means I'm not letting you go." He paused and gave her a look that sent heat all the way through her.

Then he grinned. "At least not until the girls head off to college."

SILENTLY, THEY RODE back to the barn. The implications of what he'd done and said sank in and Jon called himself an idiot in about a hundred and one different ways. He needed to handle this carefully. First, he needed to figure out what "this" was exactly. He knew he wanted Lydia to stay. That didn't have anything to do with the kiss. He'd already made that decision before he'd kissed her. *Which should have been the hundred and second reason not to kiss her, you idiot.*

She's the nanny.

Why had he kissed her? That was the question plaguing him. He was attracted to her. Obviously. He'd known that almost from the beginning. But it wasn't that. It was all of it, all the ways he'd expected her to fail when she'd succeeded. Being amazing with the girls was at the top of the list. Excelling at her other nanny duties was a bonus. The ranching chores hadn't intimidated her; she'd cared for the chickens and the goats in a pair of sandals for more than a week. Without one single word of complaint. She truly seemed to love it here and she was seamlessly transitioning into country life like she'd been born to it.

Jon realized now that riding had been the moment he'd expected to see her shortcomings, and if she didn't fail, then at least show her true colors. He realized now how desperately he'd wanted her to succeed, or at least to enjoy it. When he'd seen her climb on that horse and take off, he'd been struck silly with a different kind of wanting. He wanted Lydia. It seemed that underlying, persistent yearning for a life he couldn't have was back. And now that he'd seen all that she had to offer, now that he'd tasted those lips, how in the world was he going to stuff that wanting back where it belonged? The fact was, he didn't really want to.

Zach had been right when he pointed out that he and Sofie had made it work. Maybe…?

The ringtone coming from his phone told him Katie was calling. He slid the phone from his pocket and answered it. "Hey, Katie. What's up?"

"Jon, thank goodness I reached you. I'm sorry. I know it's Easter Sunday. I didn't know they were coming today. I gave some of the guys the day off it being Easter and all."

"Are Big E and Zoe back?"

"What? No. Jon…" Katie paused. "I think you need to accept the notion that Big E isn't coming back anytime soon. I'm talking about the piglets."

"The piglets? For the petting zoo?"

"Yep. They're here and the pen isn't finished. You know what pigs are like—if I don't get something secure set up for them we'll have pigs running around all over the place." It was common knowledge that it took some strategic construction to properly secure pigs. They were smart as well as expert diggers.

Jon sighed. "Unfortunately, I do. I thought the guys we hired were supposed to be done with it by now."

"They haven't been back for the last three days. One of them texted and said they were taking a long weekend for Easter. It started on Thursday."

Jon huffed out an irritated breath. "Okay. I'll be there as soon as I can. I'm out at the Carneses' so it shouldn't take me long." The Carnes place was closer to his grandfather's than the JB Bar was. "I just need to round up the girls."

"Oh, good. I'd love to see them and no doubt they'd love to see the piglets and meet Henry and Edna."

She was gone before Jon could ask who Henry and Edna were.

BACK AT THE BARN, Jon briefly explained the situation to Zach and Matt. Lydia was waiting with Brenna, Tess and the girls near a corral, where a cowboy was working with a foal. The three men joined them.

Jon said, "Gen and Abby, do you want to go over to Big E's with me? Katie has some piglets she wants to show you."

"Heck, yeah, we do!" Gen answered, dancing around.

Abby said, "Uncle Ethan says pigs are real smart. They're clean, too. And you know how people say you sweat like a pig? Uncle Ethan says that's bogus. Pigs can't even sweat at all."

Jon looked at his nanny. She flashed him a bright smile. Tendrils of hair had come loose from her ponytail. Her cheeks were a little pink but he didn't know if that was caused by him or the sun. He thought she looked flustered, maybe even a bit dazed. He liked the idea that he'd done that to her, shaken her composure. She looked even more beautiful than normal, if that was possible. Despite his misgivings and 102 reasons, a lightness unfurled inside his chest and spread through his limbs. What would it be like to wake up to a smile like that every day? To kiss her all the time? When her brow nudged upward, he realized he'd been studying her a little too long.

Clearing his throat, he went on, "Lydia, Zach said he'd give you a ride back to the ranch. I'm not sure how late we'll be. I need to finish building a pen for the pigs."

Her smile slipped.

Zach spoke up. "I texted Sofie. She gave me the green light to head over and help you, Jon."

"Absolutely not, Zach. It's Easter. Matt's here.

Enjoy your family time. I would appreciate it if you could take Lydia home, though, when she's ready."

Zach and Lydia started talking at the same time. "Excuse me, Zach." Lydia held up a hand, then looked at Jon. "Can't I just go with you guys? Don't you need someone to watch the girls? I wouldn't mind taking a peek at those piglets myself."

Zach patted a horse as Dale, who'd helped earlier, led him away. "I'm going, too."

"Yeah, me too," Matt chimed in. "Three of us, we'll get it done so much faster. Then we can all enjoy a little family time."

"That's right." Zach clapped his hands together. "No time for arguing, Jon. Burning daylight. Let's go."

They all headed back to the house. After issuing quick thank-yous and goodbyes to the Carneses, Jon, Lydia, Trout and the girls were in the pickup. Lydia turned on the DVD the girls had been watching on the way and they slipped on their headphones.

"This is where you grew up, right?" Lydia asked from the passenger seat. She'd been asking him about places, quizzing him about the various landmarks, houses and ranches they passed.

"Yes, ma'am."

"And it's a cattle ranch like yours?"

"Yep. Well, it's like mine in that it's a cattle ranch. Mine are a heritage breed called Devons and Big E has Angus. Like I mentioned before, I go about it a little differently. I'm all organic, where Big E is more traditional. That's what prompted me to build my own place."

He glanced at Lydia and realized she was waiting for him to continue. Feeling self-conscious, he tapped a thumb on the steering wheel. "Growing up, I didn't like the way so many of our cows needed assistance with labor. More money can be made in producing calves that are larger at birth and grow fast. I don't know when I learned about it exactly, but as I got older I realized that it hadn't always been that way. Cows used to have their babies with only occasional assistance. Larger, unnaturally large calves mean more problems. On some ranches, all the cows need help.

"And most cattle end up in feedlots, where the conditions can be atrocious. On the JB Bar, other than some occasional bovine mid-wifery—" he paused to give her a wink "—it's all-natural births and no feedlots. There's a great and growing market these days for natural pro-duction methods and grass-fed beef. My way is healthier and more nutritious."

Lydia nodded. "I've been watching videos and

reading about cattle ranching. The footage from some of those feedlots brought tears to my eyes. The filth, the disease, and then the antibiotics and hormones they shoot them up with...? All I can say is, I don't plan on eating any beef but grass-fed for the rest of my life. And I wish the same for your girls."

He shot her an approving look. "These are points on which Big E and I could not agree. Every time I suggested anything that could conceivably affect his profit margin in a negative way, it turned into an argument. We would argue around and around. Eventually, I realized that I couldn't win. Ever. One day, I had enough. I walked off to start my own ranch. Big E did make a change in breeds over the past few years, which in my opinion, is a big step in the right direction."

Jon could feel her staring at him now.

"Wow. That's so...brave."

"I don't know about that. Mostly, I was fed up with arguing. I always wished I had my brother Ben's negotiating skills. He's an attorney. And brilliant. And impossible to win an argument against."

"I know what that's like. One of my friends back in Philadelphia is an attorney."

"I swear, Ben was born to it. Even when he was a kid, he thought everything was negotiable.

When he and Ethan were in high school, this new principal came back from a seminar and instituted a rule that kids couldn't gather in groups of more than five students at a time. Which is silly. The football players couldn't even get together at lunchtime and talk about the game. The drama club couldn't practice. It seemed to affect everyone in some way. The stated goal was to prevent bullying, which, to my knowledge was not a problem at Falcon Creek. Ben was outraged. He went to the school board and argued it violated the students' right to free speech and freedom of association and a bunch of other legalese. He was citing laws and documents and articles... It was amazing. He won, of course. Someone filmed him, and he made the national news. The following year, the school hired a new principal."

"How old was he?"

"Sixteen."

"Wow..."

"Yeah. When Ben gets fired up, he is a force to be reckoned with."

"When I meet him, I will do my best to get on his good side."

Jon liked how she said "when" and not "if."

"You should probably know, because it's bound to get mentioned somewhere along the line, that Zoe was engaged to Ben when she and Big E ran off and got married."

"Ouch," she said.

"Yeah, it was bad. It's a long story but he blames Ethan and me for having a hand in it. Which is accurate in that we knew she wasn't right for him. But when I look at it from his view, how can I fault him for never coming around? I don't regret that part of it, that he didn't end up with her. But it's going on five years now…" He sighed. "I don't know, sometimes I think so much damage has been done in this family that to try and repair it would just rip open all those old wounds and leave it worse than it was before. Does that make sense?"

"It does." Lydia nodded. "I know a bit about families falling apart myself."

CHAPTER FOURTEEN

"THAT'S THE HOUSE my brothers and I grew up in." Jon stopped the pickup where the long driveway forked. He pointed toward a large, white two-story home with forest green shutters. It was more like she'd imagined Jon's house would be the first day she'd arrived. A wide, welcoming front porch wrapped around the house—it was the kind that begged for rocking chairs and tall glasses of iced tea. Several outbuildings dotted the grounds. It was fronted by a generous expanse of velvety green yard.

"I'm envisioning five little boys out front, catching frogs, playing hide-and-seek, baseballs flying."

"Many, many stick-sword-fight battles were waged in that yard."

Lydia grinned. "Which window did you sneak out of?"

"By the time I was old enough to want to, I was too busy working to do much sneaking, but I did catch my brother Tyler sneaking back in one time." Jon paused to chuckle at the memory. "He tried to tell me he was sleepwalking."

"You didn't buy that?"

"Not hardly. He was covered with mud, smelled like skunk and had a broken wrist. To this day, he won't confess what he was up to. He still owes me, by the way, because I never told Big E. Took him to the doctor myself. And then we made up this story about how he fell in the hay barn stacking bales."

Lydia laughed and looked toward the house again. "It's really charming. I love the porch."

"It is. On the outside. The inside used to be, when we were kids and Grandma was here. Now it's been remodeled several times and since Zoe got a hold of it, it looks like… Like it belongs somewhere else.

"Over yonder on that rise, you can see the guest lodge for the tourists. Along with the cabins." The huge log-cabin-style structure had a grand entryway and tall windows. It looked inviting. Like tiny offspring of a more majestic parent, the cabins around it were simpler but constructed with the same rustic charm.

Taking the fork toward his old home, Jon steered the pickup toward a scattering of barns and outbuildings, all painted a bright, friendly red. He parked on one side of the largest structure. A huge sign hanging on the end of the building read The Blackwell Family Guest Ranch.

A woman stepped out of the barn and waved to them from the doorway. A marled cattle dog stood attentively by her side.

"Daddy, there's Katie. Can we go look at the pigs?"

"Sure."

Jon, Trout and the girls got out. Gen and Abby tore off toward the barn. Jon signaled something to Trout and he took off after them. Lydia followed a bit more slowly, her attention sweeping here and there and taking it all in. The buildings appeared much older than those at the JB Bar Ranch, but everything looked neat and orderly.

Lydia walked around the pickup to join him. She pointed up at the sign. "So, this is different from the sign at the entrance. The Blackwell Family Guest Ranch is like a dude ranch?"

"Mmm-hmm."

"But it wasn't when you were growing up?"

"No, it was not. We just had the cattle ranch."

"When did the dude ranch start?"

"A few years back, after Big E married Zoe."

"Your grandparents are divorced and your biological grandma, Dorothy, lives in Texas?"

"That's right. Zoe is my fourth stepgrand-mother."

"Your grandfather has been married five times?"

"Unfortunately."

"Is he like a total jerk or something?"

A flash of what look liked pain was there and gone in his eyes so quickly Lydia couldn't be sure she'd seen it. "Mmm. That's a tough one. Not really. He's a good man in a lot of ways. Or at least he was..." His voice trailed off and Lydia could see he was uneasy discussing this topic. She was wildly curious but didn't want to push. She watched him, tried to think of what she could say to ease his discomfort.

"He just kind of went off the rails when my parents were killed. There was an accident and they drowned and our brother Tyler... He took it exceptionally hard. Big E and his second wife divorced. I did my best to keep us boys together and grounded but..." He leaned a hip against the vehicle. "It was tough. I was a teenager. I'm their big brother, not their dad. I felt a huge responsibility to the ranch after Dad died. Tried to step up and fill that role, too."

Lydia felt her stomach dip. No wonder he wasn't sneaking out of windows like he should have been. She could only imagine the effect this tragedy and the ensuing family drama must have had on him, on all the boys. Big E, too. The Blackwell name seemed a heavy load to bear around here. No wonder his brothers had taken off. That's what Lydia would have done, too. That's what she had done with her own family. Lydia hadn't been able to handle her parents' divorce. She couldn't imagine how it would have felt if they'd died and left her with four younger siblings and a ranch to run. Suddenly she felt exceedingly immature for leaving the way she had. But to be fair, she'd been a child. Like Jon.

"You were only a kid yourself. You're what, three years older than Ben and Ethan?"

"Yep."

"There's no way you could have been all that to everyone." Lydia had to stop herself from stepping forward and wrapping her arms around him because of everything he'd gone through—losing his parents, a grandfather with relationship issues, strife with his brothers, starting his own ranch, marriage to a woman who was nothing but wrong for him and had ultimately abandoned him. And now he was trying to raise his girls all alone. Lydia was overwhelmed with sympathy and compassion and besieged by this impossible desire to…stay.

His lips curved up at the corners as his eyes roved over her, the affection there making her limbs feel numb. The way his gaze lingered on her mouth had the blood whooshing through her veins. That kiss wasn't going to be easy to forget, and too easy to repeat if she didn't stay focused.

He seemed to reach the same conclusion as he finally shifted his gaze. Granting her a small smile, he said, "Don't be too sorry. We had a lot of fun growing up. Worked hard, played hard. There were plenty of good times. I just wish…"

"You miss them," she said simply.

He nodded. "I do. My brother Ethan was here for a visit a couple of months ago. I don't know… Hanging out with him and spending time here lately, it's brought back a lot of memories."

"Ah, yes, Uncle Ethan." Lydia gave him a knowing smile. "The girls adore him."

He chuckled. "He's an easy guy to like. And you know the girls. Ethan being a vet means he knows everything about animals, probably more than a normal person would want to know. And the twins aren't normal in that way," he joked.

"You got that right." Lydia laughed. "If it has fur, Abby wants to cuddle it and Gen wants to ride it."

"That was me and Ethan. He was always trying to help every critter he came across. Me, I wanted to ride it or rope it. He adopted this batch of ducklings one time who showed up in the creek without their mama. Took care of 'em, even dug a pond by the chicken coop. And this one day I was practicing my roping and… Well,

let's just say that he did not appreciate me roping his ducks."

They laughed together.

A pretty, red-haired cowgirl emerged from the
barn. She pulled a pair of leather work gloves
from her hands as she strode confidently toward
them. The dog fell into step beside her. Lydia
felt a tug of envy. Could she ever look that comfortable in jeans and cowboy boots?

Jon said, "Lydia, this is Katie Montgomery.
Katie, Lydia. Katie runs the Blackwell Ranch."
He pointed at the dog. "And this pretty lady
is Hip." He reached down and gave her ears a
scratch.

Katie flashed an affectionate grin at Jon before focusing on Lydia. "Not formally. My dad,
Lochlan, is the foreman here. It's nice to meet
you, Lydia. Gen and Abby can't say enough
good things about you."

"I've heard plenty about you, too. Gen wants
to be you. She says no one rides a horse like
Katie." The dog moved closer. Lydia bent over
to greet her. "Hey, Hip, you're a sweetie, aren't
you?"

Katie's eyes danced with a mix of warmth and
humor. "Gen acts just like I did when I was her
age. Jon once caught me trying to ride a green
stallion when I was about, what, Jon? Nine or
ten?"

Jon chuckled and shook his head. "Yep, right around there. And you weren't too pleased when I thwarted your plan." To Lydia, he added, "She was standing on the inside fence rail coaxing him close with sugar cubes. I honestly don't know what would have happened if I hadn't found her."

"Um, duh, Jon." Katie playfully threw up her hands. "I would have gone for a ride."

"A ride to the hospital most likely. That stallion was named Diablo for a reason."

Lydia enjoyed the camaraderie between them. The way they interacted made them seem like family, but then again, from what she understood they'd grown up here together.

Zach's pickup came into view.

Katie shielded her eyes from the sun. "Nice of Zach and Matt to help. I need to get back to the cows, but all the building supplies are by the pen. Tell Gen and Abby the donkeys are named Henry and Edna."

"Donkeys?"

"They arrived on Friday."

"Where are they? With the horses?"

"No. They're miniature donkeys. They're in the small corral for now but they'll need their own pen. I'll put them in a stall at night until we figure something out."

"Miniature donkeys?" Jon repeated flatly.

"Mmm-hmm."

Jon shook his head and walked to his pickup. He opened the toolbox in the back and grabbed his tool belt. "All right. We'll get it done."

"Jon, I can't thank you enough. I know you don't have time for this."

"There's no need to thank me, Katie, for helping to clean up a mess that you didn't cause. I'm grateful you're here. I can't figure out what he's thinking. Not that he'd care about inconveniencing me, but he has to know how much grief he's causing you."

Katie's smile looked strained. "We'll get through it. Big E doesn't deserve you, Jon, you know that? He doesn't deserve for you to be here."

"But you do. That's the point."

"Thank you. It means the world to me to hear you say it." Stepping forward, she wrapped her arms around Jon for a quick hug. "Just know how much I appreciate this and everything you've done. I couldn't do this without you right now."

Katie moved away and called out a greeting and a thank-you to Zach and Matt. She smiled at Lydia. "I'll see you later, Lydia. Feel free to bring the girls out for a look at our calves. I'm sure Gen and Abby will want to compare them to the JB Bar's."

"I'll do that. Thank you. I'm so glad to meet you finally."

Katie and Hip departed. Abby appeared in the doorway of the barn, a baby pig nestled in her arms. "Daddy, Lydia, look! Isn't it so cute? Can we get pigs?"

Jon and Lydia shared knowing grins.

He whispered, "I swear I will find a way to get even with Zoe." They walked toward Abby, who led them to a stall where Gen was inside with five more piglets. Abby opened the door and joined her sister.

"Lydia, wanna hold one?"

"I do!" Lydia went inside. Abby handed her a gray-and-white piglet. It made the cutest noises, then snuffled her armpit and nuzzled her neck. "Goodness, they are adorable, aren't they?"

Lydia could feel Jon watching her. She looked at him. Her smile faded while his went a little wider. Now that she knew what his lips felt like, it was torture to look at them.

"Daddy, what do you think?" Gen asked. "They could live next to the bunnies."

"Girls," Jon announced, tearing his gaze from Lydia's, "we are not getting pigs."

"Darn," Abby said. "Katie asked us to come over whenever we can and hold them."

"I bet she did," Jon responded flatly. To Lydia, he added, "The more they get touched and han-

dled the more docile they'll be for the tourists."
He rolled his eyes.

"Something tells me these pigs are going to
have a nice life here." Lydia handed the baby
back to Abby and joined Jon outside the stall.

He took a few steps and turned to lean against
the wall. "Yeah and the tiny donkeys." He gave
his head a disgusted shake. "And every other
critter on its way here. I found the plans Zoe
sketched out for this little zoo of hers. She's got
at least eight different enclosures, maybe more."

"For what kinds of animals?"

"The drawing doesn't specify. There are ini-
tials on a few of them, but they could mean anything. That woman is indecipherable on a good
day."

"Why are you so against this?"

"From a ranching perspective, it's pointless.
It's an expense that's unnecessary. And it's
not only the cost of the feed, someone has to
maintain the pens—clean them, make repairs.
There's feeding and grooming. Animals get sick,
which means vet bills. If you're going to feed
and board an animal there should be a payoff at
the end—it's a food source or a tool."

"But bunnies are okay?"

"Ah, but see, there's a point there. It's teaching the girls responsibility. The bunnies belong
to them. They're invested. Eventually, they'll

move on to taking care of the horses and help-ing with the cattle. And bunnies aren't expen-sive to feed."

Lydia offered him a teasing smile. "Ah, but from a city-girl perspective this is fun. Most people I know don't get the opportunity to see animals close up like this. That's the first time I've held a pig and I loved it. I'm already plan-ning to bring the girls back and do it again. We'll have a science lesson and try to learn something new about pigs. I know you don't want to hear it, but I think Zoe might be onto a good thing here."

"Maybe so." He grinned at her, but didn't look anywhere near convinced. "I'm still glad it won't be me who has to contend with it."

He said goodbye and left to join Zach and Matt at work. Lydia and the girls played with the piglets for a while and then went to meet Henry and Edna. Jon might think they were pointless, but Lydia and the girls agreed they were about the cutest things they'd ever seen. They stopped to visit with Katie, admired the horses and cud-dled the piglets some more. When Katie had a break, she brought the girls some carrots to feed the horses and Henry and Edna. The remainder of the afternoon, she and the girls hiked around the ranch. The girls had a blast and Lydia enjoyed every second of exploring the place that had shaped Jonathon Blackwell.

THE SOUND OF Lydia's knock and soft voice filled Jon with a longing so painful he almost didn't want to look up for fear she'd see it in his eyes. "Hey, Jon? Can I talk to you for a sec?"

She stood in the open doorway of his office. All he wanted to do was kiss her again. That wasn't true; he wanted to spend time with her and then kiss her. Even with the unexpected trip out to the Blackwell Ranch, the day had been as close to perfect as he'd had in so long he couldn't even remember. But today was special. It couldn't happen again. He couldn't get involved with her. She was the nanny. What would it do to the girls if it didn't work out and she left them? What would it do to him?

"It's fine."

"Are you sure? I don't want to interrupt. You can say no."

"Lydia, I'm sure." He motioned her forward. "Come in."

She moved into the room and that's when he realized how quiet the house was. "Are the girls asleep already?"

"They are. They were beyond exhausted. They both argued about having to go to bed because they'd hardly gotten to play with their new Easter toys. My counteroffer was to read two extra stories. They agreed, and I let them each pick one out. They were both snoozing before I finished the first ones. Which reminds me, I told them you'd be in to kiss them good-night so don't forget to stop by on your way to bed."

"Unfortunately, that won't be for a while," Jon commented, hearing the frustration in his own voice.

Lydia looked alarmed. "Is it one of the cows? Do you need to go? We can talk about this later."

He liked how much she'd come to care about his herd, the pregnant cows and the newborns. He liked how she cared about all his critters and his people, too.

"No. Sort of. And no, I don't need to go. But I am trying to write an email and it's possible I might be in here all night. Have mercy on me and bring me coffee if my light's still on in the morning."

"Will do. I'll slide a pancake under the door, too." She winked. "How could an email possibly take you all night?"

"It's kind of an important email."

"Can I help?"

"As if you don't already have enough to do."

"Is that your way of saying you don't need help or that you'd like some help but don't want to ask?"

"Possibly the second. I'm not great at asking for personal favors, although I'm not sure there's anything you can help with, anyway."

"Try me."

Scratching his chin, he said, "I have this interview coming up. I don't know… I guess I'm…"

"Nervous?"

"Yeah, a little. There's a lot at stake for me."

"What kind of interview is it?"

"It's a television piece with a national cable show."

"Wow. No wonder you're nervous."

"Yeah. They're doing a feature about the natural-food craze. They've chosen the JB Bar to highlight the organic-beef industry."

"What is this going to entail?"

"A camera crew tromping around the ranch for a couple of days. This reporter, Bethany Stouffer, asking me a million questions. This email—" he gestured at his laptop "—contains a bunch of them. Supposed to help me prepare."

Eyes wide, Lydia sank down into the chair across from his desk. "Bethany Stouffer? You're being featured on *Good Day USA*?"

"Yeah, you know it?"

"Um, Jon, everybody knows it. The only people who don't know it are the ones living in the dark ages without a TV…" She trailed off as if realizing what she'd implied. "Sorry. But honestly, that would be you and about fourteen other people in this country."

"Do you want me to get you a TV?" Jon could hear the tightness in his tone.

"What?" Her face scrunched with confusion.

"Lydia, I don't want you to be unhappy here. If it feels like you're living in the dark ages, I'll get you a TV."

"Umm…" She appeared genuinely baffled by his statement. "I'm not complaining about the fact that you don't have a TV. In fact, I like that the girls don't depend on it. Besides, I have a computer and you have the internet."

Jon frowned at her.

"I'm sorry if I offended you. I didn't mean to. Honestly, I like the no TV, especially where the girls are concerned."

Huh. He shifted in his seat. He may have over-reacted a bit here. "No, I'm sorry. That was stupid. It's not you…" How did he explain without explaining? Then again, maybe she deserved to hear the truth. "My ex-wife was very unhappy here so it's difficult for me to imagine that a woman like her ever could be."

"Wait… So, you think I'm like your ex-wife? That's a crushing thought."

"No!" This wasn't going well. The problem was that Lydia was so different from Ava he still couldn't believe it. That was part of the problem.

How could a woman like her, softened from city life, take so quickly and easily to life on a ranch? "That's not what I meant." He needed to make her understand. "She used to say stuff… Make these little digs about my life, putting it down. I'm still a little touchy about it apparently."

"I see…" She worried her lip for a second.

Despite the misgivings still eating away at him, he'd hired her, and now he found that he wanted her to be happy here. He knew in his soul she was the best thing to ever happen to the twins. "Lydia, honestly, if there's anything you need, I hope you feel like you can ask."

"Thank you. That's actually why I'm here. I want to ask about the girls."

"Okay." He'd assumed she was going to want to talk about that kiss.

"Remember how I was saying that the girls could maybe use a bit more socialization?"

"Mmm-hmm." If she didn't want to talk about it, then maybe they could just forget that it happened. Forgetting was unrealistic. Pretending was more apt, as difficult as that would be.

"I was wondering if you'd given it any thought."

"Not really." He hadn't. Jon and his brothers, and every other ranch kid he knew, including the Carnes clan, turned out fine without "socialization." That sounded like a citified term if he'd ever heard one.

"What do you have in mind?" He was wary, he had to admit.

"Four-H."

"Four-H?" he repeated flatly.

"I know they live on a ranch and everything and probably know a lot of this stuff. But I was thinking it might be a fun way for them to learn more about their rabbits and how to handle them and take care of them. They'd get to hang out with other kids their age, and it's interactive so it wouldn't be like Gen would have to try and sit still the whole time like she does in Sunday school. They could even show them at the fair. The woman who runs the group is a rancher, too—Deanne Swift. Do you know her?"

"I know Deanne. Her daughter, Rainie, is the same age as the twins. I have no problem with 4-H. It sounds great." First the bunnies, now 4-H? This wasn't the first time she'd made more work for herself where the girls were concerned.

"Yes! Thank you."

He liked how her eyes sparkled when she was happy, and he liked when he was the cause.

"Now let's get back to your TV thing."

"Do we have to?"

She laughed. "Yes, we do. But don't worry. I'm going to help you prepare. Can I take a look at the email?"

CHAPTER FIFTEEN

DRESSED AND READY for a day of ranching in his jeans and flannel shirt, Jon startled Lydia when he strolled into the kitchen late the next morning. A few minutes past 6:00 a.m. was late for him, anyway. She'd assumed he was already gone.

"Something smells good."

"Hi, I didn't know you were still here."

Mouth hooked up on one side, he said, "Is it not okay to stick around and have breakfast with my girls?" The way he said it, that *my* combined with his lingering gaze made her throat go dry. Picking up the whisk, she pretended the pancake batter needed a little more mixing.

"Of course, the girls will be thrilled. I'm, uh, making animal cakes."

She felt his heat as he came up next to her. Inhaling a deep breath didn't help because it only filled her head with his delicious and already familiar scent. All she could do was hope that by ignoring what had happened, this attraction would fade away. In the meantime, she just needed to keep her distance. She could do that. Although, it would be so much easier if he wasn't so masculine and attractive.

He edged a little closer. "Animal cakes?"

And if he didn't smell so good. "Here." She shoved a plate at him. "You can have the amoebas."

He studied the pancakes. Fighting a smile, he repeated, "Amoebas?"

"Fine, they're my failed horse-cake attempts. Horse cakes are tricky. Amoebas sound more fun, I think, than blobs."

He wasn't moving. Why wasn't he moving? Reaching out, he tucked a lock of hair behind her ear. Her pulse took off like a high-speed train. "Lydia—"

"Jon," she whispered, turning serious. "We can't. You can't touch me. Or watch me or stare at my mouth anymore. We have to stay focused on the girls. And the fact that you're my boss and I'm your nanny and—"

"I know. You're right." The longing and pain in his expression matched the ache in her heart. "But—"

"Are those pancakes?" A sleepy-eyed Abby strolled into the kitchen, clutching her plush bunny. "Daddy!" She skipped toward Jon. "You're still here."

"Hey, bunny girl." She stopped beside him.

He picked her up. "Can you believe this? Lydia made us a bunny breakfast." Lydia felt herself melt. Yep, masculine and attractive and tender and caring and sweet—with his girls, with his dog, his horse, his friends, the cattle. He loved his brothers and Katie. Even his grandfather was the object of less animosity than the circumstances seemed to warrant.

"What's a bunny breakfast?" Jon picked up another plate and showed it to Abby. Her face transformed as the bunny shapes registered in her brain. She graced Lydia with a billion-watt smile. More melting ensued.

"Good morning." A gravelly-voiced Gen emerged into the kitchen.

"Gen, look, Lydia made bunny cakes."

Gen came closer. "Aww... Those are so cute. I want one."

"You can have as many as you want. Or, Genevieve..." Lydia slid the spatula under the best horse cake on the griddle. She flipped it onto a plate and presented it to her. "You can have a horse cake."

Gen's eyes lit up. *"H-O-R-S-E."*

Lydia gasped and gave her a squeeze. "That's right. That's exactly right, smarty-pants."

"It sure is," Jon added. "Way to go, Genevieve."

The look of pride and happiness on his face

mixed with her own and filled Lydia with a kind
of joy she couldn't remember ever experiencing.
Jon and the girls headed to the dining room,
where butter and warm maple syrup waited.
Lifting the remaining pancakes from the griddle, Lydia carried them to the table and slid into
the seat next to Gen. Across the table, she and
Jon locked eyes. She could only imagine how it
must feel to be a mom and share moments like
these every day with a husband who loved her
as much as she loved him…

Lydia went still for a few seconds as joy vibrated through her, like the strum of a perfectly
tuned guitar. Her heart seemed to stutter before
redoubling its efforts and battering hard against
her ribs. She nearly winced from the force of
the realization—she loved him. She was in love
with him. She loved all three of them. There
was no point in trying to deny it anymore, not
to herself.

"Are you okay?" Jon asked, and the concern
in his gray eyes had her wondering how he felt
about her.

"Perfect," she answered with a bright smile.

It was important, she told herself, to acknowledge how she felt. That way she could safeguard
them all. She would do that by keeping some
distance between them. No more intimacy. Just

friendly and platonic. Boss-employee, rancher-nanny, Lydia-Jon.

Lydia forced herself to tune back into the moment. She told a joke about giraffes and laughed with the girls. She asked Jon his opinion on organic milk. Abby and Gen talked bunny names for their new pets. They enjoyed a nice long breakfast.

Afterward, Jon kissed the girls goodbye. Lydia stood by the sink. She reached out to take his plate and glass. It made her smile when he ignored her, rinsing the dishes and stowing them in the dishwasher.

"When I am too spoiled to put my plate in the dishwasher, please push me over a cliff. Besides, I need to set a good example for the girls. I want them to know how to take care of themselves and their home. This is their home, too. You're not a maid, Lydia."

"All right." She smiled at him and wiped her hands on a towel.

"I won't make it in for dinner. Dusty saw a herd of elk in the upper fields when he was riding fence last night. I'm going to head out and check for damage. After my loafing around yesterday and this morning I want to give the guys a little time off." He'd already mentioned that he'd need a lunch today, so Lydia added an extra apple and two of the energy bars she'd made and froze a few days ago to the pile of food she'd prepared.

"No kidding, *slacker*," she said wryly. "I think I'm going to call Sofie and see if she wants to join me in a little pigpen building on my day off."

He chuckled as he tucked the lunch into a bag.

"I'd like to see an elk." She handed him a thermos full of coffee.

"Really?"

"Um, yeah. I've never seen one in real life."

"They're beautiful, no doubt about that. They're also a menace. Bust right through our fences."

"Can't you make a bigger, stronger fence?"

"I could, yes, but I don't want to stop them from getting where they want to go. They were here first. I just wish they were better about jumping over or crawling under, like the deer. Most times they'll jump 'em. But they have a strong herd mentality, and when they are running hard, especially when they get spooked, our fences take a real beating."

"Huh. That's fascinating."

Jon tilted his head, studying her. "Maybe, one of these days, we could go for a ride, see some more of the ranch? It's extra pretty in the back where the property borders government land."

"I would enjoy that," she answered immediately. It pained her that he asked so hesitantly. She was trying not to hate his ex-wife, but the more she learned, the more difficult that was.

"Okay then. Are we, uh, still on for tonight?" he asked.

"Yes, for sure. By the time I'm through with you, Bethany Stouffer won't know what hit her."

LYDIA STEERED THE SUV into a parking space in front of South Corner Drug & Sundries and glanced in the rearview mirror. Their first 4-H meeting had gone very well so she'd suggested ice cream.

"Ready?" she asked.

They climbed out. Gen and Abby held hands and skipped toward the shop. Once inside, they took a moment to study the choices through the glass case. Lydia urged them to place their orders on their own, which they did, and so politely it made her ache with pride. Chocolate chip and rainbow sherbet for Gen, chocolate mint and bubblegum for Abby. Lydia smiled inside—kids and their odd flavor combinations.

She placed her order with the sweet teenaged boy working the counter. "And I'll have two scoops, maple nut and peanut-butter pie on a waffle cone."

The girls got their ice cream and Lydia settled them at the long diner-style counter with extra napkins. She walked over to collect her cone when she heard a voice behind her. "How can you eat like that and stay so slim?"

Lydia turned to find Marilee standing behind her. Hands on hips, she looked Lydia up and down. Today she was wearing tights, sneakers and a snug tank top that showed off her defined shoulders and arms. Clearly, Marilee's dry-wick workout clothing was getting its intended use. Lydia's yoga pants had never even seen a tree pose. A taller woman with long blond hair stood smiling next to Marilee.

Lydia grinned and gestured at her curves. "I can't." *But I don't care*, she wanted to add, but didn't. In Lydia's experience, people who were as dedicated to their workouts as Marilee couldn't hear about your lack of commitment without trying to convert you to their ways.

"Hmm. Some ladies and I, we do dance fit and circuit training at the high school on Monday and Wednesday evenings and Saturday mornings if you're interested."

Not on your life, she thought. "That sounds fun," she answered noncommittally.

Gesturing at her companion, Marilee said, "Peyton and I just got back from working out. Lydia, this is Peyton. Peyton, this is Lydia. Peyton is new in town, too."

"Oh, hi." Lydia asked, "Where are you from?"

"Phoenix."

"Excuse me a sec?" Marilee said. "That's Vance Bonner, the new principal at the school. I need to ask him a quick question." Marilee power-walked across the store toward a tall, broad-shouldered man who looked like he might be doing dance fit, too, while bench-pressing the other participants.

"*That's* the principal?" Lydia asked, taking a bite of the creamy heavenly mix.

"Yep. Education is highly valued in Falcon Creek, I've noticed. I'm a waitress over at Clearwater Café and he eats there often. A lot of the women in town have important school-related questions to ask him, especially the single ladies."

Lydia snuffled out a laugh and almost choked on her ice cream. "I bet. How are you liking Falcon Creek?"

"Honestly?" Peyton smiled at her. "This place is kind of a culture shock. City girl to country girl in the blink of an eye."

"Oh, Peyton," Lydia said with a laugh. "I sympathize. I'm from Philadelphia."

Across the store, Marilee patted Principal Bonner on his muscled forearm.

Peyton said, "We should have coffee or lunch sometime. You know how they have those expatriate groups where people from the same country get together and miss their homeland? We could start our own—two city girls getting together and sharing stories and reminiscing about take-out food and rush-hour traffic."

Lydia chuckled, even as she realized that she didn't miss much about Philadelphia aside from Meredith and Tanner. But she liked Peyton and felt a connection. She found herself agreeing. "I'd like that. I know someone else who might like to join us," she added, thinking about Sofie.

Peyton pulled out her phone and Lydia quickly rattled off the number at the ranch. Lydia said goodbye and joined the girls. She found herself hoping Peyton would call. It felt nice making friends, even though she knew she couldn't confide in them. She couldn't confide in anyone. Because no matter what happened, she never wanted Jon to know the truth about what she'd done and why she'd come here. She'd never want him to think her love for this place, for him and the girls, was anything but genuine.

JON READ FROM the paper in his hand, "'How does it make you feel when you look out over this pasture filled with your cattle, cattle you so lovingly care for, knowing that one day they'll be someone's cheeseburger?'" He shook his head. "This is the stupidest question yet. I'm not answering it."

"Jon—"

"No, Lydia, seriously." He stood and stalked over to the window. "What do people like this Bethany and her citified producer think? That their hamburger grows on Styrofoam plates wrapped in plastic? Or it's like broccoli? Someone picks it in clumps and stacks it in the refrigerated section?"

Lydia tipped her head back and laughed. Despite his natural reserve, Jonathon Blackwell was extremely articulate and incredibly intelligent. She enjoyed making him laugh and he continually slayed her with his dry sense of humor. They'd been taking a few of the interview questions each night and fine-tuning Jon's responses. It was fun trying to draw him out. Even though that post-kiss awkwardness still lingered between them, she loved spending time with him.

"Hey, I'll confess I never gave those tidy little packages much thought myself until a few weeks ago. People are curious about how you reconcile raising an animal, that you obviously care about by the way, with the final product. I mean, I know ranching is about the bottom line, too. But face it, Jon, you wouldn't be doing this organic thing if that's all you cared about. You'd still be working for Big E on your family's ranch. So, just answer the question like I was the one asking it. Forget about Bethany."

He blew out an irritated breath, turned around and focused on her. "All right. Uh, let's see… It makes me feel proud and accomplished to raise a healthy herd free of artificial hormones, steroids and unnecessary antibiotics. I like that my cows get plenty of fresh air, sunshine and all the green grass they can eat. I like knowing that they have the best quality to their life that I can give them. Every living creature deserves that. It's real and it's tangible and people can see it in my cattle when they visit my ranch. Ultimately, it's a difference they can taste and one that's healthier, too. For cows and people."

Lydia's mouth dropped open into a gape. She was gaping. And her blood was humming. Good grief. She was absolutely positive no one could be more attractive talking about cattle than Jon Blackwell. "Wow," she breathed.

"Too much?"

"Um, not exactly. Well," she drawled, "that depends on your perspective." She picked up a sheaf of papers and fanned herself. Realizing what she was doing, she dropped the stack in her lap. "You are *amazing*. Seriously, talk like that and you're going to nail this thing. Pretend like you're talking to me the entire time."

Smiling cautiously, he said, "Really?"

"Really. You're so…eloquent and charismatic. Not to mention it's difficult to look away from your cowboy gorgeousness. Is your phone number on your website? Women are going to be calling you and… Oh, no, I'm going to have to answer the phone. That's it," she joked, "I'm telling them all that you're spoken for."

Lydia watched him move around the desk until he was standing in front of it. He leaned back so he was half sitting against the edge. She registered the tense expression on his face—desire meets trepidation. And that's when she realized what she'd said and how it sounded.

"Oh, Jon, I'm sorry. I didn't mean by me. I mean I wish it could be me. Wait…that didn't come out right, either."

Keeping his focus on the floor, he hissed in a breath before hauling up his gaze. Lydia froze as it traveled over her like he hadn't seen her in a good long while. And, she supposed, he hadn't, because to her mind he hadn't really looked at her like this since that morning after Easter. She realized now just how careful they'd both been at sliding glances, minimal eye contact and leaving a more than a necessary amount of personal space. *Stupid, Lydia. Why did you flirt with him?*

Her entire body suddenly felt heavy, like it was poured from concrete. It was almost painful to stand. When she made it to her feet she inhaled a deep breath of her own.

It took every ounce of her strength to untangle

her gaze from his. Squeezing her eyes shut, she whispered, "Jon, I'm so sorry." Without another word, she turned and walked from the room.

CHAPTER SIXTEEN

"A BARN DANCE?" Lydia stared at Sofie, who was sitting across the table from her and Peyton at the Silver Stake Saloon. Lydia had dropped the girls off with Willa and picked up Sofie for her doctor's appointment. Zach had a sick horse and Sofie insisted he stay with the mare. Willa encouraged them to take some "girl time."

After the appointment, Lydia treated Sofie to a pedicure at Jem Salon and then arranged to meet Peyton for lunch. Peyton hadn't wanted to dine at the café since she worked there, so they'd headed over to the bar. Silver Stake was quaint and spacious with roughhewn floors, a high ceiling and soft lighting. Axes, picks, shovels, candlesticks and other vintage mining paraphernalia hung from the walls and rafters.

"You mean like a hoedown?" Peyton asked, her lips twitching with laughter.

Sofie chuckled. "Sort of. But it's not like you think. There's music and dancing, yes. There won't be square dancing at this one, but I have to say square dancing is a lot of fun. This is more like a country jam. Lots of people play and sing. The music is phenomenal, mostly country and bluegrass."

A blue-jean-clad waitress with a large silver belt buckle and a cheerful, dimpled smile sashayed over to their table. The Silver Stake boasted a wide variety of sandwiches and burgers, served with your choice of French fries, sweet potato wedges, potato salad, or a dish called "silver-dollar slaw." The menu said that the original owner of the Silver Stake had once won first place in a coleslaw contest with this very recipe, the prize for which was a silver dollar. Every order came with beans baked in a "secret cowboy sauce." They all requested burgers and fries. The foodie in Lydia couldn't resist asking for a side of the slaw.

Peyton didn't seem thrilled by the barn-dance idea. "You would think these people would want to spend time away from their barns."

Sofie grinned. "It's actually very cool. After most of the hay is gone but before the new crop arrives, sometimes people will clean up their barns and have these get-togethers. There might be a birthday or an anniversary party, or even a wedding. Sometimes it's a music jam or just a party—any excuse to get together and have a good time with friends after calving season and before the spring planting begins.

"Trudy Inez goes all out, twinkle lights, paper lanterns and the most delicious homemade Mexican food you've ever tasted. I think it would be good for you to get out and meet some people, Lydia. Everyone is so curious about you."

Lydia grinned. "You had me at Mexican food."

Sofie sat up a little straighter. "Really?"

"Yeah, sure." Sofie was right. Lydia knew she was supposed to lay low, but she'd already learned that it was simply not possible in Falcon Creek. It felt wiser to fit in. It felt good to fit in. Plus, it was dancing.

Peyton said, "I've never done the boot-scootin' boogie. I have no idea how to line dance."

Sofie laughed. "It's not all line dancing, there's plenty of two-stepping and plain old dancing." Peyton looked far from convinced. Sofie added, "Don't worry, there'll be plenty of cowboys who will be happy to show you."

Peyton let out a dreamy sigh. "There are a few cowboys around here I wouldn't mind giving me some dancing lessons."

"Jon didn't mention this to you, Lydia? He'll be playing, but I'm sure he'll make time for a dance or two." She added a wink.

Jon played? What did he play? Why was Sofie winking? Had Jon told Zach they'd kissed?

"Did you say Inez?" Peyton asked. "Any relation to Marilee?"

"Oh. Yeah," Sofie said flatly and took a sip of her water. "Juan and Trudy Inez are her parents."

"That woman is a piece of work."

"I know, but her parents are very nice people—nothing like Marilee. No one can figure out what happened there."

"What's wrong with Marilee?" Lydia asked.

"She's a mean girl," Peyton explained.

"Yes, she is." Sofie fiddled with a napkin and looked at Lydia. "Has, uh…has Jon said anything about her by any chance?"

Lydia frowned. "No… Why?"

Peyton said, "She's got it bad for JT Brimble."

"She's sowing some postdivorce oats, that's for sure. But she's got it worse for Jon," Sofie said.

"What?" Lydia's stomach dipped as she thought about the perky little hard-body. Marilee probably knew everything about ranching.

Sofie leaned forward and said, "You don't have anything to worry about there. Zach told me they dated a little back in high school. After her divorce, she and Jon went out again a few times. But she didn't like the twins."

"Deal-breaker," Peyton quipped.

Lydia thought about the way Gen and Abby

had acted that day in Brewster's. "How could she not *like* them? They're five."

"Peyton's right about her being mean." Sofie made a face and said, "Jon said she squeezed Gen's arm so tight it left bruises."

"Are you kidding me?" White-hot anger flamed inside of Lydia. "What did he do about it?"

"He didn't know it happened until Gen told him later. He was furious. Confronted Marilee. She denied it. But I saw the bruises. Perfect finger marks. Right here." Sofie curled a hand around her biceps. Lydia was speechless. Genevieve was an innocent child. Her child. Not literally, but still…

Peyton gave her head a disgusted shake.

Sofie and Peyton kept talking. Lydia checked out while she thought about giving Marilee a squeeze of her own, nice and tight, right around her windpipe… Slowly, she became aware of the fact that Peyton and Sofie were watching her.

"What?" Lydia said.

Peyton's grin held an edge of mischief. "I was just inquiring as to why Lydia would need to worry about Marilee, anyway?"

Lydia felt her cheeks go warm. "Lydia wouldn't, Peyton. I don't know why Sofie worded it that way." She shifted her focus pointedly to Sofie. "Sofie?"

Sofie drew one shoulder up into an innocent shrug. "Um, well, Zach says that Jon seems... Jon said—"

"Uh-oh," Peyton said under her breath.

"What did Jon say?" Lydia said.

Peyton said softly, "Speaking of JT and cowboys, I think he and his friends at the bar are gearing up to make a move in our direction."

Lydia glanced over. The men had swiveled on their stools and indeed seemed to be looking in their direction. Lydia recognized the one with the long blond hair as the guy she'd seen talking to Marilee in Brewster's.

He slid off his stool and ambled over to their table. Up close, the blond curls were a little too fluffy, like a 1980s rock star. His pants seemed kind of tight for ranch work. His boots, however, were beautiful—multicolored leather and shiny clean.

"Good afternoon, Sofie, Peyton. How are you lovely ladies this fine day?"

Sofie's smile wasn't exactly warm. "Hi, JT. We're doing fine. How 'bout yourself?"

"Oh, you know, busy as all get out. Long mornin'. It's that time of year, calving and all. I'll be back on the bull-riding circuit with Matt next month. Can't wait for that."

Lydia wanted to roll her eyes. Busy drinking beer in the middle of the day more likely.

JT focused his attention on Lydia. "I don't believe I've had the pleasure of making your acquaintance."

Peyton said, "This is our friend, Lydia."

"Hel-lo, Lydia," he drawled, his expression just shy of a leer. He hitched a thumb over his shoulder to where his buddies now stood a little behind and to his left. "This here is Marshall and Denny."

They all greeted the men politely.

"Can I buy you all a drink? Or maybe my friends and I could interest you in a game of pool."

Peyton smiled. "That's a nice offer, but no thank you. We're just enjoying some girl time. You know how that is."

"I sure do," JT drawled suggestively. "I enjoy me some girl time, too. And if that's what you two are angling for, I'd be happy to oblige. There's plenty of me to go around."

Sofie let out a gasp.

Peyton looked equal parts shocked and disgusted.

Irritation boiled inside Lydia. She had plenty of experience with men like JT. Apparently, it didn't matter if you were in the heart of the city or in the middle of ranching country, they turned up nonetheless. She and Meredith dealt with inappropriate advances every time they went out dancing. Lydia knew how to shut them down.

She scoffed. "JT, you cowboy poser, what is the matter with you talking like that to a table full of ladies? If that line ever works on a woman, which I doubt, then I'm ashamed for my entire gender. Now take yourself and your cute curls and do-si-do right back over to that bar stool that has the imprint of your scrawny butt embossed on it. And enjoy it. Because I suspect that's the only circuit you're ever going to be riding with any success. What would your mother say if she was sitting at this table right now?"

Lydia realized that the room had gone graveyard-quiet. Oh, shoot, it was possible that her voice had gotten progressively louder with each word of her speech.

Then, a deep, clear voice called out from across the room, "You sure 'nuff kicked a hornet's nest there, JT."

His friends howled with laughter. The table of cowboys in the booth behind theirs erupted with cheers and hoots. Other patrons joined in. Scattered clapping ensued.

Steely-eyed, JT peered at her like he was trying to figure out how badly she'd insulted him. Finally, he seemed to realize the whole bar was watching, waiting for his reaction. Cheeks red, he gave a respectable effort at laughing it off.

With a salute, he turned and moved off toward the pool table in the back.

JON WATCHED THE pickup with trailer pull up next to the barn at the Blackwell Ranch. A big, shiny green-and-yellow tractor was chained down on the trailer. Two men got out and strode toward him. He recognized the passenger as Elbert Goode, the owner of Goode Deals Farm & Ranch Equipment & Auction House. Elbert really was a good guy who took pleasure in scoring deals for local farmers and ranchers. Jon had bought all his best equipment from Goode Deals over the years. The driver was his son, Cody.

Meeting them halfway, Jon reached out a hand to each of them in turn. "Hey, Cody. Elbert, how you boys doing?"

"Fine and dandy, Jon. How 'bout yourself."

"Just fine," Jon lied. He wasn't fine at all. He didn't appreciate having another afternoon interrupted with Blackwell Ranch business. Not to mention that here he was, staring at a piece of equipment he had no prior knowledge of. "How's business?"

"Really picked up lately. Got that tractor Big E won at the auction. He around?"

"No, he's not here right now." Jon purposely kept things vague. "When was that auction?"

Maybe Jon could track down his grandfather that way.

"Oh, it was a few weeks back, I guess. Couldn't make it in person, so he phoned in his bid. It needed new brakes and I had one needed some work done, too, so I told him I'd do a pickup and delivery for him. Dropped it off at Gil's and now here it is. Got a heck of a good deal on it." Elbert winked, pulled a slip of paper from his inside coat pocket and handed it to Jon.

Jon studied the invoice, feeling the concern settling like a cold rock in his gut. How many more surprises was he going to have to contend with around here? And it wasn't even the surprises so much as the fact that this purchase, good deals and puns aside, would bring the bank-account balance to a dangerously low level.

When Katie had called and asked if he could be here to accept a delivery, he'd assumed it was the load of hog wire he'd ordered for Zoe's zoo. Jon wrote Elbert a check. Cody unloaded the tractor. They shot the breeze for a while longer. Jon asked about Elbert's wife, Rhonda. Cody asked about the twins.

Elbert squinted over Jon's shoulder toward the donkey enclosure. "What are those critters there, like little dinky donkeys?"

"That's exactly what they are, Elbert."

"What are you using them for?"

"Believe it or not, they're just to look at."

Brow puckered, Elbert scratched his head. "Like pets?"

"Yep. Zoe is putting in a zoo here at the guest ranch."

"Huh. They're kinda cute. Grandkids would love 'em."

Jon tried not to roll his eyes. "Katie would welcome a visit from your grandkids, Elbert."

Elbert strolled over to the pen.

Cody shuffled his feet and looked at Jon. "Hey, uh, I heard that Lydia gal is your nanny?"

"That's right." How would Cody know Lydia?

"Boy, she's something else, huh?"

He could guess what this was about. Keeping his tone neutral, he said, "She is an excellent nanny."

"Did you hear what happened at the Silver Stake yesterday?"

Silver Stake? What was Lydia doing at the bar? His answer was a slow head shake. "Nope."

"You should have heard the set-down she gave JT." Cody added a chuckle. "What a moron."

"What happened?"

"I was there having a burger with some friends, sitting at the table right behind her and Sofie Carnes and Peyton, that new pretty blonde waitress from the Clearwater Café. JT came up and made this crude comment and Lydia, she…

she clocked him with words. Called him a cowboy poser with cute curls." Cody took a moment to laugh.

Jon wondered why she hadn't told him even as the urge to throttle JT overtook him.

"Do you know if she's single?"

Jon tensed. The thought of Lydia dating Cody, or anyone else, was out of the question. "No," he lied. "She's not."

"That's too bad. I was hoping to steal a dance at the Inezes' party this weekend."

Elbert ambled back. "They're real friendly. I think I'm gonna take you up on that offer and bring the little ones out."

Jon said goodbye to the men and went looking for Katie, but his mind was still on Lydia. Lydia was going to the Inez party? How would Cody know Lydia was going? He should have told Cody the truth. That wasn't fair to Lydia. But the thought of her dancing with anyone but him left him feeling a bit nauseated. This is what he was reduced to? Lying and conniving to keep Lydia from spending time with another man?

Jon needed to face the fact that Lydia had the kind of shine that wasn't ever going to wear off. He couldn't go on like this. And if he didn't do something about his feelings, then some other cowboy would. But what if he told her how he felt, and she didn't return the sentiment? Or worse, what if they gave this a shot and it didn't work out? Would they be able to live together under the same roof for the sake of the girls? It felt selfish to risk the best thing that had ever happened to the twins.

Jon found Katie in one of the ranch's riding arenas working with a horse.

"Katie, we have a problem." Jon pointedly said "we" rather than "you" because he didn't want her to think she had to face this alone. Although Jon now believed the two of them alone couldn't tackle it, either, not for much longer.

Katie led the horse toward him. "What is it?"

Jon patted the sorrel mare. "Did you know Big E bought a new tractor?"

Katie sighed. "No."

"It's in the barn. I just paid for it."

"Okay. Well, we needed one."

"The problem is, we… The ranch is going to run out of money. When I called the bank a few weeks ago and looked at the monthly bills I figured there was enough in that account to get by for several months. But between the building supplies for Zoe's petting zoo, their feed, payroll, the overdue bills we didn't know about and now a new tractor, it won't last another month."

"Can't you just write checks out of another account? Or transfer money from savings? Big E is always doing that, moving money around and stuff."

"I would if I could, but I can't find any other banking information."

"What do you mean?"

"I can't find his records or other bank-account information. I called the bank and they won't tell me anything. If I'm not on the account, they won't release any information."

Katie paled. "Jon, what are we going to do?"

Jon blew out a breath. "I don't know. The guest ranch is due to open in a few weeks. How does the pay structure work for that?"

Katie frowned and stroked the horse's muzzle. "When guests register, they pay a deposit and then the rest is collected when they check out."

"So those deposits are probably already spent. There might be enough money to get by until the guests start checking out. But who knows what else is going to pop up."

Katie's phone rang. Removing her leather gloves, she swiped her finger across the screen and answered it. The frown on her face made Jon think it was a serious matter.

Hanging up, she stared at Jon, her expression confirming his supposition.

"Katie, what is it? Is it your dad?"

"No, no, nothing about Dad." Raising a hand, she gripped her forehead like she was in pain.

"I'm, uh… We're in even worse trouble than what you just told me. That was Jess Kearns."

"Jess of Jess and Marie?" Jon knew Katie relied on Jess and his wife, Marie, for a lot of the guest-ranching duties. Jess was one of their best guides and Marie oversaw housekeeping duties for the lodge.

"Yep. They're not coming back."

"What do you mean? Why not?"

"They took a position at another ranch, making more money."

Jon let out a frustrated groan. "Information we could have used weeks ago. You need to put word out as soon as possible. I know it'll be rough to train new people right now, but we'll—"

"Jon," Katie interrupted. "We need way more than two."

"What do you mean?" Jon felt the anxiety in his gut bunch tighter.

"No one is coming back. Someone hijacked our entire crew. Bob Tucker called yesterday but I didn't think that much of it. This morning I heard from Will Peterson and I thought, huh, that's odd. But now? This is more than a coincidence." The phone rang in Katie's hand. She read the display. "This is Kyle Gibbs. He teaches the guests how to rope, among other things. Any guesses what he's going to tell me?" Katie took the call. The conversation was brief.

When she finished, she shoved the phone into her pocket like she couldn't stand to hold it any longer. Jon was a little tired of it himself. "What are we going to do?" she asked. "We've got reservations. If I cancel them, we have to return those deposits. How are we going to run two cattle ranches between us plus a guest ranch?"

Jon shook his head and heaved out a sigh. "We're not. Not for much longer, anyway. Give me a few days and I'll think of…something." He'd already thought about it and he had an idea. He didn't want to discuss it yet. Not until he could figure out how to get Ethan to come home.

CHAPTER SEVENTEEN

"THIS IS KIDD." Jon patted the rump of a handsome bay gelding.

Lydia slid a foot into the stirrup and swung her leg over. "Kidd and I are already friends." Leaning forward, she patted the horse's neck. "It's possible I may have been buying his affection with carrots."

"I'll spare you the pointers today," Jon joked, adjusting her stirrups.

She smiled down at him. "Pointers are always appreciated."

Jon's insides felt like a mass of tumbleweeds. Telling her how he felt was probably a terrible idea. But every time he stopped to reconsider, an image of her in Cody's arms or JT's or some other cowboy's appeared before him.

"I'm so excited for this. Are you sure you have time for it?"

"Don't worry," Jon said, tucking a few tools into his saddlebags. "We'll be working while we're at it—ride fence along the way, check on cattle. You might not know this, but multitask-ing was perfected by ranchers."

"Is that a fact?"

"It is. We have another name for it."

"What's that?"

"Ranching." Jon gave her a wink and mounted his horse.

Lydia's response was a half groan, half laugh. "And I thought I was the one with the bad jokes."

Jon urged his horse into a walk. Lydia did the same and Kidd soon found his stride next to Jon's horse. Trout jogged in front of them like he already knew where they were heading. Which, Lydia acknowledged, he probably did.

"Joking aside, that makes me feel better. Like I'm not taking up too much of your valuable time."

"I think that would only be fair seeing as how I've been taking up yours every evening for the last week or so."

"That's different. Plus, we can go over some of your interview questions while we're riding." The *Good Day USA* crew was arriving in two days. He was prepared. And even if he wasn't, Jon didn't want to waste this afternoon talking about it.

"Or we could just go for a ride," he countered smoothly. "You didn't tell me that you met one of our local cowboys."

"Well, Jon," she said in a playful tone, "I've met several. Can you be a little more specific?"

"JT Brimble."

"Oh… *Him*. He's a cowboy? He doesn't look like a cowboy to me. He looks like he wants to be a cowboy. What kind of a cowboy wears tight jeans and shiny boots?"

Jon chuckled. "A poser?"

She grinned. "My goodness, you've got good sources, don't you? He made a crude comment."

"Why didn't you tell me about it?"

Lydia shrugged. "I don't know. It didn't seem like that big of a deal. Meredith, my friend back in Philadelphia, and I used to hear comments like that all the time when we'd go out. Different phrasing, same meaning."

"Where are you going that men are talking to you like that?"

"Dancing."

"Dancing?"

"Mmm-hmm. I like to dance. I love music. My friend and I like to go out and enjoy them both together."

"WHAT KIND OF music do you like?" Jon had noticed that the radio was almost always on when he came inside, a habit he indulged in himself.

"Most kinds. Punk rock is a little shouty for my taste. And I'm not a huge rap fan, don't care for a lot of the lyrics. But some of it I love." She shrugged a shoulder. "Speaking of music and dancing, Sofie said there's a music jam on Saturday night."

"That there is."

"Are you going?"

"I was planning on it."

Her grin was mischievous. "Were you going to tell me about that?"

"Uh…"

"Spit it out," she teased.

"Saturday is supposed to be your day off. I guess I didn't think it would be something you'd be interested in." Not until Cody prompted him, anyway.

"And why's that?"

Jon thought about the one time he'd taken Ava to a music jam at the Carneses'. She'd acted fine while they were there, but Jon had seen the misery lurking behind her smile. On the way home, she'd cried. When he'd asked what was wrong, she'd said, "Homesick," and stared out the window into the moonlit night.

"Uh, well, it's not exactly a fancy dance club like you're probably used to."

"How would you know what I'm used to?"

Jon adjusted the hat on his head. "Umm…"

He could see she was fighting a smile. "You assumed because I'm from the city that I'd think your barn dance was too provincial and unso-phisticated?"

Guilty. He grimaced. "Maybe."

Lydia shook her head. "You realize, don't you, that this assumption makes you the narrow-minded one?"

He liked the way she called him out on this. He liked how she called him on everything, even his grumpiness. "Maybe." How could just chatting with someone be this much fun?

"If you could see some of the clubs my friend and I have been to in the name of good music, it would frighten you. The neighborhoods..." She shook her head. "We saw a knife fight once."

Jon felt a flicker of alarm. "Why would you go to a place like that?"

"It's all about the music. We'll brave anything to get our groove on, everything from Irish pubs to swing-dance clubs to trendy techno discos to biker bars. If the beat's on, we're in." She added a laugh.

"Lydia, biker bars? That can't be safe. Then again, cities aren't safe."

"Hey." She pointed a finger at him. "Most bikers are nice people. Besides, I know how to take care of myself."

Jon didn't want her to have to take care of herself. He wanted her to stay away from places that were dangerous.

"You miss it? Going out with your friend?"

"No." Cocking her head thoughtfully, she added, "A little, maybe. But I've been too busy since I got here to do much missing of anything."

Jon thought about how much of herself she'd given to this job, what she'd done for him, for the girls especially, since she'd arrived. Aside from a single afternoon with Sofie and Peyton she hadn't taken much time for herself.

"The music will be good. I'm not sure if it's the kind of good that you're used to. But I am going, and I would like for you to come with me if you're interested."

"Hmm… Are you sure? It wouldn't be uncomfortable for you if I went?"

"Why would it be uncomfortable for me?"

"I don't know. Socializing with the nanny—would that be awkward?"

Jon wanted to laugh out loud. He wanted to do a lot more than socialize with his nanny. Deadpan, he answered, "No. We ranchers socialize with everyone around here, even the hired help."

"Funny." She laughed. "What about the girls?"

Jon liked how Gen and Abby seemed to always be on her mind. "The girls are going to come for a while and then they're going home with Willa and Pete to have a sleepover. Garret and Raelynn and the kids will be in town and staying the weekend."

"They'll love that."

"I know. I'm going to tell them tonight. Willa called this morning, but I didn't want to tell them too soon. Their excitement is going to drive us crazy as it is."

"Good thinking. So," she said eagerly, "Sofie said you were going to be playing at this shindig. What do you play?"

"Fiddle."

"Are you any good?"

"Fair."

"What kind of music do you play?"

"Punk rock mostly. Some rap."

She burst out laughing. "Your humor still surprises me sometimes. It's fun."

He slid her a grin. "I play mostly country, bluegrass and Southern rock. I like Irish folk music, too. But my brother Chance is the real musician in the family."

"Wait a minute... No way! Your brother Chance is *that* Chance Blackwell, the singer?"

"You know him?"

"Sure I know him! I told you I know all the music. Oh, man... 'Butterfly Blue' rocks my world. I literally remember the first time I heard that song. I was working at the bakery and I was carrying this cake that my boss had just finished decorating to the walk-in fridge. That song came on the radio and I froze. And then…" She laughed at the memory. "One minute I was holding it and the next it was sliding off the turntable… *Plop*. All over the floor."

Jon laughed. "Chance would be thrilled to hear about your ruined cake."

"My boss wasn't, so much. But that song is one of my all-time favorites. Now that I think about it, I haven't heard much music from your brother lately."

"He's had a rough go of it since his wife, Maura, died. Found out she was pregnant, had baby Rosie and died a few months later. Maura was Katie's sister. It was hard on her, too, as I'm sure you can imagine." Jon felt a sharp hit of grief. They had all loved Maura. It was difficult enough to raise a baby girl on your own, Jon couldn't imagine adding grief to the mix. Chance had the added struggle of a strained relationship with Maura and Katie's dad, Lochlan. Then there was the fact that he had his own turmoil with Big E. As much as Jon wished Chance would come home, as much as he wished all his brothers would, he couldn't blame them. But that didn't stop him from missing them, from wanting it to be different. He'd give just about anything for the girls to grow up knowing their uncles, and their cousin Rosie.

"You know, I think I remember hearing some-thing about his wife passing away. That's so sad."

"It is. And I don't know how to help him." Or Tyler. His heart already a little tender at all the brother memories he'd been reliving lately, he rubbed a hand over his chest. "I'm not sure there's a lot you can do to help with another per-son's grief, even your brother's."

That felt so true, especially for Chance and Tyler, despite how much he hoped otherwise. "I'd like you to meet him some day." Jon enjoyed a vision of taking Lydia to one of his brother's concerts.

"Me, too. Will it embarrass you if I ask for his autograph?"

Jon laughed. "No, ma'am. He deserves to be asked. He is that extraordinary."

As they rode on, Jon relayed information about the ranch and pointed out landmarks. When they neared the back of the property, he dismounted and opened a gate where the trail led out of the upper pasture. The terrain was scattered with trees and there was more brush. Patches of spring wildflowers bloomed in the bright green grass.

"This is my property line," he explained, sweeping an arm toward the hills. "From here up is federal land, but I have some grazing leases up the basins."

"This is where you put the cattle in the summertime, right?"

"Yep. Summer is the easiest time of year, cattle-wise. We don't have to feed them or water them. We drive the cattle up here and let them graze. There's a big creek running down that way." He pointed. "Lots of water. In the winter, we have storms. Trees get blown over, branches break off and come down. That's the cleanup I mentioned. We have trails through here and we keep them cleared so the cattle can move through more easily. And us on horseback."

"So, you just turn them loose all the way out here? All alone?"

"Yep. We ride in now and then to check on them, do a head count, make sure they're healthy and safe. They pretty much stay in the valleys and basins, where the food is. We have mountain lions, wolves and the occasional grizzly."

"Bears?"

"Mmm-hmm. Mostly, they'll leave an adult cow alone. But they have no problem bringing down a small calf or a lame cow. Wolves can be a bigger concern."

"For sure," she remarked sarcastically, "it's the cities that aren't safe."

He laughed.

"Seriously, Jon, you do realize that people from the city would be terrified to be out here right now all alone with no people around?"

"Hmm. You think so?"

Dipping her chin, she gave him a pointed look. "I know so."

"That's hard to believe." He looked around, feigning surprise. "No one is going to mug you here."

"Let's argue the merits of a mugging versus a mauling."

He laughed. "We could. Although I think I'd win because a mugging is way more common than a mauling."

"I'd be willing to bet the survival rate is higher in a mugging."

"You might have a point. Or, there's a nice view of the river and the ranch from up on this ridge. We could ride up there if you're up for it?"

"Absolutely."

Jon climbed back on his horse and led the way on the trail. They rode through heavier timber, eventually coming to a wide, flat shelf.

"We can get down and walk a little closer to the edge if you'd like."

Lydia agreed. They both dismounted.

"Will the horses be okay?"

"Yep, they're very well trained. Trout will

keep an eye on them." Trout moved closer to the horses.

"Amazing, that dog," Lydia whispered.

Jon led her toward the edge. She was quiet for a long moment. "This is your idea of a *nice* view? I'm telling you, Jonathon Blackwell, I've never seen anything so gorgeous in my life. I *would* argue that it's way more beautiful than any city I've ever seen, or country, either, for that matter. And I've seen a bit of the world."

"Have you?"

"Yep. Before I—" She halted the sentence and started again. "Before my parents got divorced we did some traveling—Europe, Australia, Thailand, Japan."

"And after they got divorced?"

Her short laugh held a bitter edge and Jon knew there was a story here. He'd been curious ever since she'd made that comment about families falling apart. "After, not so much."

"What happened after? Did you live with your mom or your dad?"

"I lived with Nana. For two years on her little farm in upstate New York. I use the term *farm* loosely." She bent to pick up a rock. "She had a huge garden and an orchard. She canned vegetables, cooked, sold stuff at the farmer's market. That's how I learned to garden and cook and sew—the basics, anyway. Nana is also the one who taught me how to ride. She had two horses."

"Why only two years?"

"That's when she died."

"I'm sorry. You mentioned her in passing but not that you'd been living with her at the time. That must have been terrible."

"It was. My mom was—*is*, as far as I know— busy living the single life she claimed she deserved because she never had it. My dad married Tina and started a new and improved family."

Jon didn't like where this was heading. "So where did you go after your nana passed away?"

"I moved in with Dad and Tina. Moved out soon after."

"And then what? You went to live with your mom?"

"No. I…left."

"You left? How old were you?"

"Fifteen." Blue pain-filled eyes met his look of concern. "Yes, technically, I was a runaway. But my dad never reported me as one. He knew where I was but he didn't care."

"Lydia… How…" Anger shoved at him, jostling his thoughts and words. How could a man not care enough about his fifteen-year-old daughter to go fetch her from wherever she'd gone? He'd go to hell and back for the twins. Gen and Abby were only five and he already dreaded their leaving home someday. "How did you survive?"

"Friends, at first, bounced around. Lived in shelter for a while, several shelters. Then I landed at Hatch House, this incredible group home for teens. It's privately owned, nonprofit. I lived there for almost two years. I got a job as a seamstress apprentice, but couldn't work full-time because of the labor laws about minors. I worked for cash on the side, babysitting, cleaning, dog walking, house-sitting. That was enough to pay the rent on an apartment with three other girls. Four of us in a one-bedroom apartment." She chuckled at the memory. "I saved and kept getting different jobs, learned some skills. Got new jobs that paid more and more until eventually I could support myself."

Jon felt guilty for ever thinking she was spoiled. "What about high school? College?"

"A friend and I studied together and I got my GED. No college."

"When did you decide to become a nanny?"

THAT WAS THE moment Lydia realized that she'd talked herself into a corner. She didn't want to lie to him. Of course, she was sort of lying to him by being here as it was. But that was different. She'd had no idea that she'd fall in love—with him, his girls, the ranch, Falcon Creek.

"I just kind of fell into it. All the jobs and experiences I've had seemed to point me in this direction. When my friend saw the position available, he encouraged me to take it." That felt good, truthful. "And I'm so glad I did. It's the best thing that's ever happened to me."

"But...how is that possible?"

"What do you mean?"

"Stuck out here in the middle of nowhere taking care of someone else's kids? This is the life you want?"

Lydia stared back at him, hoping her heart wasn't showing in her eyes. "Um..." She turned and held her arms out in front of her. "This isn't exactly nowhere. Pretty sure it's the most beautiful place on earth."

"I'm not trying to put you on the spot here, it's just that I'm wondering why."

In that moment, she wished she could tell him everything. But what would he think of her? There wasn't a situation in the world that would cause Jon Blackwell to run from his problems the way she'd always run from hers. Maybe, she could tell him a little, though. Tanner's warnings surfaced but she brushed them away. She'd keep things vague.

"Well, Jon, I've made some mistakes. I haven't had great luck with relationships." With a little grimace, she went on, "There's no luck involved. It's more that I get involved with the wrong guys. The last one was a real piece of work. I had a difficult time getting out of the relationship." Gripping the rock she'd gathered, she continued, "That's part of the reason that I took this job, to get away from him. I needed to get out of Philadelphia."

Jon's eyes homed in on her like a laser beam. "Lydia, did some guy...? Are you talking about abuse? If someone hurt you, I'd like to know about it."

Lydia's heart fluttered helplessly in her chest. She couldn't help but wonder how it would feel to have a man protect her for once, or at least to not want to hurt her. And not just any man, but this man, who was strong and smart and good. Too good, maybe, because he ended up with a woman who took advantage of that goodness. She ignored the little voice that reminded her that she was currently doing the same.

But she didn't want to be. She wanted to protect him, too, from the wiles of Ava and Marilee. She wanted to help him in every way that she could—take care of his girls, support him on the ranch and keep him from working too hard. She wanted to be his partner. And love them all in the way they deserved.

"Um...he didn't hurt me physically." Lydia had often thought he wanted to. She suspected he'd been abusive in other relationships. "But he could be rough and the threat of more was always there. Verbal abuse, yes. I worked for him so that made it all worse." She sighed. It was so difficult to explain without explaining. "At the end, I lived in constant fear."

Lydia watched his mouth flatten out to a thin, angry line. "You deserve so much better."

"Thank you. I know I *want* better."

"What do you want?" His voice was low and deep and somehow made her want to cry a little.

You, her heart answered immediately. It hurt that she couldn't say it, so she looked out at the view again. Doing her best to lighten the moment, she tossed the rock from the cliff and answered in a teasing tone, "Oh, I don't know. Not much really. Just love, safety, security… And someday…maybe my own horse."

Her attempt at levity didn't work.

Jon looked out toward the horizon. He was still and appeared calm. But Lydia knew him better now. Tension radiated from him and she knew it wasn't anger. Her breath stalled as her pulse began to pound fast and hard. His expression was pure Rancher Blackwell—grave and solemn and almost unreadable. Almost, because she could see the vulnerability there. She knew he had feelings for her, too. The attraction between them had been simmering hotly since he'd kissed her on Easter. What she hadn't known was what those feelings entailed or how strong they were. But now she did. And at that moment, all of the reasons why they couldn't be together flew out of her head. Which left only her heart, aching and craving his love. *Just say it*, she silently pleaded. Because no matter what happened long-term she wanted to hear the words at least once in her life from a person she wanted to hear them from.

He faced her again, his gray-blue gaze ensnaring hers. Her heart jumped into her throat. "What if I told you that I want those things, too? And what if I told you that I didn't ever want to let you go, not even when the girls leave for college?"

CHAPTER EIGHTEEN

LYDIA STEPPED INTO his arms. He gathered her close, his lips finding hers. The kiss was different this time. With feelings clearer, there was less desperation and so much more sweetness.

Jon adjusted his hold and trailed kisses along her neck. When he whispered, she could feel his lips brushing against her skin. "I've wanted to do this for so long. Kiss you right here. You smell so good. You always smell so good."

"So do you."

"Ha. Like cows?" He drew back to look at her face and Lydia felt her heart clench when she saw the uncertainty there. He was such a steady, rock-solid guy that these flashes of insecurity from him always surprised her. And they made her despise his ex-wife.

Cupping his face in her hands, she kissed him. "Yes, like cow and horse and hay and sweat and Jonathon Blackwell and sweet Montana air. You could bottle it and call it Sexy Cowboy and sell it for an ungodly amount of money."

"Sexy cowboy," he repeated and then Jon

pressed his forehead to hers. With a groan he closed his eyes. "Do you really mean these things that you say to me? About the girls and me? And the ranch and Montana?"

"Jon, look at me."

He did. "Ava was one woman. I know for a fact you've had others. I can name at least five women who'd like to join them and one who's dying for another chance. And another one who is standing right in front of you wearing her heart on her sleeve. Why is Ava the one that you remember? Why do you let her ruin this for me? For us?"

"I don't want her to… I hate that she does. I guess because it was such a failure. I don't like to fail. Usually when I try hard enough, I succeed. I gave her everything I had and plenty that I didn't. And it wasn't enough. I wasn't enough. Then we had these two beautiful, perfect children together. How could they not be enough?"

"I don't know." Lydia blinked and then swallowed her tears. Because this was important, and he needed to hear it. "But you have to let her go. You don't need her. The girls don't need her. If what I hear is true, you're all better off without her. Honestly, I suspect that deep inside she knew that. Leaving you is probably the most unselfish thing she could have done. And I know it's selfish on my part, but I'm glad she did. Because otherwise I would never have had this chance."

He smiled and Lydia could feel it; she'd made a breakthrough. "Me, too." He kissed the corner of her mouth. "And just so you know, Ms. Lydia, she never made me feel this way."

"Oh, yeah? And what way is that?"

"Giddy. Like I'm losing control. No, like my mind is possessed, like you've taken over a part of it. Because you're always there. Every morning I get up and wonder how long I can loiter around the house before you get up so we can have coffee together, or I can at least catch a glimpse of you before I head out. Then I plot and scheme about how I'm going to work my schedule so that I can get back to the house and have lunch with you and the girls. Or even just see you for a few minutes. And this last week when you came into my office in the evenings, it was the unqualified highlight of my day."

Happiness roared to life inside of her. It felt like her heart had caught fire.

"When I was married, I used to dread coming in at night because I never knew what kind of mood I'd be facing. But you… You always seem to be in the moment. Whatever you're doing, it's like you try to squeeze whatever joy out of it you can. It's contagious. And I love that you're setting that kind of example for my girls. They haven't been happy like they are with you in a long time. Not since Annie died."

His expression was filled with a satisfaction that, incredibly, seemed to match Lydia's own feelings. He said, "I can't believe how different you are than I thought you'd be."

"It's nice to finally hear you say that," she teased.

"After I say this last thing, I'm not going to talk about Ava anymore because you're right— we don't need her. I'm ready to leave her behind. But I want you to know that you're nothing like her. I mean she wasn't all bad, obviously, or I wouldn't have been taken with her. But being with you is so easy. Where she was all hard edges with this cold essence, you're so soft and inviting." His hands wandered down her back to lightly grip her hips. "And I'm not talking about your curves, although I can't stop thinking about those, either." He brought a hand up and placed it over her heart. "It's this right here that I've fallen in love with. And your spirit that is warm and kind and so generous it leaves me a little awed."

"Jon…" A soft sob of joy halted her response. She swallowed it down. Then she shook her head and said, "My cowboy is a poet."

"I don't know about that, but your cowboy

is in love." Eyes shining, he went on, "And the way you love my girls… I don't even know how to say how that makes me feel…" He shrugged helplessly.

"They are easy children to love. As easy to love as their father."

"Lydia…" He paused, and she watched him swallow his own lump of emotion. He kissed her again and then held her. With his face buried in her hair, he said, "It feels too good to be true. I'm sorry I doubted you. But *you* have seemed too good to be true from the start."

Like flipping on the lights in a dim, cozy room, his words woke her up. Because he was right—it wasn't true. She wasn't true. Not like she wanted to be. Her actions were genuine, her love was real, but they had no future. She had to find a way to stay in Falcon Creek. She couldn't—she wouldn't—break his heart. Was there some solution to make this situation with Clive go away? She needed to talk to Tanner. She needed to think.

"Jon, we need to keep this between us for now. I don't want to confuse the girls and—"

"I know," he interrupted. "I agree. But I'm not sure how we're going to be able to do that."

"Bethany and her crew will be here tomorrow. Let's focus on that first and then…we'll figure this out."

LYDIA SPENT A restless night, tossing covers and turning her pillow, along with possible solutions, over and over. By morning, her heart was so heavy she had to drag herself out of bed. She realized she'd forgotten to check her phone the night before. Fishing it out from her suitcase, she discovered several missed calls from Tanner. With a shaky hand, she dialed his number.

"Lydia, where have you been? I've called you like five times."

Her already churning stomach took a hard tumble. "I know, Tanner, I'm so sorry. I can't carry the phone around with me. Everyone here thinks I don't have one. I only check it a couple of times a day and I forgot last night. What's going on?"

"You need to start keeping it with you."

"Why? Did something happen?"

"I had a visit from Wendell yesterday." Just the name of Clive's shark of an attorney made Lydia flinch. "He was cagey but he suggested they may have an idea where you are."

Panic welled inside of her as her gaze darted around the room. She focused on the closet where she'd stashed her suitcase. She could be ready to go in minutes. A stab of anguish made her knees weak and she stepped back to sit on the edge of the bed. She didn't want to go. She couldn't. Not yet.

"What do I do?"

"Nothing. Stay put for now. I bet he's bluffing to try and flush you out, get you to run. A person on the move is much easier to find. When you're traveling, people see you, you make transactions, interact, et cetera."

She blew out the breath she'd been holding. "Okay. That I can do."

"Lydia, you need to keep a low profile. You're doing that, right?"

"Yes… I mean as much as I can. There are places I have to go. I'm a nanny to two little girls. They have appointments, and there are things…" She doubted Tanner would consider a big party where practically the whole town would be in attendance a place she had to go. Hanging around a nationally known reporter and her camera crew also would not fall under his low-profile criterion, which is why she hadn't told him about it. "But I'm in the middle of nowhere and Falcon Creek is small. Trust me, if Clive was here I'd know."

Tanner sighed. "Okay. Find a way to keep the phone with you and the bundle from your suitcase."

"I'm not comfortable carrying all that cash around."

"Lydia, if I call and tell you it's time to go, you won't have time to pick up your things. You won't have time to say goodbye to your rancher or your twins. Do you understand? You will get in your car and you will drive away. End of story."

She had to ask. "Tanner, can you think of any way we can change the plan? Make this all go away? And not…run?"

He was silent for too long. "Lydia, you took millions of dollars from Clive. And it's not like you can give it back."

"What if I went to the authorities? The FBI or whoever?"

"With proof of what? You said yourself he hadn't actually done anything illegal yet." Tanner paused. "We talked about this before you took the money. I warned you about how it would likely go down. No, you're going to have to run. It's just a matter of when."

He went on, but Lydia only vaguely registered his repeated words of warning as reality seeped into her; she had stolen millions of Clive's dollars. But there was no figuring to do and there was no strategy to make it work out.

Absently, she agreed to whatever Tanner said. They exchanged goodbyes. Hopelessness and grief overwhelmed her. Her entire body felt weak. She spent several minutes staring blankly at the wall. She needed to talk to Jon, tell him… something, in case she had to leave sooner than she thought. But she couldn't. Not now, anyway, not with the interview happening today.

Still trembling, she headed out to the kitchen, where she realized the girls would be up any minute. Glancing at the clock, she noted she had roughly two hours to take care of the animals, feed the girls breakfast and get them to Willa's before Bethany Stouffer and the crew from *Good Day USA* arrived. Grateful for the distraction that this long day would provide, she started moving.

It wasn't as if Tanner had said she needed to leave now. He was being overly cautious. The term *needle in a haystack* had never meant so much to her as it did in Montana. And that's what she was. The longer she stayed, the more impossible it seemed that Clive would find her here. Other than Tanner and Meredith, she'd had no contact with her old life, much less the outside world. She hadn't ventured farther than Falcon Creek. Then again, it would be foolish to underestimate Clive.

Hurrying back to her bedroom, she dug the cash from the lining of her suitcase and peeled off 500 dollars. She rolled it and the phone inside one of Jon's handkerchiefs, tucked the bundle into the inside pocket of her jacket and zipped it shut.

BETHANY STOUFFER AND her crew descended upon the JB Bar Ranch as scheduled. It wasn't long before Lydia had a sense of why Jon disliked the guest portion of his grandfather's place. It felt invasive to have strangers poking around. On a positive note, they all turned out to be so much nicer than either she or Jon had imagined. The crew was respectful and considerate, and everyone seemed interested in everything Jon had to say.

The producer and one cameraman spent the morning riding around the ranch with Jon, shooting footage of the scenery, the fields, cattle, horses, Jon, Tom, Trout, Jon on his horse with Trout, all the cowboys on their horses, the barns and equipment. Not even the chickens were spared. The first of the one-on-one interviews with Jon and Bethany was set to begin after lunch.

Lydia headed to the bunkhouse, where she and Dusty put together a buffet that they'd planned and prepped for in the preceding days. Opting for traditional ranch-style fare, they prepared fried chicken, potato salad, baked beans, roasted vegetables, fresh-baked rolls and blackberry cobbler. To her surprise, the crew dug in. Even Bethany filled her plate. She'd imagined famous TV people from New York would be finicky and demanding.

The reporter approached her after the meal. "I don't think we've met. I'm Bethany Stouffer."

"Lydia. It's nice to meet you, Ms. Stouffer."

"Please, call me Bethany. I understand you're responsible for this delicious meal?"

"Dusty and I made it together."

"He gave you all the credit. He says his food doesn't taste anything like this. It truly was outstanding. I could eat three more helpings of that cobbler. I'm going to have to do extra elliptical as it is."

Lydia laughed. "I'm sorry about the elliptical part but I'm glad you enjoyed the food. I was excited to see that you…" Lydia struggled for the right words and finally went with honesty. "Eat."

Bethany belted out a laugh. "I know what you mean. That is a thing with many people in the TV business. Not with me. I'm a farm girl from Michigan. I love food. Grew up on home-cooked meals. This—" she gestured around her "—means everything to me. People like my folks, Jon Blackwell and his grandfather, Big E, are the backbone of this country. One generation after another carrying on the family legacy. My brother runs our family farm now."

Hmm. Bethany had obviously done her homework on Jon's family history. "I agree. Before I came here I never gave much thought to how hard ranchers work. They're on call twenty-four/

seven. This life keeps you so grounded. I love
how everyone is so close to the earth. Every day
I walk outside, and I'm stunned by the beauty
around me. And then I'm overwhelmed by the
amount of work and responsibility a rancher has
on his or her shoulders. It's incredibly important and most of it can't be put off for another
day or another time. It's… Well, for someone
from the city it's offered me a whole new perspective on life."

"You're a nanny for five-year-old twins on a
huge ranch in the middle of Nowhere, Montana.
Jon told me about everything you do for him. It
sounds like you work as hard as he does. I don't
know how you do it. Can I just say…off the record?" Lydia nodded. "With a boss who looks
like yours it's probably a little easier to take."

Lydia chuckled. "My nana always said that
was the key to life—discovering what you love
and then finding out how to do it all the time.
I feel lucky I've found that. I love this job so
much that sometimes I forget that it's a job.
And, my off-the-record response to your off-the-
record comment would be that I can't lie and say
I haven't noticed what the man looks like. But
honestly, he's an easy guy to like, in addition to
all of that…um, rancher appeal."

Bethany took a moment to laugh. Then she
peered at Lydia with the curious, measured con-

templation that had helped make her famous. Lydia feared she'd said too much. Bethany shook her head thoughtfully. "You know, you're genuine and articulate and very beautiful. The camera would love you. Have you ever done any film work?"

"Thank you. Um, no."

"Any chance we could do a short piece with you and Jon? You could give us a tour of the home? Tell us all of what you just said, what it's like to work for a cattle rancher, what it was like to move here from the big city?"

Lydia's heart nearly stopped at the suggestion. "Oh, um, thank you, but no. Absolutely not."

Bethany's brow knitted in surprise. "Seriously? Most people would jump at the chance to be on my show. And that passion I just heard from you. You could offer something special to this story."

"Not me. Camera-shy." Lydia forced out a nervous chuckle. "Just wait until you hear Jon talk about it. You'll forget all about me." *Please*, she added silently, *forget about me*.

Bethany gave her another assessing look. "You don't strike me as shy."

"I do my best to overcome it," she lied.

Lydia felt a rush of relief when Bethany reached out and gave her hand a light squeeze. "I understand. If you change your mind let me know. You're going to want to roll your eyes because people say this all the time, but I have good instincts. I like you, Lydia. If there's ever anything I can do for you, give me a call." Bethany pulled a card out of her pocket. "This isn't the card I hand out to everyone. This has my personal cell number and email on it."

From the doorway, Bethany's producer motioned to her.

"That's my cue. I'll see you later. And thank you for lunch."

"What was that about?" Jon asked, joining her a moment later.

"We were just chatting. She liked the food, she appreciates the, um, scenery here on the ranch, wondered if I wanted to film a spot with you."

"I like that last one."

Lydia gave him a sideways grin. "Not me. The only stars of this show are you and Tom. And Trout." The dog had already wowed every member of the crew. Jon had given them a demonstration on how he used the dog to herd the cattle.

He leaned down so his mouth was close to her ear. "I can't wait until these people leave my ranch. I want this to be over and then I want to sit and look at you and wallow in my good fortune."

It was difficult to imagine Jonathon Blackwell being anything but supremely confident, but Lydia realized he was nervous. No one else would ever know it. They were alone, so she slipped her hand around his and gave it a tight squeeze. "You're going to be great. You've got this. I'll be there. Remember, just like you're talking to me."

A short time later, Lydia felt her spirits soar as she watched him chatting with Bethany like there weren't cameras and a bunch of people standing around. Like they hadn't rehearsed every question a hundred times. Talk about a person who was born to be in front of a camera. He looked so handsome it made her ache. He was so charming, she hoped Bethany didn't fall in love with him, too. Pride filled her up and swamped her to the point that she wanted to weep, but in a good way.

They wrapped it up by dinnertime. The producer informed Jon they would be back the next day but expected only to stay a few hours. They wanted to film the ranch at sunrise and capture the cattle and horses in the morning light. Lydia couldn't blame them for any of that.

CHAPTER NINETEEN

WILLA AND PETE had offered to keep Gen and Abby for the night. Exhausted and grateful, Lydia agreed. The next morning, she made muffins for the *Good Day USA* crew and sent them out with Jon before daylight. Lydia prepared an egg casserole for later, when he returned to the house.

Thinking she'd have enough time to take care of the animals while it baked, she stepped into the mudroom. Boots on, she was zipping her jacket when she felt the phone buzz in the inside pocket.

Tanner. Adrenaline surged through her body. Running toward her bedroom, she pulled the phone from her pocket. She stared at the screen. Not Tanner. She didn't recognize the number, but what if something had happened and he had to call from a different phone?

She punched the green button. "Hello?"

"Lydia, thank goodness!"

"Meredith." Lydia collapsed onto the edge of her bed. "Where are you calling from?"

"Work. I'm using a line at the receptionist's station. No one else is here yet."

"Oh, good. What's going on? Did something happen?"

"Sort of… Where do I start? Okay, Clive showed up at my house last night ranting and raving about the money. The money this and the money that. I asked him, 'What money? I don't know anything about any money.' And that's when he said, 'I know she took it, Meredith. But if she was going to give it away she could have at least given me credit.'

"I had no idea what he was talking about. He was ranting and raving and totally losing it. Even more than normal, I mean. Anyway, there have been all these announcements in the news about anonymous donations to different charities across Philly the last couple weeks. I didn't think a thing about it. I'm just like, oh, some rich dude died or grew a conscience, how nice of him to do good works with his millions or whatever. Until this morning when I was watching the news. Guess who was on there? I'll just tell you it was Joanna. It seems the Hatch House Group Home for Teens received a million dollars from this same anonymous donor."

Lydia felt flush and her skin was tingling. Joanna was the house's director. The donation was supposed to be kept out of the press.

"You stole money from Clive and gave it away, didn't you?"

"Yes."

"Why?"

"It's dirty money, Meredith. And when I figured out what he was doing, he threatened me. Told me I was stupid for not realizing it sooner. He pointed out that the authorities would never believe I didn't know about it. Especially when I'd been living on the money myself and I'd better keep my mouth shut or I'd regret it. When I asked what he meant by that, he said, 'Lydia, just keep doing what you're doing and you won't have to find out. It's not that hard. Add two plus two and give me four.'"

"What a snake! I always hated how he talked to you."

"Me, too. That's why I left exactly four dollars in every account I had access to."

Meredith chuckled. "No wonder he was so ticked off."

"When I figured out how he was coming by this money, I knew I couldn't just take it from him. So, I did something better—I passed it on to people who really need it."

"That's why you left all your stuff…" Meredith paused. "I thought it meant you were coming back. But it's the opposite, isn't it?"

"Yes, I'm so sorry that I didn't tell you, but I thought it would be better if you didn't know."

"Lydia, aside from the fact that I'm devastated by the idea of never seeing you again, there is a much larger issue here. Wherever you are, I hope you are very, very well hidden. Clive made it clear that he…wants to catch up to you."

"I know." Lydia dipped her head and squeezed the bridge of her nose. "Thankfully, he wants his money more. And I'm hidden, Meredith. In fact, I'm hidden so well you wouldn't even recognize me."

They chatted for a few more minutes before Lydia ended the call. The timer beeped, and she removed the casserole from the oven. Then she fed the animals and went to pick up the girls.

SATURDAY AFTERNOON, SHE was removing the last load of laundry from the dryer when she turned around to find Jon watching her. She hadn't seen much of him since the *Good Day USA* crew had departed yesterday afternoon. After tackling some of the ranch chores he'd put off for the filming, he'd assisted a heifer with a difficult labor and hadn't come in until after she and the girls had gone to bed. He'd already left this morning by the time they'd gotten up.

Lydia caught up on housework and spent time with the girls. She also contemplated Meredith's phone call. She was going to tell him the truth. Maybe not all of it, but as much of it as she could. When she had to go he'd know why she was leaving. And most importantly, he'd know that she didn't want to leave. Now, if she could just figure out where to start.

"Hi," he said from the doorway, a small smile playing on his lips.

"Hi yourself. How's it going?"

"Pretty great. That last heifer gave birth today. Another calving season is officially complete on the JB Bar Ranch."

"Congratulations."

"Shaping up to be a good year, one-hundred-percent survival rate so far."

"That gives you something to celebrate tonight."

"Oh, I have plenty to celebrate, Ms. Lydia." He gave her a slow smile. Her pulse took off at a gallop.

"Good. It's going to be fun."

"It is. But I came in here to tell you that I'm going to have to meet you guys there. I'm sorry."

"Oh. Is everything all right?"

With a frustrated sigh, he raked a hand through his hair. "Yeah… Well, no. I have to run out to Big E's. I haven't been able to get out there the last two days. Katie didn't want to bother me because she knew how busy I was. But they've got a stretch of fence down and fifty-some head of cattle straying over onto the Double T." Lydia had learned that relations weren't exactly friendly between the neighboring ranch owners.

"I understand. Are you still going to be able to make it? I don't want to go if you're not going."

"Really?"

"Yes, really. Marilee Inez doesn't like me and—"

"Well," he interrupted, "I don't like her so that evens things up in the universe."

Lydia laughed.

Gleam in his eye, he took a step farther into the room. Lydia's throat went dry. "Where are the girls?"

"In their room, playing. Why?"

Crossing to her, he took her by the hips and lifted her onto the washing machine. Standing between her legs, he cupped her face, leaned in and kissed her. Nice and hard. And with so much feeling Lydia thought her heart might explode.

When he pulled back they were both out of breath. Jon's eyes searched her face like he was making sure she felt it, too. Then he grinned, satisfaction settling over his features. "Because I wanted to do that." He set her back on her feet. "I promise I will be there. Maybe even before you. I'm taking Trout and Tom's going with us. Trout and Hip will have the cattle rounded up and pushed back in no time. Probably take longer to splice the barb wire. We'll use Tom's pickup and head straight to the Inezes'. I might be smelling like horse, but don't worry. There's no way I'd let you be at that party without me."

"You know how much I like *Eau de Horse*. How can I argue with that plan?"

"I only have one request."

"What's that?"

"Please don't slow-dance with anyone but me."

"Jon, if I dance with you like that, the whole place is going to know how I feel. I won't be able to keep my hands to myself."

He slipped his hands into his pockets. "I don't care about that, do you?"

"Only where the girls are concerned."

"I've been thinking about that and maybe we should tell the girls. We're in this, Lydia. And I honestly don't believe there's anything we couldn't tackle together."

She'd needed to hear him say that. She wanted to believe it. She would tell him everything. Almost everything.

But not tonight. He needed this night. Successful calving season, promising interview, a woman who loved him. The girls were thriving. He deserved to relax and have fun before she took some of that joy away. Tomorrow she would figure out what to tell him, and how, and at least she'd be able to say goodbye honestly. He owned her heart and she wanted him to know it.

"I'll be able to drive you home. I'm going to leave you my phone, so I can keep you posted. I need to get you a phone."

He kissed her goodbye. Lydia checked on the girls and then took a shower. As she got ready for the evening, she felt a curl of excitement in her stomach similar to the feeling she'd get when she and Meredith ventured out to hear a new band. She couldn't wait to dance with Jon. And hear him play. She knew him, and she knew he wouldn't get up there in front of all those people if he wasn't good.

Sofie had told her people would be dressed in their "nice casuals" so she opted for the slim-fitting jeans she'd ordered online but hadn't worn yet. She paired them with a knit top that gently hugged her curves without being too tight. Comfort sat a notch above fashion when it came to dancing clothes.

That's when she realized she didn't have any suitable boots. Her riding boots were already too dirty to try and dress up. Pulling out the impractical ones she'd worn the day she'd arrived, she slipped them on and checked herself in the mirror. They looked good. And they reminded her of how far she'd come in the month she'd been here. She felt like a completely different person from the desperate, terrified woman she'd been. She just hoped there was no mud.

LYDIA AND THE girls arrived right on time. She parked on the edge of an open field in a long line of cars. Gen and Abby were bubbling with enthusiasm. Their excitement was contagious, and Lydia felt her spirits lift as they approached the crowd of people. Sofie hadn't exaggerated. The Inez barn would make the country-chic enthusiasts in Philly lose their minds. Twinkle lights adorned every edge and corner of the structure. The giant double doors were open, and Lydia could see that strings of lights decorated the rafters along with glowing paper lanterns. The wooden floor was bare. Hay bales and long wooden benches provided seating.

Outside, picnic tables sat upon a fresh semicircle of sawdust. Around the perimeter, metal stakes brandished lanterns already luminous in the fading daylight. A long row of tables overflowed with steaming dishes, and people were lined up and loading their plates with food. Laughter, conversation and the sound of sizzling meat swirled around them. Smoke billowed from three grills. Heavenly odors filled the air. Lydia recognized garlic, chili, cumin and sweet barbecue.

"Hi! You made it," Peyton said as she and Sofie appeared before them.

Sofie said, "Jon and Zach are helping set up the sound system. Let's fix plates for the girls and we can sit with Zach's family."

Jon had texted earlier to say he was on the way and Lydia was relieved to hear he'd already arrived. Looking around, she recognized quite a few familiar faces—Tom, Dusty, June and Emma from the salon, Zach's sisters, Brenna and Tess, Nell from Dr. Beazley's office. Katie was visiting with Grace Gardner, the pretty blonde woman whose parents owned Brewster's. Lydia waved at Scooter.

They followed Sofie's plan and headed for the buffet. The girls were perfectly behaved and the food every bit as good as Sofie said it would be. Scooter and Tom joined them. Zach's family treated her like one of their own.

The melodic tune of a fiddle cut through the air and made her eager to see Jon in action. Guitar and banjo joined a few notes later. People began to file inside the barn. As the girls finished their cherry crisps, the rhythmic thump of boots on the wood floor carried outside.

Brenna asked, "Hey, girls, you want to go inside and dance? Is that okay, Lydia?"

"Absolutely. I'm going to clean off our table and I'll be right in. Thanks, Brenna."

Lydia gathered up the remaining paper plates, bowls and napkins and headed to the garbage can. She'd just tossed the trash when JT Brimble stepped up beside her. "Evenin', Ms. Lydia."

He'd pulled his blond curls back at the nape of his neck, where they looked much better. Turning on a smile, Lydia said, "Hello, JT. How are you tonight? I like that ponytail."

He seemed taken aback by her friendliness. "I'm good, thank you. Uh…" Lydia waited because he seemed nervous, like there was something he wanted to say. Clearing his throat, he went on, "I'd like to apologize for my behavior at the Silver Stake the other day."

"Oh…" Now Lydia was the one surprised.

"My mama would have been mortified is the answer to your question. I was disrespectful, and my comment was crude. And I want you to know that is not how my mama raised me. Your comments made me think and I wanted to thank you for that. I'm sorry."

"Apology accepted. I appreciate you trying to make it right."

He looked relieved. "Thank you for going so easy on me."

"Well, we all make mistakes, don't we? I wouldn't want anyone judging me too harshly for mine. I learned that little nugget of wisdom from my nana."

JT had an adorably crooked smile and Lydia could see why he was popular with the ladies. "My grandpa used to say the same thing."

That's when Lydia noticed Marilee eyeing them from where she was standing by the beverage station. She reminded Lydia of the hawk who sometimes sat in the tree beside the coop, eyeing the chickens.

"Let's go inside," Lydia suggested. "I'd like to hear that music a little better." *And see Jon.*

Together, they walked toward the barn. The music stopped as they stepped inside. The musicians were huddled together on a wooden stage set up in the corner.

JT shuffled his feet a bit and then looked at her. "I'd also like to add that I think you're the neatest thing to happen to Falcon Creek in a long time. And that's not a line, that's the honest truth."

Lydia was touched. "Thank you, JT. And just so you know, you're on the right track there. Women love honesty. They value it way more than a tired old pickup line."

JT grinned. "Jon Blackwell is a lucky man."

"Why would you think—?"

He tilted his head toward the stage. Jon was watching them. Her breath caught as he granted her the full force of his smile. She waved. He winked and shifted the fiddle in his hands.

JT leaned toward her. "I think I'll go try a little of that honesty on Tess Carnes."

Lydia laughed and shooed him away. The first notes of a song resonated through the room. Lydia watched, captivated by the sight of Jon playing. She didn't care what he said about his brother having talent, which she knew to be true—Jon Blackwell had his share.

One song turned into another and the girls skipped up to her.

"Lydia, will you dance with us?" Gen asked.

"Are you kidding? I'd love to. I've been waiting my whole life to dance with you two."

FROM HIS SPOT on the stage, Jon watched Lydia step onto the dance floor with Abby and Gen. For a moment there he'd feared he'd have to watch her with JT. They were playing a popular line-dance song and it only took a few beats before she owned it. She held one of the girl's hands in each of her own. Looking down, she moved her own feet and gave them instructions. They joined her, stomping their little boots in time to the music. She beamed. Anyone could see how much she adored the girls. Jon felt a moment of happiness so intense it left him stunned.

Soon the three of them were joined by Sofie and Zach and Matt and Peyton.

Lydia was of those people who was completely comfortable on the dance floor, drawing attention to herself without trying. It was understandable as she had a natural rhythm, and danced with grace and ease and skill—he knew she'd practiced as much as she'd said. The total and complete joy she had for life shone through, like it did in everything she attempted.

As much as he wanted to dance with her, at that moment Jon decided it was a good thing he was playing. He didn't think he'd be able to keep from swooping her into his arms and telling the whole place how much he loved her.

They'd played several songs when Gordie, who was on guitar and singing the lead, signaled to him. Jon nodded. Gordie opened the song with a few soft notes. Jon picked up the tune. The soulful Irish song showcased the fiddle and was the most challenging in his repertoire.

Lydia was standing at the edge of the dance floor visiting with Sofie. When Jon started playing the first difficult section, she spun around and looked at him. She opened her mouth and closed it again, and he smiled because he could imagine her dropping that cake.

CHAPTER TWENTY

LYDIA TOLD THE girls goodbye and helped secure them in Pete's pickup. She waved as they pulled away. Back inside, she spotted Peyton in the middle of the dance floor. For a woman who claimed she wasn't thrilled about a "hoedown," she seemed to be having an awfully good time. She watched Jon and the dancing for a few more minutes before heading back outside to find a cold drink. She said hi to a few people milling around. Cup of ginger ale in hand, she turned to find Marilee standing in front of her.

"Hello, Marilee."

"Hi there, Lydia. Having a good time?"

"Yes, I am. Thank you."

Beer bottle in hand, Marilee tipped it toward her. "Would you like a beer?"

"No, thank you."

"You probably don't drink, do you? Paragon of virtue that you are." Marilee added a nasty sneer.

"Never acquired a taste."

"Hmm. Well, it seems you've acquired a taste for cowboys, though, haven't you?"

Lydia rolled her eyes. "What are you talking about?"

"I'm not stupid. You and JT? And anyone can see that something is going on with you and Jon. Nanny with benefits, maybe?"

Lydia blew out an impatient sigh. "That's none of your business."

"It is my business," she snarled at her. "Jon and I belong together."

"Marilee, I'm not stupid. Everyone knows that Jon is not a fan of yours. Not after what you did to his daughter. And I'm telling you, if you ever lay a hand on Genevieve or Abigail again, if you ever so much as look at them crossways, you'll have me to contend with. All that working out you do will be no match for my wrath."

Marilee's jaw dropped and she stumbled back a few steps.

"Now, I need to go. Jon and I have a date for a dance."

Lydia noticed a few heads had turned but she didn't care. No one was going to mess with the girls or Jon on her watch. She was almost to the barn when she felt the phone vibrate in her pocket. Hating the rush of panic the sensation caused, she veered around to the side of the building and pulled the phone out of her pocket. "Tanner, hi."

"Where are you? Why is it so loud?"

"I'm at a...dance."

His voice vibrated with tension. "You're out dancing? Perfect. Well, why not? Since your face is already splashed all over TV what could it hurt? Did you forget to tell me that you're going to be on *Good Day USA*?"

"No, not me. Jon is. How do you know about it? It's not supposed to air until next week."

"Yeah, Thursday, that's what the teaser said," Tanner said calmly before raising his voice. "Lydia! Your face was on national TV. What were you thinking? I can't even... It doesn't matter. The damage is done. You need to go. Now. Clive could be there anytime. He could be there now for all I know."

"When, Tanner? When did you see it?"

"Meredith called and said Hailey saw the preview tonight. I have no idea when it first aired."

"Oh, no... What did she see?"

"Your face, Lydia. Hailey DVR'd the show. Meredith went over to her house and watched it. She says it's a pretty quick flash of you in the background, but Hailey recognized you. Which means someone who knows you and Clive will recognize you, too."

"Okay, um... Let me think." It seemed un-

likely that the teaser could have been aired before today. Clive probably couldn't get here this
quickly. Still, she'd have to leave tonight. She
would explain to Jon and say goodbye, throw
her suitcase in the car and drive all night to put
some distance between her and the ranch. But
what was she going to tell him?

"Are you getting in your car right now? I'm
afraid Clive will have people at the airports in
Montana so you're driving to Boise, Idaho. A
ticket to California will be waiting for you when
you get to the airport."

She didn't want to run. Lydia was tired of running. That's when an idea that had been forming
in her mind officially became a plan. Her own
personal Hail Mary pass. "Tanner, I want you to
know that no matter what happens, I love you.
You've been more than a friend to me through
all of this. Thank you."

"Lydia, you can thank me later. When you're
out of there and safe."

LYDIA WENT BACK inside the barn and leaned
against the wall behind her to watch Jon. A short
man with a pot belly and a big sweet voice was
singing about fishing and Friday nights. She
needed to find a way to tell Jon…something.
How was she going to explain all of this? His
gaze found hers as the final few bars of the song

resonated through the room. He moved toward the lead singer and spoke a few words. Stepping off the stage, he placed the fiddle in its case. Another cowboy whom Lydia didn't recognize took his place.

The music started again. Lydia recognized the song immediately—"Butterfly Blue" by Chance Blackwell. Jon's gaze captured hers. Her rancher. Heart full, soul alight, she pushed away from the wall and walked forward to meet him. Jon was weaving between couples who were pairing up to dance to the poignant song about love and regret and chasing your dreams. Knowing Jon, hearing Chance's story, realizing she had to say goodbye… The lyrics burned and made her want to cry. But she refused to spoil this perfect moment because they also made her want to tell him how very much she loved him.

They met on the edge of the dance floor.

"Hey," Jon said, taking her in his arms and drawing her close. He enfolded one of her hands in his. His other hand rested low on the curve of her back. They fit so well together.

"Notice how I made sure there was no cake in the vicinity?"

She laughed, and the knot of despair loosened. "I appreciate that. When you started playing 'The Silver Spear' I almost passed out." Satisfied grin in place, she shook her head in disbelief.

"Can't believe you know that song."

"I told you how it is with me and music. I can't believe my rancher is a musician."

Eyes twinkling, he said, "Oh, yeah? Well, my nanny is a dancer. But I'm not—"

"Please don't tell me how much more talented your brother is than you because then I'll have to name all the famous dancers who are better than me. You have a beautiful gift, Jon."

"All right. I'll just say thank you then." Mouth barely crimping a smile, he whispered, "You have a beautiful everything, Lydia."

They stared into each other's eyes and Lydia hoped he could see every bit of the love overflowing from her heart. She felt certain that the combination of this moment and Marilee's drunken ramblings would result in her and Jon's relationship being the talk of Falcon Creek by tomorrow. She felt a stab of regret that she was leaving him here to make up excuses about why she'd left. But maybe her plan would work, and she'd be able to come back and they could…

Across the room near the back door, among the swell of people congregated there, a flash of coal-black hair caught her eye. Fear and anger and reality pierced through her fantasy. *No. Please, no.* Not before she had a chance to explain. The air froze in her lungs as the crowd parted to offer a clearer view. There, standing out like a sore thumb in a suit and tie, was Clive. His beefy minion, Gary, glowered next to him.

"Lydia, what's wrong?"

She became aware of the fact that she'd stopped moving. The song had ended and was replaced with an upbeat tune.

Jon's hand tightened on her hip. "Are you going to pass out on me after all?"

"I think I could use a drink of water and a breath of air. And I need to tell Sofie something before she leaves. Will you meet me by the bar outside?" What she needed was a distraction.

"Sure. I could use a drink myself."

Jon leaned in and pressed his lips against her ear. "I love you." He gave her hand a gentle squeeze and turned to walk away.

Her fingers tightened around his and he looked back at her. "Jon…" She could hear the desperation, the panic in her voice. Swallowing down tears, she softened her tone. "I love you, too."

His smile echoed her declaration. Deliberately, he let his gaze fall to her mouth. "I'll see you outside, where I'm going to kiss you." He walked away.

Clive had his back to her and was probably scanning the faces of the people seated along the wall and at the smattering of tables. A fresh blast of fear left her body tingling. Now was not the time to break down. Lydia noticed JT standing off to one side talking to Matt, Tom, Zach and Scooter.

She approached them. "Hey, guys," she interrupted firmly.

A chorus of greetings rang out and Lydia lifted her hands to halt any conversation or teasing. "Listen, guys, please don't think I've lost my mind. I'm going to ask you to do something for me, okay? I know it's a lot to ask but please do it, if not for me, then for Jon. I love him and the girls. I want you all to know that. So whatever happens next, or whatever this guy says, don't believe it."

"Lydia, what are you—?" Zach said.

"Please, Zach, just listen. There are two men in suits standing over by the back wall. One of them is my ex-boyfriend, Clive Howard. The other guy is his bodyguard, Gary. Clive is a dangerous man and an abuser and he's here for me. He's going to try and make me go with him. I don't want him anywhere near Jon or the girls. But I have to go."

Scooter's shrewd gaze narrowed.

"Did he hurt you?" JT asked. "I'll kick his—"

"Yes, JT, he's hurt a lot of people, including me. And he'll hurt more to get to me. I need to leave. Jon is waiting for me outside and I'd like a chance to say goodbye." Zach was glaring, looking furious, and she couldn't blame him. "I know what you're thinking, Zach. But I never meant for this to happen. I didn't want to put Jon or the girls in danger. I have to—"

Scooter said, "Lydia, if this man has broken the law then you and me need to have a conversation."

"Scooter," she said, giving him a beseeching look, "it's way more complicated than that." Lydia glanced at Clive, who'd sidled up to a crowd of women that included Marilee. It would only be seconds before Marilee gave her away. "I appreciate your concern more than I can say. But this all happened in Pennsylvania, before I ever moved here. It's so much bigger than Falcon Creek. I—"

"Lydia, darlin'," Tom interrupted, "I suspect it's too late to get into all that now. He's here. We've got this. Go on and do what you need to do. Jon will be okay. We'll make sure of it."

"Thank you, Tom. I hope I…" Lydia choked on a sob, pulled it together and said, "Thank you, guys. I love you all, too. Goodbye."

Lydia hurried outside, where she saw Jon waiting. What could she say to him to make him understand? She should have written him a letter in case this happened. She'd been in denial, she could see that now. And before that, she'd been so convinced running was the answer. She knew now that safety was just an illusion. The only way to face her problems was head-on, the way Jon did. He tackled every challenge that life threw at him. She wanted to do that. Starting now.

Approaching him, she said, "Jon, I need to tell you something." But Jon was scowling over her shoulder. Squeezing her eyes shut, she knew what she'd find when she turned around. But she wasn't afraid anymore. Anger and determination fueled her now. Perfect. Finally, she'd found her courage. And it was too late.

Jon kept his focus on the man in the suit. Like fog creeping across the pasture on a cold fall day, an unsettling feeling engulfed him. He'd be hard-pressed to name many people in Falcon Creek who even owned a suit. He didn't know any who would wear one to a music jam.

The guy kept coming, until he was way too close. He stopped, looked oddly at Lydia and said, "There you are, *honey*. Finally found you."

Jon felt the words like a punch. Lydia grimaced.

"Lydia, you know this guy?"

"Yes, unfortunately, I do." Lydia pivoted, so

that she faced the suit. "Clive, I want you to leave."

"Ha. I bet you do. And I'm going to, but you're coming with me." With a smirk, he looked Jon up and down. "Hey, cowboy, didn't your nanny tell you she had a fiancé?" Jon kept his face blank. The guy went on in a wry tone, "No? Well, I'm not surprised. She's a thief and a liar. But you're probably starting to figure that out already, huh? At least the liar part. Let's go, Lydia. We have a plane to catch."

"I'm not going anywhere with you."

"Oh, you're going. You're going or your country-boy hick here and his little twin dolls will pay."

"Lydia, what's going on? Who is this?"

Clive ground out a bitter-sounding laugh. "You really didn't tell him anything, did you? I wondered. Does he think you're just some pretty, innocent gal from the city who *wants* to be a nanny?" He looked at Jon. "She's playing you, cowboy. Just like she played me. She stole twelve million dollars from me. Do you seriously believe she plans to stick around Podunk, USA, with a farmer like you?"

Jon couldn't think for the buzzing in his ears. This wasn't true. It couldn't be. Was this the ex she'd alluded to that day they'd went riding?

Should he deck the guy? And yet, Lydia was just standing there. Not denying any of it.

"It's over, Lydia New-*bury*." He tossed another disparaging look at Jon. "That's not even her real name. I'm guessing you didn't know that, either. It's Newton. Lydia Newton. It was almost Howard but then she decided to take my money and practically leave me at the altar." To Lydia he said, "You thought you were so clever with that four-dollar thing, didn't you? You could have had everything, Lydia. Come with me now and none of your country bumpkin friends get hurt."

Jon saw Zach, Matt, Tom and JT emerge from the darkness beside the barn. Lydia had been standing with her back to Jon. Now she turned to face him, her eyes were flashing with what looked like fury.

Her voice was calm as she spoke. "You're right, Clive. It's over. I knew it couldn't last. I was just biding my time trying to figure a way out of this. Let's go."

"Lydia?" Jon said and then watched helplessly as Clive flashed him a victorious smile. The man stepped next to Lydia and draped an arm over her shoulder to lead her away.

Reaching up with both hands, she grabbed hold of his wrist as if to acquiesce. Jon heard a crunching sound as she gave it a twist. At the same time, she stomped hard on his foot with the spiked heel of her boot. Clive howled with pain and crumpled to the ground.

She leaned over and in a voice rigid with contempt she said, "He's a rancher, you idiot. Not a farmer."

Her gaze locked on to Jon and all he could do was stare at her in shock. "Jon… I'm so sorry about all of this. I wish we had more time. I wanted to explain before I had to leave. I'm going to…"

In the distance, the howl of a police siren reverberated through the night. Zach, Matt, Tom and JT descended on them. JT produced a length of bailing twine and proceeded to tie Clive's wrists behind him.

Tom looked pointedly at Lydia. "Scooter's got the other guy handcuffed out back. He took a swing at JT. That's good, because it'll buy you a little time. But you best scatter before the cops get here and start asking questions."

Expression resigned, she said, "Thank you, guys."

Then Jon watched as the woman he loved walked away into the night. Except, he realized, he had no idea who she was. He did know that he couldn't let her leave. Not like this.

He caught up with her as she was climbing into her SUV and said a silent thank-you for the not-so-stupid boots that had slowed her down and helped save her from that thug.

"Lydia, wait."

She faced him. He could just make out her features in the glow of the moonlight. The music playing in the barn sounded like it was coming from miles away.

"Jon, I don't have much time."

"So, it's true? That guy is your fiancé? You stole his money and you were hiding out here in Falcon Creek?"

She looked up at the sky for a second before focusing on him. "Yes, it's…true. Except for the fiancé part. I never intended to marry him. But I—"

"But you never intended to stay here, either, did you? You let me fall in love with you. You did whatever you could to make me fall in love, didn't you? I said all that stuff to you. You told me you loved me. You said you loved the girls. You told Genevieve and Abigail you weren't going to quit… And all along you knew you would only be here for a little while?"

"Yes, to most of that," she whispered. "But—"

"That's why you wanted to keep the job so much. It didn't have anything to do with us." He cursed and took a step back. "I am such a fool."

"No, Jon, you're not. It's way more complicated than that." Tears sparkled in her eyes, but

Jon didn't care. He was done caring. "Jon, you and the twins—"

"Not from where I'm standing it's not. From here, it's not complicated at all." She'd used him. He felt the heart that she'd so painstakingly and deviously thawed freeze all over again. He could only hope that it would stay that way this time. "Goodbye, Lydia. I'd tell you good luck, but I know you'll be fine. You've got millions of dollars and you are hands down the best liar I have ever met. What more could a woman like you need?"

With those last words, he turned and strode away.

CHAPTER TWENTY-ONE

GRIPPING THE STEERING wheel so hard her fingers ached, Lydia drove past Falcon Creek toward the freeway and hoped that all available law enforcement was on their way to the Inez place. She felt nauseated. She wanted to pull over and throw up. She wanted to give up. This was all so pointless. If she couldn't have Jon and the girls she might as well have nothing. Even if this plan worked and she could get Clive off her back, how could she convince Jon that she really loved him? That she'd never meant for any of this to happen?

She didn't know the answers, but she did know she had to try. She was through running from her mistakes. Picking up the phone, she dialed Meredith.

Her friend answered tentatively. "Lydia?"

"Yep, it's me, Meredith."

"Oh, thank you, thank you. Are you okay?"

"I'm okay. For now."

"Where are you? Did you talk to Tanner?"

"Yes, Tanner called. But Clive got here before I could get away."

"Oh, no! Where is he?"

"He's indisposed at the moment. But probably not for long." She had no idea how much of a head start Scooter, Tom and the others had given her. Or if Clive had people staked out at the airports, gas stations and rest stops, or wherever. Lydia could only hope he'd done something the police could charge him with. "Meredith, I need your help."

"Of course. Lydia, anything."

"I don't have a credit card. I need you to buy me an airplane ticket from Missoula to LaGuardia. It would be even better if you could use Hailey's credit card or someone who doesn't have the last name Blumen."

"I'll do it right now. But you're going to New York? Shouldn't you be heading in the other direction? Or possibly toward Australia or Jupiter even?"

"I'm going to New York City and then I should be back in Philadelphia in two days." It was the weekend, so she wasn't sure how long this would take. There was also the possibility that it wouldn't work at all, at which point she would have to try for Jupiter. "Can I stay with you?"

"Lydia! Yes, of course. I can't wait to see you."

"Don't tell anyone I'm coming. I'll call Tanner when I can. I shouldn't talk anymore because I don't have a car charger for this phone. Text me the flight info, okay?"

They exchanged love-yous and goodbyes and Lydia ended the call, silently thanking Tanner for making her put the cash in her jacket. Even though it was only 500 dollars, it should be enough. She wondered if Jon would look through her things and what he'd think when he found the rest of the cash, gift cards and bundle of odds and ends. Her passport was there. She cringed. It would be further evidence of her deception, of her intention to not stick around. Not that it mattered because she wouldn't contact him right now, anyway. Not until she knew this plan was going to work. Which was a long shot.

And even if by some miracle it did work, she was pretty sure Jon would never want to talk to her again. She knew how bad this looked. How bad it was, really, when you viewed it from his perspective. She'd deserved everything he'd said to her. She'd earned his trust—trust that he didn't give easily, and rightly so. But she'd done it. And then she'd shattered it.

AT LEAST AVA had been honest about her feelings, Jon thought. She hadn't wanted to be here, so she'd left. Lydia hadn't wanted to be here, either, but she'd lied about it. Not only had she lied about it, but she'd also used him and the girls.

The shock had worn off, leaving Jon with a sense of disappointment so intense he could barely speak. Most of it was directed at himself. He should have trusted his instincts that first day and sent her away. He could see now why she'd fought so hard to keep the job. Jon had been her cover. A place to hide. That in itself was dishonest. But she'd made it so much worse. She'd made him fall in love with her. The girls had fallen in love with her. He would survive, but using Abigail and Genevieve the way she had was unforgivable. What was he supposed to tell them?

Zach had brought them back this morning from an overnight stay with his parents. They'd immediately asked where Lydia was. Staring into their innocent, eager faces, Jon was overwhelmed with sadness and frustration. He'd chickened out and told them there'd been an emergency and Lydia had to go back to Philadelphia. He didn't like lying to them, but he needed time to figure this out, to get his zigzagging emotions under control. Soon after they'd returned, Tom had taken them over to the Blackwell Ranch to visit the pigs and donkeys.

Jon appreciated how Tom, Zach, Matt and Scooter had his back. Even JT had been great.

Later, he'd informed Jon that he was a changed man, due in large part to Lydia. Funny, Jon thought bitterly, that the day before Jon would have said the same about himself.

As it turned out, they had Lydia's back, too. Scooter had placed Clive and Gary in separate sheriff vehicles while the deputies questioned witnesses. JT wanted to press charges against Gary for assault. Scooter radioed Harriet at the sheriff's department asking her to run every conceivable check on the subjects, which she did. Clive's turned up a Vermont bench warrant for a traffic citation. Both men were arrested and transported to the county courthouse, where they would wait until court convened on Monday. Scooter said they'd be gone by noon. No one expected to ever see them again.

Zach walked into the living room and handed Jon a cup of coffee. He placed a plate of scrambled eggs on the table and settled on the sofa opposite him. Jon couldn't eat the eggs. He picked up the coffee and attempted to smile at his friend. Beside him on the sofa, Trout sighed softly and laid his head in Jon's lap. Jon scratched his ears.

"Thanks, Zach."

"What are you going to do?"

Jon shrugged. "Not much to do from where I'm sitting."

"Do you believe what that guy said? Did Lydia steal twelve million dollars?"

"She didn't deny it. Clearly, she lied about a whole lot of things."

"She told us that she's in love with you. Did she tell you?"

"Yeah."

"Are you in love with her?"

"I thought I was."

"What do you mean you thought you were? You either are or you're not."

"She's not even who she says she is, Zach. How can I be in love with her? How am I supposed to know what's true? What I can safely deduce is that she was using the ranch to hide from her thug boyfriend. She used us all. She didn't really want this job." *Or me*, he added silently.

"Hmm." Zach was quiet for a long time. "Well, all of that might have been true. At first. But from where I'm sitting, it seems to me, if she was planning on leaving anyway, falling in love with her boss would only complicate matters exponentially for her. And if she has twelve million dollars, why didn't she go to Morocco or Argentina or wherever rich people on the run go?"

Jon had puzzled over that last part himself.

"And I understand that she was trying to keep her job, but did she have to do it so well?"

"What do you mean?"

"Did she have to do *all* of those things that she did for the girls? Teaching them, sewing their dresses, getting the bunnies, signing them up for 4-H. You told me yourself she went above and beyond every day. Making everyone happy while she made more work for herself."

Jon stuck with his argument. "She didn't care about us, Zach, not really, not…in the same way we cared about her. She would have done anything to stay here, to stay hidden."

"I don't know, Jon. It seems a little over-the-top, doesn't it? You said yourself you don't know how you would have gotten through that interview without her. And, if you think about that, she took a risk even being here with those cameras around. She made friends all over town, doing nice things here and there, things she didn't have to do knowing she was leaving. And, did she have to take on Marilee like she did? At least ten people heard it. Are those the actions of a woman who doesn't care?"

LYDIA DISEMBARKED AT LaGuardia on Sunday afternoon and braced herself to find Clive or one of his goons waiting for her. Afraid to hang out for hours in the airport the night before, she'd spent a cold night in her SUV in the parking lot of a grocery store in Missoula. Shaking with terror, she'd headed to the airport just in time to walk on to her 6:00 a.m. flight.

If they'd somehow gotten to Meredith and figured out where she was going, Lydia's plan would probably die right along with her. But she knew Clive wouldn't kill her until he had his money, or at least until he was satisfied that he'd recovered as much of it as possible.

Coast seemingly clear, she stepped outside the terminal and dug the card out of her wallet. She caught a cab to the address listed, which turned out to be a mammoth skyscraper that housed the network's offices. It was Sunday. Lydia had no idea what she'd do if no one answered. She didn't want to waste her cash on a hotel room.

With trembling hands, she pulled her phone out and dialed the number.

"Hello?" Bethany Stouffer answered her own phone.

"Bethany? Hi, it's Lydia Newbury, nanny at the JB Bar Ranch?"

"Lydia! Hi! How are you? The footage of the ranch is glorious. The producers love it all. We're beyond excited for that segment to air."

"That's wonderful news. But actually, Bethany, I'm calling for a different reason. I have another story for you. Different topic entirely. One that you might find rather unbelievable."

"I'm listening."

"Have you heard about the anonymous philanthropist in Philadelphia who has been in the news lately?"

"Of course. The person who has been donating money all over the city? At last count the total was over eight million."

"That's the one. Soon, it will equal close to twelve and a half million. Did I mention that I'm from Philadelphia?"

Bethany paused. "Lydia, do you know this person?"

"Yes, Bethany, I do. I know him very well."

"Where are you?"

"I'm in New York standing outside your offices. I know it's Sunday but—"

"Wait there. The building is closed but I'm here. I'll be right down to let you in."

THE NEXT DAY, Jon walked down the sidewalk in Falcon Creek, greeting friends and ignoring curious glances from others. He wouldn't be in town except for the fact that Abigail and Genevieve had gotten into a patch of poison ivy again. They were almost out of cortisone cream and he needed to get some at South Corner Drug. Grace had called and said the "special" rabbit feed Lydia had ordered was in, so he'd head over to Brewster's and pick that up, too.

On his knees as he scanned the shelf in the skin care section, he was about ready to give up and ask for help when he located the cream. Shaking his head over the fact that the repackaging phenomenon wasn't even safe where itch medicine was concerned, he headed to the pharmacy checkout register and took his place in the short line.

It was located right next to the UPS and FedEx counter. A woman stepped up there and it took him several seconds to recognize Rachel Thompson. Rachel's parents owned the Double T Ranch. Rachel was an attorney, the only attorney currently practicing in Falcon Creek. She and Ben had gone head to head regarding the water-rights issue and, as with most things Ben tackled, he'd come out on top. Rachel was also Zoe's best friend. Jon braced himself for a bout of uncomfortable small talk, but maybe she'd heard from Zoe.

Mandy, the woman who worked behind the counter, handed her a thin package. "Here you go, Rachel. Sign here. Like I told you on the phone, there's no name or return address on it. Who do you think it's from?"

"I have no idea. Thanks, Mandy." Rachel picked up a pen and scrawled along the bottom of a sheet of paper. She slid it across the counter and exchanged it for the package. Stepping to one side, she opened the envelope and pulled out the contents. Brow furrowed, she studied the documents before stuffing them back inside.

She spun around, noticed Jon and stopped in her tracks. Even in his own miserable state, he could see that Rachel didn't look herself. Like Zoe, she'd always been slick and perfectly assembled. Now she looked more like an unmade bed—no makeup, bluish circles under her eyes, hair askew. She had a stain on her jacket.

She startled, then seemed to recover but kept the package clutched to her chest, arms folded tightly across it. "Hello, Jon."

"How're you doing, Rachel?"

"Just fine. How are you?"

"Been better." He held up the tube of medicine. "The twins got into a bit of poison ivy."

"Yikes. That itches."

"Yes, it sure does."

"I'm only familiar with diaper rash at this point."

Jon recalled hearing that she and her husband, Ted Jackson, had a baby together before they split up. Empathy stirred in him. It also explained her rumpled state. Ted was an alcoholic. Rachel's father had recently suffered a heart attack. Jon doubted she had much help where the baby was concerned.

"That can be rough, too. How's the baby?"

"It is," she said quickly. She glanced away for a few seconds before meeting his gaze again. "I guess you know all about that, huh? Single parenthood?"

"Yes, ma'am, I do."

"I can't imagine what it's like with twins… Which reminds me, I heard you got yourself an awesome nanny."

Jon nodded because that part had been true.

Rachel went on, "And the baby, my baby, Poppy is her name. She's…perfect." Her face transformed with a love-filled smile. "Thank you for asking."

"I do not doubt that. Enjoy her while she's young. I know you can't see it right now when those nights are so long. But it goes faster than lightning. Gen and Abby are five now."

Her smile wavered a little. "I'm sure trying to. Thanks."

Jon felt another stir of compassion, wished he could offer his help, but knowing she wouldn't want it, he asked, "Have you heard from Zoe lately? I'm trying to track Big E down."

"No, I haven't. Zoe and I aren't…as close anymore."

"I see. If you do hear from her, I'd appreciate it if you'd let me know."

"I'll do that."

"Thank you. It was nice running into you, Rachel. Take care."

"You, too, Jon." She walked away, and her voice sounded stronger, more confident, as she added, "We'll be seeing you soon."

Jon paid for the medication and exited the store. Trout, who'd been waiting outside, fell in beside him as they headed toward Brewster's. They met June on the sidewalk.

"Jon, hey," she said. "Hi, Trout."

"Hi, June. How are you?"

"Great. I'm glad I ran into you. We heard that Lydia had an emergency and had to return to Philadelphia. Do you know when she's coming back?"

All Jon could do was shake his head.

"Okay, well, can you tell her our first prom is coming up, the second week in May?"

"I'll pass that along." He had no idea what she was talking about. But he wasn't ready to do any explaining where his former nanny was concerned.

"We're so happy she agreed to help us out. When are you going to stop in for a free haircut?"

"Free haircut?"

"Yeah, didn't Lydia tell you? We worked out a trade in exchange for her doing some prom hairstyles for us. She gives us updos, we do her hair, plus haircuts for you and the girls. And the leave-in conditioner. You are using it on the girls while she's gone, right?"

"Um, yeah." He would now, anyway. Lydia had been gone for two days. They were probably due for a hair washing.

They chatted for a few more minutes before June moved on. Jon continued toward Brewster's. Hmm. Lydia had agreed to help June and Emma in their shop. She'd negotiated haircuts for him and the girls. He couldn't help but wonder what her strategy was exactly. How long had she planned on staying?

He approached Brewster's. Pops waved. Jon stepped onto the porch.

"Hey, Pops."

"Hi, Jon. There's super dog." Trout moved closer so Pops could offer a proper greeting. "When are you going to teach this dog to play chess?"

"Only thing holding him back is me."

"Ain't that the truth." Pops chuckled. "I heard Lydia had an emergency and had to go. Hope everything's okay?"

"Me, too."

Pops winked at him. "Finally got yourself

a good one there. That woman makes the best chocolate-chip cookies I've ever tasted."

That was a fact. But when had Pops tried them?

"She brought some by one day when she was in town. Just out of the blue, sweet thing that she is."

Jon could only nod.

"Sofie told me her mac and cheese is like heaven."

"Sofie did not exaggerate."

"You know, I've been thinking…" Pops leaned back in his rocker. "Those Devons are working out fine, huh? It's been a while since I've seen your place."

"Yes, they are. I'm flat-out sold on the breed. And you're always welcome, Pops, you know that."

"I think I'll take you up on that. If the timing is right, I wouldn't be averse to a dinner invitation."

Jon couldn't help but chuckle. It felt good. He tried not to think about the fact that Lydia wasn't even here, and she was inadvertently making him laugh.

"That could be arranged. The girls would love it." Jon didn't currently possess the will to break it to him that the meal would not be up to the standards he was anticipating.

Pops gave him a satisfied grin. "I hope she's back soon. She promised to let me beat her at chess."

Jon said goodbye and went inside to collect the rabbit chow. Grace and Belle both inquired about Lydia. Belle asked him to tell Lydia that they could get the poultry supplements in that she'd wondered about. He pretended like he knew what that was about, too.

Errands complete, he and Trout climbed into his pickup and headed to the Carneses' to pick up the girls. The entire way he pondered his visit to town. He replayed the conversation with Zach over again in his mind. Apparently, Lydia had made everyone in Falcon Creek fall in love with her. Except for Marilee, who he was pretty sure wouldn't be calling him again anytime soon. He could thank Lydia for that, at least. And about a million other things, if he was being honest.

No matter how many ways he analyzed the situation, he had to admit that Zach had a point; why had Lydia needed to be so good at her job if she was leaving anyway?

TANNER HIT THE play button on Meredith's DVR. They'd both watched Lydia's interview with Bethany Stouffer, but Lydia hadn't seen it yet. After two emotional days of travel and non-stop terror, followed by filming the interview, she'd been exhausted when she finally arrived on Meredith's doorstep in Philly. She'd crashed for hours and then woke to find Tanner in Meredith's living room.

Now she focused on Bethany's words. "A spokesperson for Philadelphia-based multimillionaire businessman Clive Howard has announced his responsibility for the millions of dollars in anonymous donations that have been made around the city in the last month. Lydia Newton, a friend and former employee of Mr. Howard's, says circumstances and opportunities compelled him to come forward. Here's what Ms. Newton told me in an exclusive interview."

The camera panned to Lydia. "Mr. Howard feels like he can do even more good if he makes his identity known. Clive is passionate about certain issues—women's rights, helping troubled teens, healing sick children, to name just a few. He's also a gifted financier. Capitalizing on the attention his donations have received, he wants to meld those passions and become a spokesperson for these causes."

Bethany went on to ask Lydia about her time as Mr. Howard's personal assistant. Lydia kept those answers brief and ambiguous, emphasizing Clive's "generous nature, unfailing dedication to helping others and overarching desire to improve the world."

"That was…wow," Tanner said when it was over. He stopped the DVR and flopped back against Meredith's sofa. "Lydia, I am blown away. That was brilliant."

Pride and relief washed over her at Tanner's words.

"What gave you the idea?" he asked.

"Meredith, unintentionally. Clive told her if I was going to give all his money away the least I could do was give him credit for it." She grinned at her friends. "Thank you, Meredith, for relaying that nugget when we talked. It reminded me about what a huge ego he has and it got me thinking. Maybe if he was faced with the good that money is doing, he would embrace it."

"You're welcome." Meredith added a surprised laugh. She scooted forward to look at Tanner. "But that money—his money—is gone. Doesn't he still want to go after Lydia?"

"Nope, I talked to Wendell and he said that while Clive is very angry at Lydia, he seems to be enjoying the attention more. The spotlight is on him and he's reveling in it. As of now, he's the most celebrated man in Philadelphia. Heck, in all of America for that matter. He's been given a humanitarian award by the city council, asked to serve on the board of the children's hospital. And he's even been invited to throw out the first pitch at a Philadelphia home game." Tanner chuckled.

Lydia couldn't help but smile at the thought. "He does love his baseball. So, this is his opportunity to become the man the world now thinks he is. The man he doesn't know he can be."

"He should embrace it," Meredith said drily. She gave her head a shake. "If Clive stays on the straight and narrow, it will give me hope for all of humankind.

"But what about you being in the teaser for your rancher's interview? Isn't that going to look weird now? You going from Clive's assistant to a nanny with a different name?"

"Oh, yeah, after I told Bethany the whole story, she pulled the clip. At the time, I asked not to be filmed, but they rushed the teaser and made a mistake. She apologized and promised to double-check the footage for my image before Jon's interview airs. Since I didn't say anything in that snippet, we're going to hope that no one notices."

Meredith looked thoughtful. "That should work. Who would put it together if they didn't know you? People in Falcon Creek, maybe?"

"People in Falcon Creek won't care." Except for one person, she added silently. The only one who really mattered, and he hadn't returned her phone calls. "And if someone does notice, I'm going to say that I quit working for Clive because I was tired and ready for a change. I wanted to spend some time in the country. Which is true. But because of my firsthand knowledge of Clive's philanthropy, I decided to come back and handle the press release."

"That's pretty good." Meredith looked thoughtful. "At the end of the interview Bethany says that you're no longer working for Clive due to health issues. And all questions for and about Clive are being referred to Wendell. So maybe people will leave you alone."

Tanner agreed. "Clive is the real story here. And, Lydia, to give you added peace of mind, I have a dinner meeting set up with Wendell, who's already given me assurances that Clive has no intention to press any charges. In fact, Clive intends to be at our dinner."

"Just like that?" she asked.

"Yes, just like that. This money was a handful for Clive, but he's got plenty more handfuls to play with. Plus, all this press and publicity is going to be nothing but good for his businesses. In the long run, he might even thank you, Lydia."

CHAPTER TWENTY-TWO

"ETHAN, I NEED you to come home." Jon walked closer to the fence enclosing the cows and calves. He watched two babies rip across the field kicking up grass and dirt.

"Sorry, Jon. No way. You know I love you, brother, but I can't come home right now."

"Ethan, listen to me, I need your help. *We* need your help, Katie and me. It's not just the fact that I'm trying to run my own cattle ranch here. There's Katie and Lochlan to consider, and the rest of the employees. We will not be able to make payroll if we don't come up with a plan. The future of the Blackwell Ranch, the Blackwell name, is at stake here. The guest ranch opens soon and—"

"Where's the money, Jon?" Ethan interrupted. "You and I both know Big E has a stash somewhere. You need to find his other accounts or his cash hoard or his gold bars or whatever."

Jon barked out a laugh. "You don't think I've been looking? You're going to have to find it. Ethan, I am asking you to please, come home

and help. I am barely holding it together as it is
with trying to run my own ranch, helping Katie,
who shouldn't have to deal with all this by herself, and taking care of the twins." That wasn't
an exaggeration now that Lydia was gone. The
last few days had been rough.

Somehow, he had to convince his brother that
he was needed. Maybe pulling the single-dad
card would help. Ethan adored the girls. If anything could soften that shell of stubbornness, it
was the twins. And animals. That was his next
move.

"Plus, I, uh… I have to do some traveling. Not
sure how long I'll be gone. It would be nice if
you were around for the girls' sake."

"Traveling? Now? You're leaving Gen and
Abby?" Ethan's voice had risen to a concerned
pitch, leading Jon to believe he might be waf-
fling. "Where in the world are you going?"

Then again, if he needed to hint at his personal problems to get his brother home, then so
be it. "Philadelphia."

"Philadelphia? Isn't that where your nanny
is from?"

"Yes, it is. But she's no longer my nanny."

"What happened? I thought everything was
working out great."

"It was. And with any luck, it will be again."
There was a pause on the line while Jon

imagined his brother piecing things together on his end.

"Ah," he finally said. Then he sighed. "Fine. I can leave tomorrow, day after at the latest."

"Great! Thank you, Ethan." Jon felt a rush of gratitude and relief so great it left his legs a little weak. He leaned against the fence in front of him. "My plane leaves tomorrow morning. The girls are staying with Willa and Pete. Katie can fill you in on the mess that Big E has left us with. You'll be bringing all your vet gear, right?"

"Of course, why?"

"Because Big E has two pregnant mares, one is high-risk. And that place is turning into a zoo."

Ethan chuckled. Undoubtedly, he didn't believe how literally Jon meant that statement. "All right. Good luck, Jon. Go get her."

"That's my plan, little brother. That's my plan."

THURSDAY MORNING, LYDIA and Meredith made breakfast. Tanner came over. He filled them in on his dinner with Clive and Wendell, which went even better than he'd predicted.

"Suffice it to say, he'll never bother you again, Lydia."

After breakfast, they all sat down to watch *Good Day USA*. Lydia knew it was going to be difficult. The night before, she'd prepared herself for an onslaught of emotion, including crying and missing Jon and the girls and the ranch, as she replayed precious memories over and over in her mind. She thought she was ready. But as soon as Jon appeared on the screen she started sobbing. And once she started, she couldn't stop.

"Oh, Lydia…" Meredith cried in sympathy, good friend that she was.

Tanner sipped his coffee and checked his watch. He typed out a text on his phone.

Lydia snuffled out words "I hope you—*hiccup*—set the—DVR. Because I can't—*hiccup*—hear what…he's saying."

"I did."

"Isn't he—*hiccup*—gorgeous?"

Meredith dabbed at her eyes with her shirt, and answered, "Yes, he is."

A knock sounded on the door. Meredith glanced over her shoulder. Tanner got up. Lydia ignored it, wiping at her snotty nose with her sleeve. How dare someone interrupt her time with Jon? She heard murmuring. Irritation stirred inside of her. Tanner needed to get rid of whoever it was.

"But it's not even…that. He's just…the best man I've ever met. Men like him are so…rare. Like…mermaid-riding-a-unicorn rare. I love him so much. I wish…" She trailed off as another painful wave of sorrow and longing tore through her. "I wish…"

"What do you wish, Lydia?" A deep voice sounded from the doorway.

Meredith leaped to her feet.

Lydia squeezed her eyes shut. Hope bore down on her so fast and hard, it was painful. She forced herself to open her eyes and look at him. "Jon, what are you doing here?"

"Right now, I'm doing some wishing of my own."

"Wh-what…" she muttered helplessly. "About what?"

"I'm wishing I wasn't the one to have made you cry. But from the looks of the television there, I'm guessing I'm too late. But I wish never to make the woman I love cry again. And I wish I could have my Nanny Fantastic back for certain and for good. Except, hopefully, with a slightly different title."

"Oh. Wow…" Meredith cooed dreamily. "That's incredibly, unbelievably, devastatingly romantic. I feel funny. I think I need to sit."

She backed toward the sofa. Tanner grabbed her hand, pulled her forward and marched with her out of the room.

"Hey, where are we going?"

"Out," Tanner said. Lydia heard rustling

and the word *but* before the door clicked behind them.

Lydia continued to stare at Jon. She couldn't believe he was here, in Philadelphia, in the middle of a city. He had come all this way for her. He remained standing where he was like he couldn't quite believe he was here, either.

"Meredith was right," she said, "that was pretty romantic. But I already knew my rancher was a poet."

His eyes blazed. "Your rancher?"

"Yes, sir. My rancher. If you'll have me."

A few long strides and he was across the room and kneeling before her. He took her hand. "Lydia, I'll have you and I'll cherish you forever."

Lydia slid her other hand around the back of his neck. "I'll cherish you, too. And the girls. I miss them so much. I miss you, Jon. I'm so sorry. I never meant—"

"Hush," he interrupted gently. "Lydia, I know. I'm sorry, too. I told you that day we went riding that I was done with Ava, that I left her behind. But I hadn't. When you left, all I could think about was the fact that a woman like you, like her, would never choose me and my ranch over money. Especially millions of dollars. But inside, I knew the truth. My heart knew it, anyway, because after you'd gone I kept getting reminded, I kept thinking about all the ways that you're different."

"None of that money was mine. I didn't keep any of it."

He cupped her cheek. His thumb brushed away tears and then traced along her cheekbone. "I know. Tanner told me everything. You left his number in your suitcase. I called him."

"But… I called you. Why didn't you call me back?"

"You have my phone, sweetheart."

Lydia let out a groan. She'd forgotten. He'd given her his phone that morning and she'd put it…in the car. "I must have left it in the SUV. It's at the airport in Missoula."

He chuckled. "You know, I'm glad. I'm not sure what I would have said… I'm not proud of the fact that it took me a few days to get to this place, and then come here to Philadelphia. Zach and Sofie deserve a little of the credit, as do Tom and Willa, and Scooter, and Pops, and June and Emma, and everyone else back in Falcon Creek who've fallen in love with you. It was stupid of me not to see that you fell in love with all of them right back."

"I did."

"But I love you the most, Lydia."

"Oh, Jon, I love you, too." She leaned forward, drew him close and hugged him tightly. "Let's go home."

"How soon can you be ready?"

"I'm ready now."

He drew back enough to look at her. "No, I mean, for good. How long will it take you to pack? I thought we could rent a truck and drive back. It's a couple of thousand miles. That's about three days of driving. I wish we could take our time and see some sights, but Ethan is on his way home to help Katie and me with Big E's place. We could be back by—"

"My turn for a hush," she teased, halting his words with a kiss. She said, "There's no need to rent things and drive places. We will get on the first flight we can."

"You're telling me you don't need to pack?" he asked skeptically.

She chuckled. "You still don't quite get it, do you, Rancher Blackwell? Half of what I need is right here, and the rest is in Falcon Creek, Montana."

A FEW NIGHTS LATER, Lydia marched into his office. "Jon, I need to talk to you."

It had been a perfect evening. Lydia had cooked a delicious meal and over dinner they'd told the girls they were getting married. They'd squealed and hugged and danced and Jon despaired of them ever settling down. But, of course, Lydia had managed it.

Jon liked how she came in now without knocking. "All right. Come around here." He raised a hand and circled a finger.

She moved closer. "I don't know what to do about—"

Reaching out, he took hold of her hand and tugged her down onto his lap. With a little yelp, she landed on him and slipped her arms around his neck.

He tucked her close and nuzzled her neck. "What don't you know?"

She giggled. Then she drew back to look at him. "Be serious for a second."

A frisson of alarm went through him. He answered with a somber "Okay."

"My goodness," she said, eyes wide. "Not that serious. That's your Rancher Grim-Face."

Jon laughed and shook his head. "At least it's not Rancher Grouch-Face."

"Grim-Face is worse than Grouch-Face, Jon," she quipped. "Please try and keep up. It's not that difficult."

"I am trying." He kissed her, knowing that whatever she had to say couldn't be that bad if she was teasing him. "I was actually going for sexy cowboy. What has you troubled?"

"Tonight, when I tucked them in, Genevieve and Abigail asked if they could call me Mom."

Jon's chest went tight as he watched her nibble her lip. Truly, it felt like his heart might explode. He swallowed. "Lydia, sweetheart, do you think this is a good thing or a bad thing?"

"I'm not sure. That's why I'm here. I'm not their mom. I mean, I would love to be, I want to be. And hopefully we'll have more kids and I don't want the twins to feel like I love them any less. They already feel like my daughters." Jon loved the sound of that. They'd discussed their mutual desire for more children on the airplane. He was thrilled they were on the same page. "But I don't know how you feel about it."

"Honestly?"

"Yes, please. I don't ever want you to be anything else."

"I couldn't have picked a better mom for them, Lydia. I feel like it's a dream come true."

"Oh." She let out a relieved sigh. "Good." Her blue eyes sparkled as her face lit up with a smile as wide as the Montana sky. "Me, too."

EPILOGUE

Kentucky Derby—first Saturday in May

"FINE DAY FOR a horse race, wouldn't you say, Big E?"

Elias Blackwell looked up from where he sat in his plush box seat to greet his old friend, Dr. Rodney Gaither. Family and friends, and even those who didn't care to claim him as the latter, called Elias Big E.

"That it is, Rod. Fine day indeed. It's a dream come true for me to attend the Derby and I'm glad you're here to share it with me."

There, that wasn't so difficult. And if Rod was surprised by Big E's sincerity and imparting of emotion he didn't show it. That was the sign of a true friend as far as he was concerned.

"Me, too, Big E. Thank you."

Big E invited Rod to take a seat. He did, and they spent several minutes talking like old friends do, discussing horses, the bets they'd made, their wives, their wives' silly hats and the virtues of bourbon neat versus hiding its fine flavor inside a mint julep. Neither of them was impatient to get to the real business between them.

Rod said, "I saw Jon in that TV interview the other day. Boy, I gotta say that was real neat. I know you don't subscribe to his organic methods and whatnot, but he sure was convincing. I suspect his business is going to skyrocket. Demand seems to be growing for those heritage breeds, too."

Big E's response was a trio of slow nods. That was his hope. He still couldn't think about Jon's interview with Bethany without getting choked up. *Pride* was such a funny word. He'd been too proud to listen to his grandson when he should have and now that same word was oozing out of him like maple syrup and making him soft.

"I agree. I may be coming around, Rod, you never know."

Rod leaned his head back and guffawed loudly.

Fact was, he was getting old.

That interview was just one item on a long list. He'd heard it called a bucket list, and he supposed in his case it was true. But the difference was, his list wasn't only about the things he wanted to do. It was about the people he wanted to do them for, and the mistakes he needed to own. A man should do whatever he could for his family. Big E believed that even if his execution was a little rusty. "So, tell me about this opportunity at your clinic."

Rod was a doctor of veterinary medicine, operating one of the premier equine veterinarian rehabilitation outfits in the country. He only hired the best of the best. Not even a favor owed could sway him there. Luckily, Big E's grandson, Ethan, was brilliant and talented and didn't require special favors where his skills were concerned.

Rod sat back and reached into his jacket pocket. "I don't believe it's tooting my own horn to say a position at my clinic is the highest accomplishment for any veterinarian. Particularly one fresh out of school. And I think you'll find the starting salary satisfactory."

He handed over the envelope. Big E read the address:

Dr. Ethan Blackwell, DVM
c/o Blackwell Ranch
Falcon Creek, MT

"I trust you on that score, Rod. Now, if you could hang on to this envelope and mail it after you hear from me, I sure would appreciate it. It won't be long."

* * * * *

ETHAN BLACKWELL WAS surrounded by critically ill checking accounts.

Of course, up until two days ago, the only terminal checking account he'd been working with had been his own. He'd never expected his grandfather's finances to need resuscitation too. He might've suspected Big E to be up to his usual manipulation if his grandfather was still in town. But Big E and his thirty-foot motorhome had departed four weeks ago in early April, without a farewell to anyone or a return date mentioned.

Before Ethan had walked away to build his life, his own way, Big E had accused Ethan of forsaking his family legacy and the land that had raised him to pursue a pretentious career in equestrian medicine. That day, Ethan had vowed to return to the Blackwell Ranch only for the reading of his grandfather's will.

Though no funeral arrangements had been made and as far as the brothers knew, Big E was AWOL, not deceased, Ethan was back at the Blackwell Ranch, pacing around his grandfather's oversize office and scowling at the paperwork nightmare scattered across the oak desk.

Jonathon, his older brother and the only reason Ethan had come home, strode into their grandfather's office. Jon tossed his hat on one of the twin cigar-colored armchairs and dropped into the other. His dog, Trout, sat beside Jon's boots and regarded Ethan as if the border collie was the deputy assistant his brother had brought in for backup. "Please tell me I heard you wrong on the phone."

"That depends. What did you hear?" Ethan leaned against the rolltop desk.

"I thought I heard you tell me that you planned to search Big E's bedroom." There was no question in Jon's certain tone. His brother had better hearing than a bat. But his gaze zeroed in on Ethan like a rifle scope, challenging Ethan to change his own mind.

"That's exactly what I plan to do with your help," Ethan said. "The money's gotta be somewhere."

Get 4 FREE REWARDS!

We'll send you 2 FREE Books plus 2 FREE Mystery Gifts.

Love Inspired® books feature contemporary inspirational romances with Christian characters facing the challenges of life and love.

FREE
Value Over
$20

READERSERVICE.COM

Manage your account online!

- Review your order history
- Manage your payments
- Update your address

> *We've designed the*
> *Reader Service website*
> *just for you.*

Enjoy all the features!

- Discover new series available to you, and read excerpts from any series.
- Respond to mailings and special monthly offers.
- Browse the Bonus Bucks catalog and online-only exculsives.
- Share your feedback.

Visit us at:
ReaderService.com

RS16R